Let the interview begin ...

"**P**olice see so much more death and pain and evil than the rest of the world, you need to get your guard up against it. Shield yourself. You see violence every day, murder every day, drugs and thieves and rape ... every goddamned day—it gets to you."

"Oh, I understand that principle well enough. But, the shielding—why bother? Why not open yourself up to it? Let the feel and flavor of it penetrate? How can you combat something you don't understand— that you hold at arm's length?"

"What can I tell you," Madsen answered honestly. "I don't have to think like a rabid dog to know I want to put a bullet through its head rather than let it bite me."

"But," the whispering man asked, his voice holding the slightest trace of humor, "haven't you ever wanted to know what it feels like ... that rabid freedom to throw off the rules? To do exactly as you desire?"

— from "Dracula: Long Live the King" by C.J. Henderson

First Moonstone edition 2009

Vampires: Dracula and the Undead Legions
A Moonstone Monsters Anthology

Published by Moonstone

ISBN 10 digit: 1-933076-55-0
ISBN 13 digit: 978-1-933076-55-3

Cover by Dave Dorman
Back Cover And Interior Illustration by Ken Wolak
Cover Design by Dave Ulanski
Book design by Rich Harvey

Printed in the USA

PUBLISHER'S NOTE:

This is a work of fiction. Names, characters, places, and incidents either are the products of the authors' imaginations or are used fictitiously, and any resemblance to actual persons, living or dead, business establishments, events or locales, is entirely coincidental.

Published by Moonstone,
582 Torrence Ave.,
Calumet City, IL 60409
www.moonstonebooks.com

VAMPIRES

Dracula and the Undead Legions

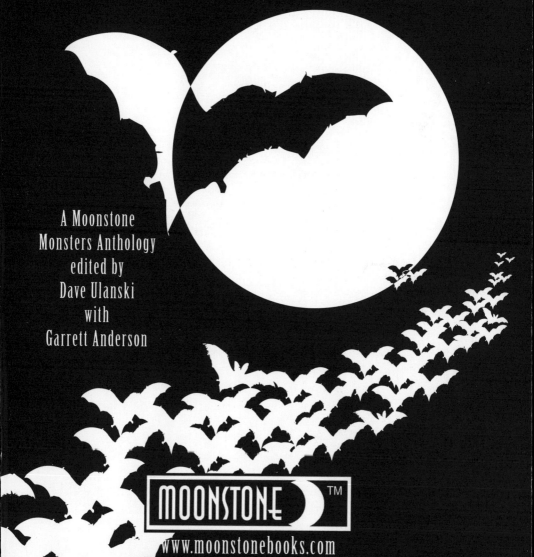

A Moonstone
Monsters Anthology
edited by
Dave Ulanski
with
Garrett Anderson

MOONSTONE ™

www.moonstonebooks.com

Table of Contents

Editor: Dave Ulanski with Garrett Anderson
Cover Art: Dave Dorman
Cover Design: Dave Ulanski
Book design: Rich Harvey
Back Cover And Interior Art: Ken Wolak

The Evil of Dracula
by Martin Powell

OVERTURE

The night fog glided in like a dimly glowing ghost, brushing wetly across the weathered window sill. A soft grey drizzle droned through the empty branches scratching against the single pane as the cottage girl hummed a sweet sigh alone in her bed.

Outside, the darkness was waiting to get in.

Through dreamy half-closed lids the girl's eyes dilated slowly, engorged with the night, sleepily shuddering in her intimate invitation. The small room grew suddenly colder, despite the crisply crackling hearth. Without a sound, except for the thunder in her veins, a looming black presence filled the bedchamber eclipsing the firelight.

She drew down the bedclothes languidly, breathless in her anticipation. A pale luminescent face separated itself from the mist as if it had been a part of it, the feral nostrils pulsing with the girl's moistened fragrance. Shining eyes the color of polished pennies smoldered in the shadows of hollow sockets. The creature bowed and poured its long black form across the bed, caressing the heaving hips and panting bosom of the girl like a carnally weighted shadow. They both wanted this.

Her delicate features winced only slightly at the sight of the sharp white teeth between livid lips the colour of bruised wine. Shuddering against the chill of the gaping mouth fastening upon her naked throat, the girl tightly curled her toes against the gentle hurt.

Hours passed and the dark thing remained with the girl, nursing at the slope of her whitening neck until she was gone. Drawing upon now hollowed veins the creature remained fixed, unsatisfied, with the life it had stolen. No matter how beautiful, how bountiful the woman, it was never enough.

Only the crow of the impending dawn slaked the passion of the daemon's thirst. The black shroud of its cloak melted and leathered into scalloped wings swimming the shadows in the sky, returning to the oppressive castle upon the jagged mountain.

Alone, within the great stone sarcophagus deep beneath the ancient battlements, Count Dracula's eyes stared wide in his unholy sleep, bloodily bloated with his spent lust. The terrible face lined with fear, knowing the horror of Purgatory which claimed his monstrous soul during the seeming eternity of the daylight hours.

There was an escape from Hell, Dracula knew. His great brain burned with the brilliance of his inspired scheme. Soon his perennial fiery tortures would cease forever. Even in the throes of agony the ancient vampire's cruel lips fixed upon a triumphant, leering smile. This much the Count was certain, more than anything else...

Time was on his side.

ACT ONE

THE locomotive emerged through the icy London fog with a pungent hissing halt of oily steam. Monsignor Russell's weathered bulldog of a face brightened immediately upon spotting an energetic wide-shouldered, reddish-haired man of forty departing the train. The passenger's fierce blue-grey eyes darted about, straining to see through the clinging mist.

"Abraham!" the Monsignor heartily waved him down, "Abraham Van Helsing!"

The two men vigorously shook hands.

"It's so good to see you again, Leslie," the severity instantly left Van Helsing's eyes, although they remained as piercing as ever. "What has it been...nine years, isn't it? As a physician and as your friend, I must say that you're not looking very well. I suspect you sent for me just in time."

Monsignor Russell hailed a cab, taking his companion by the elbow and clamored inside its relative warmth.

"I didn't bring you from Amsterdam to discuss my health, Abraham."

Van Helsing nodded and fondly tapped his friend's shoulder.

"Quite right," he affirmed. "Your cable was very sparse. I need to know more about this man before I can arrive at a possible prognosis."

The elderly Monsignor's face grew graver still.

"He's staying at the Rectory. Says he doesn't feel safe anywhere else. I dare not admit him to Saint Bart's, they would deem him insane and have him put away. Still, as I said in my telegram, I'm convinced his malady is more of the spirit than of the mind."

The suspended fog softly muffled the clatter of the hooves upon the cobblestones, and the streetlamps skulked by the cab windows looking unreal.

Van Helsing sat in silence admiring the eerie beauty of the common London street, made most extraordinary by the elemental pallet surrounding them.

"Is he still having the nightmares?" he asked at last.

The Monsignor's frown saddened and deepened.

"Worse. Now he's hearing voices."

At the Rectory, he paced the hardwood floors like a caged animal. A large middle-aged man with wild eyes, mumbling Latin incantations beneath his breath, while continuously crossing himself with madly twitching fingers. Some great, nameless fear seemed to quicken and swell within him like a living thing. Incessantly, he darted glances of dread at the dimming light behind the stained glass windows. Daylight was fading.

The Monsignor and Van Helsing had hardly stepped foot into the door before the man crumpled to his knees in front of them.

"Why did you leave me? Night is falling and I was alone!" he gasped, his eyes wilder than before."

"Calm yourself, sir," Monsignor Russell scolded gently. "I brought a man whom I believe can help you. This is Dr. Van Helsing from the Continent."

The quivering wild man shot Van Helsing a venomous glare.

"There's nothing wrong with me that your pills can cure," he spat out contemptuously.

Van Helsing's eyes hardened, then brimmed with pity. His strong, intelligent face lifted in a soothing smile.

"I am more than merely that kind of doctor and I am confident that I can help you, my poor friend," Van Helsing offered his sun-bronzed muscular hand. "Please tell me your troubles, Mister--?"

The man immediately lost much of his wildness, the glazed eyes slowly softening into brimming tears. With a trembling gesture he clasped Van Helsing's hand.

"Renfield," he murmured low. "Roderick Matthias Renfield. Forgive me, Doctor. If you can truly save me, then I am your obedient servant."

Transylvania, the Land of Phantoms.

Nightfall swallowed the Carpathian valley, letting loose all its moving, hunting shadows.

Pale things, dead by day, crawled forth, shrouded in grave-dirt as howling bristling horrors lurched through the haunted forests.

Looming over all with trident spires of diabolical majesty was Castle Dracula, whose unholy foundations were old when Eden was new. No one spoke of the dreadful place. No one went there.

Except a man with nothing more to lose.

"All is prepared for you, my Master," the peasant bowed within the gloom of the courtyard, cold sweat blurring his vision. "The Vesta sails in two days. The crew has been bribed as you directed. Your...cargo is already onboard, bound for London. The one you seek is there."

Count Dracula stood at the top of the time-worn stairs, unmoving. Only his smoldering eyes seemed alive on the grim, waxen face. For a long moment there was a terrible stillness, as if the world had stopped. Then, abruptly, the Count glided down, his boots soundless upon the cold stone of the steps.

"Master...?" the peasant dared to follow. "My...my daughters...my girls...you promised to release them if I served you..."

Dracula paused, the moonlight turning his long shadow into something unnamable. He nodded slightly toward a darkened crevice in the ancient stone, and then, inexplicably, his imposing figure shimmered into nothingness. It was as if Dracula had become the Night itself.

The peasant drew in a shuddered breath, turning slowly, following the icy prickles running down his spine. Six glowering eyes burned at him from the shadows of the edifice, followed by three emerging figures resembling young women. Their low, savage laughter was almost musical in the stillness of the castle. Flesh, pale and bloodless, took form over their ghostliness like the guttural drip of a melting candle. Voluptuous lips, purpled from famine, curled back over their glinting animal teeth.

The peasant screamed only once, as fiends who were once his daughters fed deeply and lustfully from their own flesh and blood.

"I've actually heard of you, Doctor," Renfield sat uncomfortably, repetitively glancing at the great ticking clock in the Monsignor's book-lined study.

Van Helsing listened intently through his stethoscope, nearly finished with Renfield's physical examination.

"Ah, your heart is rapid, but strong. A good sign," the doctor amiably nodded. "Please follow my finger with your eyes, Mr. Renfield. Now then... how is it that you know me?"

Renfield's face brightened suddenly, making him appear rather younger and more intelligent.

"You've been published, sir," he beamed. "I'm quite a voracious reader, especially upon scientific matters. In fact, I am something of an amateur entomologist, the species Psychodidae being a particular specialty of interest."

Peering deeply into his patient eyes, Van Helsing smiled quite satisfied.

"Of course, the common moth fly. They can be quite a nuisance, can they not?" he gave Renfield a gentle, comforting pat on the knee. "Now then, you're vision and reflexes are normal. In fact, except for being somewhat malnourished, overall your health is quite excellent."

Again, Renfield stabbed a look at the clock. His face grimaced for an instant, as if in sudden pain, then smiled sadly at the physician.

"So, Doctor," he flushed in shame, "you're telling me that this is all in my mind?"

Van Helsing rinsed his hands in a water basin, and blotted them with a clean towel. He regarded the question silently, and seriously, for a moment and then smiled again. There was something calming, something comforting in his manner. He had an inner strength about him and Renfield clearly and gratefully felt it.

"I notice that the clock worries you, does it not? Why is that, pray tell?" it was peculiar how Van Helsing's Dutch accent sometimes grew more pronounced when he was concentrating.

"The night…" Renfield started, then sadly shook his head.

"Ah, then. It is the coming of night that you fear, Mr. Renfield," Van Helsing offered at last. "Is that not so?"

Renfield nodded, reluctantly.

"You say you suffer from lucid nightmares," the doctor continued, "which I also have experienced from time to time. They can be, I know, very terrifying. However, there is something much more than merely bad dreams tormenting you. You've complained that something is following you, devouring your very thoughts. You feel weakened and empowered at the same time. You don't trust your own mind. All this started, you tell me, when your only daughter became tragically stricken with consumption. Now you feel something has, how again did you say it? 'Invaded your soul', you said. You feel as if someone, or something, is looking out through your own eyes. Spying on the rest of us. Yes?"

Renfield's haunted eyes glazed with tears.

"Am I…am I quite insane, Doctor?" he managed, at last.

Van Helsing frowned, narrowing his eyes. The sudden hush in the room was jarring.

"You'll find that I differ considerably from my esteemed colleagues, sir. I believe a metaphysical explanation may be in order, something along the lines of clairvoyance or precognition," Van Helsing turned grimly to Renfield, his strong, bronzed face grown a bit grey. "In all truth it is even possible that you may be possessed."

"I refuse to believe in such rot," Renfield flushed, defensively.

"These things, and more, exist in this world as few others would ever begin to suspect. I have spent my lifetime, such as it is, in pursuit of these obscure truths about the world. I have journeyed far and wide, seeing things with my own eyes that defy intelligent explanation. To those ends, I have, myself, become convinced of the reality of the unearthly and the unnamable. The Supernatural will not go away simply because we disapprove, or even disbelieve in it, Mr. Renfield."

Van Helsing paused a moment, then clasped Renfield by the shoulder.

"Tell me about these voices."

Renfield peered at the clock, stood and took to pacing. He hesitated for a full minute, then Van Helsing's patient smile brought out his trust.

"Only one voice!" he, at last, stated desperately. "Something dark, terrible…it's knows all my secrets. God help me, Dr. Van Helsing…it promises that after my daughter dies— she will live forever!"

"You needn't be so shy about it, Dr. Van Helsing…I know that I'm dying."

Miss Adelaide Renfield smiled with blind, beautiful eyes. Though weak, her voice had retained a bit of the music it must have possessed before her illness. She scarcely moved in her hospital bed, but her faded pallor still bloomed with some of its delicate sweetness. Although she could not see him, Dr. Abraham Van Helsing couldn't take his own saddened eyes off of her.

"I am so sorry, my dear young Miss," he managed, pressing her forehead with his palm. She was burning up.

Adelaide smiled again. It was both uplifting, and heartbreaking, that smile.

"There's nothing for you to feel sorry for, Doctor," she gave his sinewy wrist a whispered squeeze. "Death is a natural thing. I find it almost comforting now. I only wish my poor father was not so direly affected. I know he feels guilty for not visiting me. He shouldn't. I understand. When my mother died, it nearly killed him."

Van Helsing studied her shining grey-green eyes which, despite their sightlessness, warmed with an inner light.

"How long have you been blind?" he presented his comforting, professional tone. The girl very visibly responded to its quiet strength.

"Almost since birth," Adelaide's pale lips curled in a bit of humor. "I had scarlet fever as a baby. You'd think there could be nothing more wrong with me, wouldn't you?"

Van Helsing lightly stroked her hair, which fell so very dark and silken about her shoulders, with spun threads of blued sapphires.

"What I think," he said after a long moment, "is that you are a very brave young lady."

Van Helsing continued speaking with quiet, paternal patience as he answered the girl's grim questions considering her consumptive illness. He held nothing back, telling her everything of what to expect. She never flinched, not even at the worst of it. Afterwards, they passed a peaceful silence for a number of minutes. Then, for the first time, Van Helsing saw a fretful frown crease her supple brow.

"Doctor…I'm fearful for my father," she whispered at last. "When Monsignor Russell comes to give me Holy Communion, I feel he is trying to protect me from something. Is my father ill?"

Van Helsing took her hand, warming the chilled fingers.

"What makes you ask that?"

She stared passed his shoulder at nothingness and her eyes slightly rounded.

"I…I've been having dreams. I suppose you could call them nightmares. In my sleep, I sense something following him. Something wild and vicious, like a thing from the jungle. It…wants something from him. Something terrible."

Dr. Van Helsing leaned forward a bit. Her voice was getting tired and fainter with every fitful breath. The sudden shift of anxiety alarmed him.

"Sometimes a dream is just that, my dear Miss," he gave her wrist a gentle pat, keeping her father's similar malady to himself.

Adelaide's eye grew wider, more pronounced in their catlike glimmer.

"But—sometimes, Dr. Van Helsing…sometimes my dreams come true."

"Oh? In what form does this happen?"

She took a slow, hurtful breath. Van Helsing much too casily noticed the fluid rattle from her chest.

"Last night…I dreamt of a sea vessel. A rank, creaking ship pushed by evil winds toward our shores. There was a hideous stillness on board. Hushed voices of the crew stammered in horror. The Devil was on that ship."

"Ah, yes. You heard the grim news about the unfortunate Vesta, which docked late last night with its crew of madmen."

The girl winced, painfully swallowed, and then coughed a bit of blood into her hand.

Van Helsing was glad the girl couldn't see his sudden apprehension. Her slight consumptive hemorrhage quieted and he spoke soothingly to her. Just the sound of his voice seemed to take away much of the pain.

"Sister Charles reads the morning papers to me," Adelaide finally managed, nearly recovered from the spasm.

Solemnly, Van Helsing reached into an inner pocket of his coat.

"I have just the cure for these nightmares," he withdrew a small silver crucifix and draped its thin golden chain around her neck. "This was blessed by his Holiness in Rome himself. Never take it off."

Adelaide's unmoving eyes gained more brightness as they moistened.

"I must leave you, my dear," Van Helsing lightly caressed her flushing cheek, renewing its warmth. "However, I will return again tomorrow, to be charmed by you all over again."

The girl's questing fingers caught at his sleeve.

"Doctor," she asked with an expression like a child, "is it still daylight?"

"Yes, Miss. It's late afternoon. A beautiful day."

Her face lifted again in a girlish smile.

"Could you open the curtains, please? Although I've never seen it, I can still remember the sun on my face. It always felt friendly."

Left to herself, Adelaide Renfield was softly smiling, privately treasuring her own wild imaginings of what colour might be like.

Van Helsing arrived at his room at the Northumberland Hotel some hours after sunset. He had walked long and thoughtfully through the rattling, humming London streets pondering the events of the past few days. As the long shadows cast themselves across the cobblestones, a chill of dread crawled over his skin. Somehow the great city was different. Tainted, he believed. Something unnatural had mixed itself into its thundering swirl and rush of life.

Twice, Van Helsing felt certain he'd heard a voice softly speak his name. Two times he turned, and no one was there. For the first time in his observant life, the eminent scientist took intimate notice—and was unnerved by—the darting shadows of the moths fluttering around the streetlamps.

He felt colder than he should as he turned the key and stepped into his rented flat.

He was not alone.

The chamber was well-lighted, but somehow Van Helsing needed to strain his eyes in order to fully take in his unknown visitor. He observed the towering figure of a man all in black, without a single speck of colour about him anywhere. Motionless as an obelisk, only the figure's unblinking eyes looked alive.

Finally, the bruised lips curved and spoke.

"Dr. Abraham Van Helsing...the great scientist, whose name we know even in the wilds of Transylvania. I have crossed land and sea to make your acquaintance. Only in you may I find salvation."

Van Helsing took an uneasy step forward, toward the invader.

"How did you get in here?" he demanded. "Who are you?"

White wolfish teeth smiled.

"I am Count Dracula."

ACT TWO

VAN HELSING studied the uninvited visitor with a quick sweeping study. Although peculiarly pale, and possessing fiercely probing eyes, the stranger seemed normal enough at first glance. In fact, despite an undeniably commanding demeanor, the gentleman seemed quite congenial, even cultured in his manner. Still, there was something oddly foreign about him that even the worldly Van Helsing couldn't quite place.

"I have never heard of you before in my life, Count," Van Helsing said curtly. "Yet, you say that you know me. If that is so, then you must realize that I am a man pressed for time with many other duties. May I ask why you have disturbed my privacy this evening?"

Dracula took a single silent step forward, suddenly a prowling black-draped panther of a man, losing some of his amiable comportment.

"Physician, anthropologist, attorney, theologian, student of the occult, and master of a dozen different scientific disciplines...I am fully aware of your accomplishments and reputation, Doctor," he spoke excellent English, though with a strange intonation as if unpracticed in speaking aloud.

"Indeed?" Van Helsing scowled.

"I know, for example, that many years ago as a curious student you investigated an infamously haunted monastery in Tibet. Although your initial purpose was to scientifically disprove its supernatural reputation, you came away from that terrible place a very changed and enlightened man. You had learned...too much. Although kept largely secret from your learned brethren, your true life's work is the scientific pursuit of the unnatural, the unearthly, of Life beyond Death. It has become the engine that drives you."

The scientist was stunned.

"How...do you know these things? I never wrote of my Tibetan explorations. Never spoke of them to a living soul."

Count Dracula paused for a brief moment, a sinister smile on his sensual red lips.

"Rejoice, Dr. Van Helsing, your long search has ended," he moved nearer, black cloak writhing. "I am your obsession personified."

The floor seemed to sway and the gaslight faded. Van Helsing caught the edge of a chair to steady himself. There was something about the stranger's eyes, with their weird ruby illusion reflecting the firelight, which pierced and drained the doctor's strength. He felt suddenly drugged.

"I...I don't understand," the doctor found it difficult to speak as the Count continued to stare with his knowing, animal smile.

Dracula glided closer still, placing a sharp-nailed hand upon Van Helsing's shoulder, inducing an involuntary shudder.

"Don't you, Doctor? Then, allow me to help clarify what you oddly fail to realize. There is an old adage, I believe, very close to the heart of every scientific man," the Count explained, indicating the large heavily framed mirror behind them. "Behold—for in seeing there is believing."

Van Helsing breathlessly gazed at his astonished reflection. The Count's hand had continued to grip the doctor's coat. He was fully aware of the uncannily controlled, hideous strength contained in that white bloodless talon.

Yes, there was no doubt, Van Helsing still felt that dreadful grasp, and yet, somehow, unbelievably...Count Dracula's own image was utterly absent in the glass!

The scientist's blood pounded icily in his temples. There was but one implausible explanation.

A single, weighted, alien word escaped Van Helsing's learned lips.

"Nosferatu...!"

"Van Helsing has betrayed me," Renfield couldn't remain still, stalking a visible trail across the rug.

Muttering and constantly crossing himself, he was persistently in motion, twitching and agitated like a beast in pain. No less than three times during the past quarter hour Renfield stabbed a hated, frantic glance at the clock, and contemptuously shook his head. He had grown leaner and wilder-eyed during the past several nights.

Monsignor Russell frowned for a long moment, finally forcing a kindly smile.

"Dr. Van Helsing said that we might not see him for a while," the elder priest offered. "His last telegram spoke of some great emergency, but he also prescribed that you remain safely here in the Rectory. Above all, he accentuated that you should never lose hope. He will find a way to help you, Mr. Renfield."

"Ah, yes, of course. 'Hope Springs Eternal'…" Renfield growled, beneath clenched teeth. "But Eternity scoffs back at us, Monsignor. It mocks me with its empty promises. Just as Van Helsing humiliates me by his negligence."

Renfield spun, savagely tearing open the curtains to stare up at the moon. Almost at once, his breathing slowed, his nervousness diffused. Monsignor Russell had seen this effect before with Renfield. Sometimes the moon alone seemed to be the only thing capable of calming him, if only for a moment.

Renfield continued his reverie of the shimmering orb for several minutes, his lips moving without noise.

"Did you know, Monsignor," he finally spoke low, trance-like. "That the moon doesn't possess any actual light of its own? Moonlight is merely reflected sunlight…no matter what else we may choose to call it."

The Monsignor didn't recognize the subtle shift in Renfield's voice. The hysteria had dimmed, and something of the man's former scholarly nature returned. It was a welcomed, if sudden, change after many nights of wild proclamations and tremulous seizures.

"Why, that's quite interesting, Mr. Renfield," the old priest sounded relieved. "I didn't realize that you included astronomy among your other many areas of scientific expertise."

The moonlight felt cold upon Renfield's skin, raising gooseflesh along the hackles of his neck. When he turned again to face the Monsignor, the icy light of madness glowed silver-blue upon his twisted face.

"Merely pointing out one of the innumerable ways that this world lies to us, Monsignor," he said, lurching toward the old man.

"Mr. Renfield…what…what're you doing? Stop—stay back! For the love of God—"

Monsignor Russell sought retreat, but the madman's hands were already at his throat. Renfield wanted to wrench and wring, but he released his grip once the old man ceased to struggle, letting him flop unconscious on the hard floor.

"I'm doing what your God will not," Renfield flung on his cloak, emerging out into the blue moonlight. "No matter the price, no matter what I must do...I am going to save my daughter."

It was a little before midnight when Adelaide's demon awakened her, both boiling lungs erupting into her throat. She coughed up a spasm of pink fluid, certain for many long minutes that she was drowning within herself. Ever paler and trembling, she fought fiercely for breath. Dr. Van Helsing's crucifix offered only a cold weight upon her breast.

Adelaide fought the compulsion to call out for Sister Charles, knowing it could all be over much sooner this way. Perhaps, at last, this was the end. Death was only a door, all the priests had said. She had been chained as a prisoner in its terrible threshold for much too long.

Concentrating persistently against the pain, Adelaide struggled hard to think of happy little memories as a small girl, and finally found a few. Unlike her daydreams, desperately uttered prayers only seemed to sink impotently away into the ether.

Adelaide was more than half-dreaming of the briny, gull-fluttered air of Dover when she perceived a tiny cry. There! She heard it again, now fully awake. Was it reality, she puzzled, not merely the pleasured caw of the seagulls of her girlhood? There, again! More like the cottony coo of a dove. And it was real, was it not? She had to know.

The cold floor bit Adelaide's bare feet, her dressing gown remained at the end of the bed. Both of her dancing hands traced the wall to the door, and with a weakened wrench she opened it. Again, there were the stifled sobs, this time very near. Adelaide's practiced, sensitive fingers found a soft-tressed, quietly quavering child curled into a corner of the icy corridor.

"Poor thing! Why, you're only a little girl," Adelaide gasped. "Hush now, don't be frightened. What's your name?"

There was a pause as the child gathered courage. Looking up in the dim light she was comforted by Adelaide's sweetness, though was puzzled that she didn't quite look at her.

"Lucy...Lucy Westenra," she sniffled prettily. "I awoke and was lost."

"It's all right, dear. I'm Adelaide Renfield, you're not alone now. Are you a patient here, Lucy?" she lightly touched the girl's trembling cheek.

The girl nodded, but then sharply realized that Adelaide couldn't see her.

"I was...walking in my sleep, Miss. I do that a lot...during bad dreams. That's why I'm here," Lucy admitted, her shoulders slumping.

"Sleepwalking is no reason for shame."

Both turned to the low, cultivated voice behind them. Little Lucy looked at the gentleman standing in the arched corridor, and she smiled.

Warily, Adelaide stood slowly upright, sensitive to the abrupt drop in temperature. She tightly clasped the girl's small hand.

"Your voice is unfamiliar, sir. Are you the physician on duty?" she felt, for some reason, quite unexpectedly apprehensive.

There was much too long a pause.

"Not a doctor at all, are you? I think you are a king," Lucy offered, bravely stepping a bit forward.

A shorter pause.

"How cunning for one who has not yet begun her own lifetime," he replied, amused.

Adelaide tilted her head, mystified. True, the cultured masculine voice was unknown to her, but the stranger's silent stately presence seemed to stir half-forgotten memories of her own untold dreams. Was she dreaming now? Who was this man?

"Count Dracula!"

Van Helsing clamoured before them, his boot heels creating a chorus of hollow echoes.

"Dr. Van Helsing?" Adelaide felt flushed, and suddenly warmer.

The scientist darted quick nervous glances at the odd trio in the arched hall. Jaw muscles flexing, he glowered at the Count, then back to Adelaide.

"Miss Renfield…this child…what on earth—"

"Please, don't be cross with me, Doctor," Adelaide held Lucy close. "This gentleman and I are merely escorting little Lucy back to her room."

Again, Van Helsing studied both patients, then looking down at the pretty dark-eyed child he forced a smile.

"Allow me to accompany the both of you, my dear," he gently clasped their elbows, again narrowing his eyes at Dracula. "Meet me in the laboratory, as we had previously arranged, Count. I will join you presently."

Van Helsing could feel the vampire's stare through the back of his collar. He was careful not to return the gaze. Adelaide found comfort in the doctor's firm grip. Little Lucy couldn't help but glance back at the tall, black-clad figure behind them.

"Where is he from, Doctor?" Adelaide wanted to know. "There is something so strong, yet also so sad in his voice."

He frowned a long moment, then patted her hand.

"The Count is quite ill," he offered. "He has come here from a very great distance seeking a cure."

"Then, why don't you make him better?" Lucy scowled, snatching her hand away.

The doctor nodded seriously, his face reflected a steely inner strength. "I will, my dear young lady. As God is my witness. I swear it."

Something that wasn't blood drew slowly from Dracula's veins into the hypodermic syringe. Repressing a shudder, Dr. Van Helsing forced himself to focus on the routine of his examination. Count Dracula had stood in stilled silence for several hours, like the stopped hands of a clock.

Van Helsing's highly trained concentration finally snapped, broken by the eerie atmosphere radiated by this macabre patient.

"I must insist upon punctuality, Count," he warned, finally finding his nerve. "We were to meet here at sunset. Did you not agree upon your honour to place yourself in my hands, when I granted to help you? You must never again be late for these appointments. If I am to have any effect here, any at all, I must be master or I can do nothing. Do you understand?"

Dracula remained motionless, at certain moments he seemed more shadow than man.

"I understand that you don't trust me, Doctor."

The scientist attempted to face the creature, but could not endure the piercing glare of the red eyes.

"I know what you are," he said, flatly.

Returning to the laboratory work, Van Helsing handled the specimen with all the reverence of a religious artifact. He had lost all perspective since his initial encounter with this most rare and unusual patient, disregarding many others. How long had that been? Days, at least, surely. Possibly more than a week, he couldn't be certain. He'd hardly eaten, or slept. Blindly absorbed with each impossible fact he had discovered, the great scientist grew ever voracious for more knowledge. The existence of Dracula had become both Van Helsing's greatest passion and also, possibly, his most profound weakness. He realized this painfully. Still, he couldn't stop now.

Meticulously smearing the vacuous fluid on a glass slide to scrutinize under the microscope, Van Helsing again audibly gasped peering into the eyepiece.

"Progress, Doctor?" the Count's words were like low, distant thunder.

"It's nothing less than miraculous," Van Helsing shook his head in disbelief. "You are without blood pressure. No respiration, except when you speak. There is no pupil contraction under the influence of bright lamp light. And, I have never seen such anemic blood cells as these. There is no life within you, yet the presence of decay is also extinct."

Van Helsing rose from the instruments and slowly, warily, circled

Dracula as he would a savagely caged animal.

"Dead and yet immune to Death. You are truly not of this world, Count Dracula," he admitted in whispered awe.

The flickering gaslight played strangely upon the vampire, moving shadows into macabre shapes that exist only beyond the wall of sleep. He remained in his ghostly silence.

"You possess the physical strength of more than a dozen mortal men," Van Helsing spun upon his heels, lecturing as if to further convince himself. "There is something akin to mesmerism about you, as well. Frequently I have found it difficult to see you, except in my direct line of vision. I've also detected biological evidence indicating that you are indeed just as staggeringly, unimaginably ancient as you've attested. Inexplicably, the elements of fog, wind, and storm seem enslaved by your mental command. I am frankly astounded. And yet, I also suspect that you possess even more supernatural prowess, which you have decisively kept secret from me."

At that the Count smiled, slightly.

"I confess it," the doctor continued, wearily defeated one second, fervently vibrant the next. "This unprecedented investigation has given ponderous weight to my own ignorant arrogance. Obviously, we scientists are fools—understanding very little of the true world and we have, all of us, long believed in many wrong things. Now, however, I begin to see the light. I am admittedly…very much in your debt, Count Dracula."

Van Helsing offered a brief, formal bow to the vampire.

"You have learned enough, then?" Dracula glided forward, his expression and inflection suddenly more human.

The room itself seethed with tension. Dr. Van Helsing pondered the question thoughtfully. There was still so much he didn't understand.

"Before I answer," he rubbed his chin, "there is something more I must know. I'm afraid that it's a philosophical query, rather than a physiological one. Yet I sorely need to understand before we continue forward."

The Count nodded, pensively.

"Ask your question."

Van Helsing drew in an excited breath.

Why should an immortal being," the scientist began, "himself not subject to the established laws of nature or society, wish to become…human again, even if such a thing was essentially possible?"

Dracula moved closer, his flowing cloak a living part of the room's gloom.

"I would think that was obvious to a theologian brilliant as yourself, Doctor. You see before you a semblance of a man who has roamed the world for centuries, seeking the ruin of souls, feeding upon Christian blood," the Count said, hollowly. "My long-past human life seems now little more to me now than a dimming dream. Suffice to say that certain secrets must forever remain my own, however, I have indeed succeeded in surviving my own grave and have buried many, many enemies...but now the wars of old are over."

Van Helsing started to speak, but Dracula raised a commanding hand and continued.

"Make no mistake, I fully acknowledge that I am a monster," the vampire stated. "And, as such, I am aware of much more, besides. What you take on mere blind religious faith, is unrelenting reality to me. The soldier that I am has long accepted the inescapable inevitability that I will one day be destroyed, most likely by a learned man of knowledge such as yourself. Much more than any mortal man, I know that literal Hell is waiting for me."

The chamber resounded a moment, the vampire's pronouncement ringing in the stone walls, although the words had not been of great volume. Dracula remained impassive and proud, seeming now even taller, a magnificent devil in black.

"Yes...yes, I see. I believe I am dimly beginning to understand," Van Helsing nodded. "You hope for redemption, Count Dracula."

Rising autumn wind scratched a tree branch across the window pane with a scuttling cackle, pouring through a crack with a low lonely howl. The lights dimmed, the fire dying in the hearth. Palpable evil smothered the chamber.

"I seek only Escape," the creature corrected.

The scientist lurched backwards, feeling the dampness of the grave from the Count's whispered hiss. He wanted to flee, to dash wildly into the London back-alleys, losing himself to madness. Then shaking his head sorrowfully, he ached with a sudden pity. A monster, a daemon stood before him, truly. Yet, the doctor's own faith taught that no soul was lost which also sought mercy, whatever its stains of sin. No one was past hope or beyond forgiveness. Van Helsing could not do less than follow that testament.

"I know not how this terrible curse came to you, Count," he began, softly. "Only you know the full degree of your own liability for the many, many terrible things you've done. I will not—I cannot judge you. We physicians are blessed, sometimes we are permitted by Providence to heal those who are sick in body or even in mind. However, your disease is a malignancy of the spirit, quite outside the realm of my meager influence. It is not in my power to help you."

Livid rage twisted the Count's waxen face, only to gnarl into a mask of such anguished passion as Van Helsing had never before witnessed. He found himself clasping Dracula's shoulder, in an unconscious effort of comfort.

"Do not despair," he said softly. "True, my poor methods are limited in these matters, but there is another scientist, a colleague, whose own metaphysical experiments have shown great promise."

Dracula's eyes flashed.

"Bring him to me."

Van Helsing gestured slowly, speaking low as one would to calm a wild animal.

"Never fear, I have already sent a telegram, and today I received a response," he explained. "He will arrive tomorrow evening. We are very fortunate, indeed, to have such a mighty brain on our side. In all of London there is no scientific adventurer more brilliant than Dr. Henry Jekyll."

ACT THREE

RENFIELD anxiously prowled the midnight London backstreets, his unusual sensitivity leading him into the darker places like a death's head moth to a glowing gaslight. In the midst of stench-soaked alleys, reeking of bile and sour wine, he could almost smell the iniquity in the oily fog. The gloomy, dimly-lighted labyrinth of Whitechapel was always a wicked place, but tonight was somehow different. The air itself felt filled with devils.

"Master...?" he breathed, dimly watching a lone stunted figure skulking toward him from across the street.

Furtively, Renfield concealed himself within a doorway, continuing to spy in silence, his pulse pounding in his ears. He'd been witness to many awful things this evening, including a suicide at London Bridge and a drunkard knifed over a shilling in the East End, but the aura emanating from this hunched, malevolent shape was far worse as it grew nearer, stamping its way with a heavy walking stick wielded like a club.

To Renfield's unnaturally-tuned senses, there was a psychic bestial stench reeking from the figure, although it looked like a man, well dressed in immaculate, but ill-fitting evening clothes. This was not at all what he'd expected. He'd imagined someone more regal, more cosmically perfect. There was something not quite right about the dwarfish, disfigured frame. Perhaps, Renfield reasoned, he wasn't truly a man at all. Perhaps, indeed, this was the Master.

Just then, a thin waif of a girl, about eleven or twelve, padded toward the cane carrying ogre as they both neared a flickering streetlamp. She gazed hopefully at the orange-lighted windows of the Mermaid Inn, hearing the raucous laughter from within. Maybe someone would come out to buy one of her wilted flowers. The girl and the fiercely stalking figure were, unknowingly, about to meet at the corner.

Renfield watched the collision in horror.

The urchin had barely stuttered a weak apology before the villain savagely struck her down with his cane and trampled her under his heavy boots, leaving the girl screaming on the damp cobblestones. The cries of the child quickly aroused a mob from the inn, cursing and staggering after the deformed figure in hot-blooded hast.

When Renfield saw the cretin run for his mortal life, he lost interest. The hunchback was an evil brute true enough, but he was just a man. This was not the Master. God would not help his daughter and he knew, somehow felt deep in what remained of his soul, that the Devil himself walked the earth this night.

Turning up his collar, Renfield moved on, doubting his anomalous intuition for the first time. He had searched hours throughout London, channeled by an incomparable sense of Evil. Renfield had pursued this perilous path easily as following the street signs. He'd been so sure the loutish dwarf was the one he sought, but he'd been dead wrong. Was his accursed sensitivity, a facet that had tormented him from his boyhood, merely be a delusion created in his imagination? Was he as mad as others had longed believed?

His doubt was to be short-lived. The faintest sound, like the whisper of a feather, immediately caught Renfield's hyper-senses causing him to look upward. There, unbelievably, impossibly, was that which he sought descending from an upper floor window, crawling down the sheer face of the outer wall with reptilian silence.

Black and terrible, its cloak spread like the great predatory wings, somehow defying gravity, the figure crept downward like slowly pouring ink. The pale face, almost silver in the moonlight, was nearly human, only its horrid expression and unblinking garnet eyes betrayed its true nature. Something dark smeared the fiercely gnashing mouth, and Renfield felt a dribble of wetness fall across his cheek. Alarmingly, the salty scent of the gory droplets stimulated his own saliva.

For an instant, their eyes met. The chalk face shimmered, the flapping cloak writhed. Something dragon-winged and swift took to the wind. Renfield ran like a madman, keeping the flying devil in sight. Finally he watched it drop again to the earth, like Satan falling from Heaven, seeking the sanctuary of a long abandoned crypt in the anciently neglected Brookwood Cemetery.

"O my dark Lord," Renfield dropped to his knees. "You are truly the Resurrection and the Life. Whoever believes in you, and serves your will, shall not die! My daughter will live forever!"

Van Helsing slid the needle from his elbow, dabbing at the budding splotch of blood with a bit of sterile cotton.   He paused a moment, leaning slightly in his chair, bracing himself against a brief wave of dizziness and nausea.   Count Dracula soundlessly rose from the operating table like a stringed marionette, nourished by the scientist's two spent pints.

"It is crude and experimental, I'll grant you," Van Helsing poured himself a fortifying glass of wine, his hand slightly unsteady despite all his effort to the contrary. "And, in time I intend to perfect it further, but for now this blood transferring apparatus will serve to feed you."

Dracula offered an icy glance at the soulless tubes, pumps, and hoses on the table, the gleaming complexity of Van Helsing's inventive genius.

"It is not enough," he said, hollowly.

Van Helsing's pulse quickened, feeling it stabbing in his temples. He knew the vampire spoke the truth. How much longer could he appease the monster, holding it at bay?

A scuffing knock at the door abruptly ended the chilled silence.

"'Knock and it shall be opened unto you,'" Van Helsing quoted and smiled, clearly relieved. "I highly suspect that the hour of your salvation is at hand, Count Dracula."

The scientist opened the door, standing surprised in the doorway. A slope-shouldered man, dressed in ill-fitting clothing, impatiently awaited entrance, anxiously glancing behind him. Van Helsing noticed a carefully wrapped parcel was clutched in one hairy corded hand, with a heavy walking stick tightly gripped in the other . The stranger seemed purposely determined to hide his features within the shadows of his wide hat brim and up-turned collar.

"Package for Abraham Van Helsing," the hunchback rasped. "From Dr. Henry Jekyll."

Van Helsing glanced over at the Count. This was not what they had expected.   He studied the nervous, disproportionate dwarf with grim interest. An odd courier, indeed. Even without clearly seeing the man's face, Van Helsing had never before meet anyone he'd so instantly disliked. The scientist nodded, and gestured the stranger to enter.

"My name, sir. I'm afraid that you have me at a disadvantage," Van Helsing stated suspiciously. "I was expecting Dr. Jekyll himself to arrive this evening."

The stranger's anxious little eyes darted about, under the low brim, cagily scanning the room. He'd felt certain upon first entering that another occupant, a black-garbed man, tall and ghostly pale, had also been there. Now it was uncannily obvious that he was alone with Van Helsing.

"Jekyll regrets that he unable to keep the appointment," he replied, his voice as distorted as the rest of him. "I'm the doctor's messenger. He instructed me to deliver this parcel, with detailed directions for the purpose of its contents also contained within a sealed envelope inside."

That sounded plausible enough. Dr. Henry Jekyll was one of London's most celebrated physicians, also well-known for frequently attending the multitude of destitute patients within the squalid wards of the charity hospitals. Still, Jekyll's response to Van Helsing's confidential, detailed correspondence absolutely affirmed that he would appear that evening in person. Something wasn't right.

"So I see. And, may I ask who you are, sir?" Van Helsing queried.

"The name is Hyde, if that's any of your damned business," he snarled intolerantly, turning to leave, an oil lamp catching full sight of his face in the sudden glare.

That was enough. There was something in the messenger's cruel face, somehow savagely simian, with the unbearable leer of a satyr, which switched Van Helsing's growing alarm into instant action. As if by magic a small, deadly revolver appeared in the scientist's grip from the pocket of his smock.

"I'm making it my concern," Van Helsing stated grimly, taking deliberate aim.

Hyde scratched the air with a sharp cackling chortle, but a nervous sweat dampened his collar.

"Don't be a fool, Van Helsing," he grimaced, hissing through ivory canines. "You have what you need. Let me go."

The longer Van Helsing looked at the man called Hyde, the more his instinctive hatred grew. Suddenly, he feared the worse for his friend, Jekyll. The scientist took a cautious step closer, cocking the pistol.

"Where is Henry Jekyll? That distinctive walking stick belongs to him. I recognized it instantly. How did it come into your possession? What have you done to him? Answer me!" Van Helsing demanded.

The dwarf again growled his ugly laugh.

"Pull that trigger," Hyde sneered, "and he's good as dead."

Van Helsing paused, fighting to quiet his hurried breath. Examining the brutish lout in closer detail, he noticed that Hyde's clothes, though poorly maintained, were of excellent quality. Did these costly over-sized garments also belong to Jekyll? What had this fiend done?

Barely had Van Helsing blinked when Hyde's weighted cane struck, sending him crashing into a corner. Still gripping the revolver, he resisted the almost irresistible urge to fire as Hyde stalked fearlessly toward him.

"You self-righteous hypocrite," Hyde gave the handle a twist, drawing an edged blade from inside the cane. "Look what you're making me do."

A film, like a blurring grey veil, suddenly clouded Hyde's vision. It was a curtain of fog writhing before him, a vaguely man-shaped mist shielding Van Helsing as would an icy guardian angel. Hyde backed away like a cornered beast. Van Helsing lowered his own weapon, looking on with awe.

Count Dracula darkly materialized, towering and terrible, right before their gaping eyes.

Hyde froze, shaking his misshaped head in shock, terror born for the first time in his brutal heart. He leaped, slashing the sword with ape-like fury, futilely slicing through Dracula harmlessly as smoke. Even with all his knowledge, all of his years of occult experience, Van Helsing had never witnessed anything like what he now beheld. The laboratory had become a madhouse.

The cloaked figure expanded into an inky nightmare, devil's wings clawing the air. Something like a monstrous bat haunted the chamber, then within a heartbeat the creature crouched into a bristling wolf-man, its long jaws jagged with horror. Dracula's dark shadow moved on its own, an undead remnant of living Hell on Earth.

Inhuman hands dug into Hyde's throat, suspending him aloft. Dracula had become his gallows.

"Stop it! Don't kill him!" Van Helsing pleaded with the vampire. "If Hyde dies, we may never know what has become of Henry Jekyll!"

Dracula dropped Hyde to the hard floor like a twitching ragdoll, red eyes blazing like lamp wicks.

Hyde started to laugh.

"Jekyll is as alive as I am, Van Helsing. Although I will admit, he is in some considerable danger."

Van Helsing got shakily to his feet, wincing at a couple cracked ribs.

"Explain yourself," he kept his revolver aimed at the wild man's heart.

"It's easier to show you, than to tell you," Hyde grinned like a gargoyle, indicating the wrapped parcel.

Van Helsing's face flushed with revulsion.

"That...that package...you didn't...you couldn't..."

"You do me credit, but you're quite wrong," Hyde smirked, ignoring the pointed pistol as he tore into the box. "Never fear, I haven't dismembered the good Dr. Jekyll. He's not in there…"

Hyde's bestial hand removed a carefully packed test tube, among several others inside the parcel. Holding it up to the gaslight, the visceral green liquid smoldered like phosphorous.

"He's in here," Hyde smirked.

Dracula loomed forward, his rapacious teeth bared.

"You dare play me for a fool?" the Count's threat was ripe with murder.

Hyde stood his ground, unflinching, before the dreadful apparition. Surprisingly, the glass vial clasped in his fingers barely trembled.

"Jekyll is going to find you particularly fascinating," he exclaimed, and abruptly swallowed the potion at a single gulp.

Count Dracula immediately sensed a difference in Hyde, an inexplicable flux in his animal scent. Van Helsing was also receptive to a sudden sensation of high strangeness within the laboratory, something akin to a discharge of ozone. Hyde's sneer grimaced into torture, pressing a hackled paw to his heart. He reeled, staggered, and a convulsive agitation contorted his dwarfish frame. Finally, he dropped to his knees, groaning in animal agony.

Van Helsing charged forward, fearful Hyde had poisoned himself. The spastic seizure increased its violence, keeping the scientist at bay, with Hyde thrashing and groaning upon the floor, swearing vile oaths between his clenched teeth, until abruptly the curses quieted to soft sobbing.

The Count noticed it first, a change was occurring in Hyde's physique. After a moment, Van Helsing observed it, too. Hyde's diminutive, disfigured frame contorted even more, swelling and bloating, filling up inside the oversized clothes. His apish features appeared to ooze and melt, bruising a livid crimson, then purple, then almost black. Slowly, with the sufferer's pained panting the only audible sound, Hyde's flesh whitened into a nearly natural hue. When he again weakly raised his head, Dracula stepped back. Van Helsing gasped in astonishment.

There, in the laboratory, the monstrous Hyde was gone and—like a man just restored from death—Dr. Jekyll stood up shakily in his place.

"Henry!" Van Helsing rushed to his friend, easing him unto a chair. "This—this is impossible!"

Jekyll, a large, ruddy fleshed, kindly-faced man in his fifties, smiled sadly. He was as unlike the feral, dwarfish Hyde as could be imagined. Remnants of pain still creased his perspiring, intelligent features.

"Forgive me, Abraham," Jekyll's voice was gentle and penitent. "To most scientists, there's no such thing as the miraculous. We know better. For you and I, everything is a miracle."

Van Helsing clasped Jekyll's trembling shoulder.

"Henry, I don't understand. That creature, Hyde...this potion... how could you dare such a risk?"

Bracing himself, Jekyll attempted to stand. Unsteady for a moment, he soon regained his balance. His nimble practiced fingers ferreted through the inner contents of the parcel, withdrawing a journal and over a dozen vials of the glowing potion.

"You knew full well exactly what I was proposing to do," Jekyll scribbled rapidly in the notebook, then turned in awe to face Count Dracula. "Successfully separating the two halves of human nature, the Good from the Evil, may be the single most benefit to the world in the history of humanity."

"But—to experiment on yourself!" Van Helsing was irate.

"Rabbits and mice cannot explain what they are feeling. Alas, it's true... I'm not as wise as you, old friend," Jekyll's eyes welled full. "The formula works, you've both seen this with your own eyes. I have every confidence that it will also succeed again, in the case of this...gentleman."

Jekyll approached the Count slowly, as one would an angry scorpion. He offered Dracula one of the vials.

"Drink this, and you'll find your soul," Jekyll stated quietly. "But, take care to heed my warning. Hyde no longer requires the potion to become himself. I...changed, somehow, without taking it, during my journey here tonight. The slightest temptation, the faintest unclean thought, and Hyde was free again."

Jekyll pressed the test tube into Dracula hand, feeling more like the appendage of a dead man, than a living one.

"After inoculating yourself," Jekyll direly cautioned, "you must avoid your inner nature, bury the devils within you at all costs. One moment of relapse, and you will lose all hope forever. Even now, as I am doomed."

Dracula deliberated on the gleaming, bubbling potion. At last, his salvation was at hand.

"To escape," he intoned.

And he drank it down.

It was true.

Count Dracula witnessed his first noontime in fifty decades, without pain and without fear. He couldn't wait inside his coffin a moment longer, risking a terrible destruction from the sunlight if Jekyll and Van Helsing's calculations had been in error. They weren't. The golden light was warm and alive upon his face, already tingeing his pallid cheeks with healthy colour.

Colour. That was a forgotten treasure. Everything was so vivid under the sun, as if touched by faerie glamour. Mighty London breathed hue and tint from his rust red cobblestones, to the billowing blue steam from the locomotives of Victoria Station. The parks were a wonderland, their trees dazzled with rich autumn rainbows of scarlet and orange and gold.

Dracula easily lost himself within the rush and flow of the great city, walking among the populous as a fellow man. The looming crucifixes and glaring stone saints of the churches instilled no further dread within him. His visions of Hell were already a nightmare to be forgotten. He felt fully alive again, and it was delicious.

Late afternoon found the Count strolling through the flower gardens of the hospital. He was to meet Van Helsing a half hour after sunset for his next inoculation, but he didn't want to think about that yet. Now ancient, haunted Transylvania and his own dark history seemed as far away and unreal as a storybook kingdom. He was determined to maintain that distance, no matter the cost.

"Good afternoon. Count Dracula, isn't it?"

He turned toward the frail, tender voice. It was Adelaide Renfield, sunning herself in a wheelchair by the fountain. She was even more weakened and wilted since the night they'd meet in the cold hospital corridor. Her colourless lips quivered with a melancholy smile, though her sightless eyes had retained their brightness and beauty.

"You honour me, young lady," Dracula bowed before her blindness.

Adelaide's smile brightened, briefly masking her illness.

"You have a most distinctive and memorable footstep, Count. Quiet as a cat. Would you keep me company for a little while? The touch of this autumn sunshine is glorious, but the whispers of the falling leaves make such a lonely sound. Don't you think?"

Dracula halted in his reply, then stepped nearer.

"I think it is unfortunate, and unjust, that one so young should entertain such melancholy notions. Such things in life should be savoured. "

Her paleness returned, blind eyes staring at nothing upon the lawn.

"Life is easier celebrated by the living," she replied, quietly.

Adelaide's face was, indeed, cast with the shadow of Death. The Count felt something gnawing and bitter in his chest, an unfamiliar and unwelcome sensation. It made him uneasy, yet he found himself oddly drawn to this sick and fading waif of a young woman.

"From birth every man and woman are cursed with the knowledge of their own mortality, Miss Renfield," Dracula responded, startled at the softness of his inflection.

She laughed, triggering a soft cough, the wet rattle muffled behind her delicate laced handkerchief. Dracula could smell blood.

"That sounds like the parish priest. I see my dear Dr. Van Helsing has not only told you my name, but has also related something of my affliction. He tells me there's only a little time left. Please don't pity me. Odd as it sounds, I'm not afraid of death. Of dying, though…well, that is a different matter entirely. The nuns often read to me of sonnets and romances and of things worth dying for. Such philosophies often seem trite and silly to someone with my fate, but I am not absolutely averse to the poetic. For myself, I wouldn't mind dying a thousand times, if I could only…well, they say if you speak a wish aloud it may not ever come true. So, I do have some hope left, you see."

"They do not know everything, Miss Renfield. Neither physicians nor philosophers," Dracula said, growing uneasy in the presence of this gentle, dying lady.

The sweet, rotted smell from her diseased lungs reminded him of the battlefield.

"Your eloquent command of our language is quite beautiful, Count. Tell me about your own country. Do you miss it? It is very different from England?"

His mind flashed back from the clamour of war and mixed with a myriad of weary, grey memories, most of them bearing much too sharp an edge to revisit for long. It was astonishing, though, how much he suddenly remembered, enough to have filled the lives of a dozen men. This was not a place where he wished to linger.

"It was worth dying for," he said with a pressed finality.

Gently, Adelaide's hand reached out and lightly found the folds of his cloak.

She sat in silence, losing all expression for some minutes. The sunlight had softened, drifting closer to evening. Finally, Adelaide smiled briefly, as if at some private humour, and then quietly wept into her hands.

Dracula's only response was to lightly touch Adelaide's tearful cheek, without knowing why. It had been instinctive, irrational. Suddenly, it had become unfathomably difficult to look at her. Why did her sadness cause him such pain? She caught hold of his hand before he could withdraw it.

"Forgive me, for such a display…I know what that is like to be so alone," she offered.

Adelaide had always seen the world with her hands, rising up, she caressed his face from jaw to temple. Dracula said nothing, but did not pull away. Her supple smile dropped in puzzlement.

"You are certainly an enigma, Count Dracula," she murmured. "I would have sworn you to be a much younger man."

At that, the Count sprang back with such a sudden violence that the blind girl was flung to the ground. An appalled glance at his own hands confirmed his horror. Adelaide cried out, groping the air helplessly. Two muscular attendants rushed to her aid. Dracula fled, sending them reeling like broken puppets.

The sun sank, lengthening soft grey shadows to deep purple-black. The London streets crammed with rushing life, increasing their claustrophobia, swelling intolerably. Nearly every passerby startled and stared at him. Many cried out. Something had gone hideously wrong.

A street woman and her asthmatic client hastily covered themselves, running for their lives as Dracula lurched into their lampless alley. Groping at his face with withered hands, he frantically felt the wizened reality of his own flesh. There he stood, frozen with the terror of it, haunting the alley as an ancient mummified apparition, garbed in black.

"Van Helssssssssing…" Dracula sounded more reptile than man, seething with rage.

He burned for revenge, for hot red blood. Hell called to him from the abyss.

And he answered it.

Adelaide Renfield slept fitfully, breathing in shallow searing wisps. A liquid, muffled cough tasted of warm salty blood. Cloud-blotted moonlight shrouded the little chamber in deeper darkness, the blooming fever gripping the girl like a burning-then-freezing tomb. She dreamt of delicious Death, finding it sweet.

Instantly, Adelaide was awake and sitting up.

"What did you say?" she whispered, half-hoping the dream was real.

No other sounds at first, only a fetid draft drifting about her. Adelaide was certain the window had remained closed as her life-long lack of sight had finely honed her sensitive ears. It didn't make sense. Dreams seldom do.

Then, she heard it again, the noise that must've awakened her, a supple scrape upon the window as if from a cat's paw. Real and pressing, a whispered Voice pushed into her mind, the soft chafing continued upon the pane.

"Who's there? Who are you?" Adelaide's moist brow creased, straining to understand the language, or languages, that pulsed against her brain.

Phantom words hummed a soothing rhythm inside the girl, promising her things. Forbidden. Impossible. Yet, Adelaide so wanted to believe.

"Yes…it hurts. It hurts so much," tears began to bud in her unseeing, fever-bright eyes.

Adelaide tilted her head, listening. The Voice moved closer, became clearer, drawing substance from the wind and moonlight, becoming real.

"Please," she wept, no longer alone. "Please…help me."

Her purpled lips slowly smiled. Clasping the delicate chain about her neck, Adelaide wrenched the crucifix away. She had let him in.

A sudden creak of the floorboards announced the new presence. Not the tread of someone walking, but rather the inexplicable mass of a man instantly before her. Sharp-nailed hands caressed Adelaide's cheek, stroking her sweat-streaked hair. Feeling the mattress slowly sink, an inky weight mounted her, holding her, feeling her. Adelaide could no longer speak, could scarcely breathe.

Then, something cold and wet and sharp fastened to her throat.

Adelaide moaned softly from the twin sting, not unlike the steely prick of a hypodermic, and then the hurt left her. A hot ribbon of wetness snaked from her neck down to her shuddering bosom. Blood. She was bleeding. She was not alarmed, feeling a sense of relief, the release of long-captured pressure finally freed.

The girl panted in short cutting breaths, but there was no pain. Small flailing hands sought something of the countenance of her unknown lover. Sensitive fingertips painted a strong, a very strong face, gliding over the firm jaw and down the sharp predatory nose, revealing to her mind's eye the sensual, grimacing living mask. She was reminded of someone, but he had been old. Not so this daemon lover, gaining youth and vitality as he drank her in.

Adelaide's thighs pressed together, undulating with each pounding pulse of her heart. Her lungs sucked and strained. Still, there was no pain.

It was a miracle, or a delirious dream. She didn't care which.

Her syrupy sweetness freely flowed into the hungry mouth at the nap of her neck, probing and pulling. She bit into her lower lip, tasting herself, growing drunk and numb with the richness of it. The Blood. The Blood is the Life.

She told him things, hissed and whispered secrets. Buried desires, resurrected. Where to touch her. Wild, wild wishes.

He promised all of it.

Wispy sensations of a feathery tingling spider-crawled its way from her curled toes, across her belly, to the dampness between her breasts. Adelaide's head pitched side to side, her ankles locking around her lover, holding him close.

Something flashed inside her head, livid and fiery. Two distant smoldering embers swelled behind the darkness of her wet, tightly clenched lids. The red spots burned brighter, closer. They became eyes, and a ghostly white face emerged through the shadows of her blindness. The strong aquiline face was there before her, more vivid than ever. The glowering eyes fixed upon her. Adelaide's heart pounded harder, her ragged lungs gasped.

She could see him!

Dracula continued to emerge from her darkness. Finally, in the space of a few practiced blinks, the Count was revealed in all his grotesque, majestic glory. The ghastly face. The dark, dripping mouth. The scarlet animal eyes.

Never could Adelaide have imagined anything more beautiful.

"Blood of my blood," the Count spoke in a low voice sounding almost human. "There is no Death for you."

His writhing hands opened the front of his frockcoat, the white of his dress-shirt stung Adelaide's new eyes like smoldering phosphorus. She watched in rapt fascination as Dracula's sharp, horned nails opened the blued flesh of his bristling chest.

"Take from me. Take..." the vampire sighed, the shining eyes rolling back.

Adelaide kissed the loathsome wounds, nausea burning in her belly. The sticky flow spilled down her throat, chilling her as she nursed and pulled with her raw, stinging tongue.

It was done.

The bed suddenly sprung back to its original mold, the added weight of her lover had vanished like a shadow of smoke.

Adelaide touched the tiny dead-white wounds on her throat and smiled, crossing her hands over her heart, feeling it slow and then stop. She breathed no more. Her dead eyes shone brightly, starved from their darkness.

She'd seen her saviour, actually had seen him, with her own eyes, just as the door burst open with blinding lamplight.

"Mein Gott...what have I done...?" Dr. Van Helsing shuddered, seeing the bed red with blood.

Dracula loomed up from the darkness.

"Behold, Van Helsing...look what your prayers and your potions have done to me. There is no hope, only the blood. The blood is the life."

The room was ripe with Death. The Vampire King circled the scientist, ravenous for vengeance, blocking any possible avenue of escape. Red-tinged mist laced the atmosphere of the little chamber, snakish ribbons of daemonic breath hissed in monstrous fury. The battleground was drawn.

Van Helsing's reflexes were excellent, but there was no time to plan, to prepare. Already Dracula was upon him. The scientist swung the weighted lantern like a hammer, but nothing touched the monster and the makeshift weapon clamoured to the floor. The Count appeared to vanish, then suddenly his blackness filled the room. Part shadow, part man, part creature, he was everywhere and nowhere at once. How could Van Helsing hope to fight him?

Abruptly, he was trapped in the vampire's iron grip, suspended from the floor, drawn closer to the deadly dripping mouth.

"Pitiful fool," Dracula snarled, "You tremble as a lamb led to the slaughter. Where is your god to save you? He has forsaken you, as well."

At that, Van Helsing was hurled into a corner, effortlessly as a bundle of empty garments. The Count loomed, glowering over him.

"I am not going to kill you, Van Helsing. Not yet. You will live to see the fruits of your failure. It is impossible to stop me. Your colleagues, your police, none will believe you. Unlike the bee, I do not die after a single sting, but grow stronger. Your fate is to be what you are, just as mine is to be what I…am."

There must be a way out, the scientist reasoned when hurried prayers were left unanswered. He must think, and dull the fear. Think!

Then, Van Helsing saw it, a glimmer of hope. The glow from his fallen lantern sparkled off a small object near the edge of the death-bed.

It was the silver crucifix he himself had given the victim, for protection. It would protect him now.

"In a century, when you are dust, I will rise with my disciples to claim your world…" Dracula stalked closer.

Van Helsing spun quickly, grasping the lantern and opened its shutter wide. The resultant effect was nothing short of miraculous . The mirror image of the tiny cross expanded into a massive gleaming reflection, engulfing Count Dracula whole, bursting into a blazing inferno.

The fiery cloak thrashed and swelled, the vampire's awful livid face blistering from chalk to blackened crimson. Dracula's scream of rage would haunt Van Helsing's nightmares for countless fitful nights to come.

"My revenge will span the centuries!"

Window glass shattered and the roaring inferno of the monster leaped into the night, a living, shrieking comet.

Retrieving the little crucifix, Van Helsing struggled to stand. The silver cross felt cool and real in his hand. He gazed at Adelaide, heaped in a lifeless tangle of red-streaked bedding.

In attempting to redeem the monster, Dracula, the scientist had wrought nothing but despair and destruction upon the innocent and the unaware. His mind burned with the weight of what he had done.

And, what he had failed to do.

Van Helsing wept.

ENCORE

THREE nights later, Van Helsing waited in the secluded churchyard. Daylight was breaking, casting its pinkish pallet against the cold, grey tombstones. The coroner, the priest, and the funeral…he couldn't be alone with her till now. To do what must be done. It wouldn't be long now.

The scientist had aged considerably, still not completely recovered from the horrifying events of seventy-two hours before. He doubted he ever would be the same. The whole world had changed.

The horizon brightened, shadows diming, losing something of their meandering menace. Cold and shivering, Van Helsing kept watch at the new grave, unnaturally disturbed from the evening before. Suddenly, the scientist broke into a cold sweat.

He heard it. The gentle pad of delicate, naked feet whispering among fallen leaves as the crickets fell silent. It was time, at last.

Adelaide Renfield had returned.

"My dear Doctor," she smiled with sharp white teeth. "I knew you'd come to say good-bye."

She was a dreadful apparition, still shrouded in a funeral gown already wet and red with the ravaged blood of her first night. Van Helsing avoided her eyes which were no longer blind, now alive and seething with unholy fire.

All that blood. The scientist didn't dare to imagine where it had come from. No matter. She would spill no more. He tightened his grip on the meter-long oaken stake, its sharpened tip charred and hardened as the point of an iron spear.

"My failure cost you more than your life, Miss Adelaide," Van Helsing said, with pronounced remorse. "Yet I can save your soul."

Suddenly, Renfield rushed Van Helsing from behind, striking him to the earth.

"No!" he screamed, his strangle-grip tightening. "Don't you see? He gave her back to me! She will live forever!"

The scientist fought back, straining against the madman's maniacal strength.

"Renfield…Renfield, you must listen…this is not the daughter you loved…!" Van Helsing struggled through gritted teeth, using the stake as a club.

Renfield crumpled, stunned among the grave-dirt. Van Helsing was astounded to discover Adelaide still among them.

It was already sunrise.

"You may do what you like with my soul, Dr. Van Helsing," the woman said. "I have no further use for it. I've seen all I want of this world."

Adelaide stood her ground, fearlessly facing the eastern sky.

"Some things," she serenely closed her eyes, "are worth dying for."

The rising sun's beckoning brilliance bathed her like a roaring furnace, flesh melting away. In the flash of a heartbeat she was gone, a gentle morning breeze caressing the ashes.

Renfield had crawled to the grave, searching pitifully through the empty shroud.

"My hopes…all my prayers…all gone. Nothing left but death. It…it is the end of everything," cried Renfield, his mind darkening ever deeper into madness.

"Not so," Van Helsing answered, sensing a low, rumbling laughter from an approaching storm.

"This is merely the beginning."

To my dear friend, Jenny Dalton.
Poet, musician, and mystic.

Bring Out Your Dead

by L.A. Banks

New Orleans… present day

CHRISTIAN stared down into his wine glass watching the merlot and blood mixture within it separate. Tendrils of the lighter alcohol substance struggled for freedom against the rich, dense thickness of human blood. Wasn't that the way of life and death; it all came down to being trapped by the blood?

Morose, not even the jubilant sounds wafting across his senses from the French Quarter bar could stir him from his decision to remain in a foul temper. He hated this era. There was no more civility left on the planet, and most assuredly not where he was now.

He peered around, wishing for a diversion. But acute loneliness claimed him instead. Another night of dining alone—so many slayers had thinned his kind, it was genocide. Modern day hunters were an abomination, no less than the plague or influenza outbreaks of his era, when the dead wagon drivers would walk the streets yelling, "Bring out your dead," and all of London… or New Orleans, as the case may be, would comply.

Then a damned hurricane with a lovely woman's name opened all caskets to daylight and the ravages of water giving humans back their city and driving the supernatural elements away. It was an outrage! Only a few of the local coven had survived the madness, living in unthinkable conditions until the waters receded. He shuddered, remembering what he'd had to consume for the duration until things had gotten back to what the humans called normal. There was no such fantasy called "normal" ever to be had again. These deplorable conditions had driven some of his brethren mad, to be sure.

Slightly tipsy, Christian sat back, petulant, wondering if it would be worth it to attempt to vote and rig a human election. He was fairly certain he could influence the sway of human cattle to pull a lever in one direction or another, or push a button on an electronic machine, although he never meddled in human affairs. Yet this time he felt utterly compelled. However, the bedeviling problem was, he didn't have a clear choice in the local election. New Orleans was still, in his estimation, a political cesspool. The rat bastard politicians were pure thieves, scoundrels; the levees never should have broken! It was a travesty that went far beyond his beloved hometown.

The ineptitude that followed the disaster had been unspeakable. Like all things, it had changed his world, changed New Orleans in a way nothing else had. Was not the only thing one could count on in this modern era the so-called technology? If a being had to accept the loss of civility and grace, then at least the modern marvels should have made the loss of basic dignity worth it all!

Christian released a harsh sigh, worrying over all the minute changes in history he'd seen like a dog worries a bone. The other changes were more gradual and easy to accept, but the flooding of New Orleans this last time just simply stuck in his craw. The entire era was intolerable.

And he hated so-called modern clothes.

However, a diversion to his morbid introspection flounced through the door causing him to arch an eyebrow.

Indeed, she was one of his kind; he was old enough to know that upon immediate inspection, but she was newly made. He released a weary sigh. Goth. From a sidelong glance hidden deep within the shadows he took in her outfit, not willing to call them clothes. She wore big black combat boots upon what he was sure were shapely feet and lovely legs, giving her a Frankenstein appeal. He shook his head. Hands clad in fishnet black gloves with the fingers of them shorn off and black nail polish. She was already the undead, in this instance less was more. Black lipstick covering what was a cherub's heart-shaped mouth—one that would have been lovely pink and naked. A handsome figure influenced by a black leather corset over a ripped sleeveless white shirt and a red bra strap hanging... now that was intriguing... and long, lovely legs shirted by plaid, mini kilt material held together with safety pins.

Finally she spied him and smiled, not bothering to even retract her fangs. He frowned. Some things just weren't done in public amid the humans. Oddly, none of them seemed to mind.

"Hey!" she said too loudly, rushing over and plopping down at his table without as much as an invitation.

"Good evening, Mademoiselle," he replied in a smooth croon, sipping his wine and looking at the way she'd turned a chair around backwards to straddle it like a Western gunfighter. "You're new."

"Yep! How cool is that?"

She beamed at him, giving him the most dazzling fanged smiled he'd seen in a long time. Her eyes were an interesting cross between slightly glowing amber and green. For a moment he studied the subtle hue variations of amber, gold, red, and brunette in her lush, auburn hair. Yes, she was very new.

He glanced around the bar and then sent his gaze mentally out to the restaurant. "So new and your maker has abandoned you to your own devices for the evening?"

"That lousy sonofabitch bit me and then, *poof*, he was out. Left me to die in a fucking bathroom at a rave and never came back. *I could have died*, ya know. I mean, like, if I hadn't come to and stumbled into a stall to throw up before I passed out, I mighta gotten fried—if somebody had called an ambulance. Then I would have been in a hospital bed near a window or something—too crazy. But since they didn't clean the bathroom and there wasn't any window, I just stayed there on the floor all day, and it wasn't until the next night, tonight, that I woke up—talk about a hangover. And I was sooo hungry, it was pathetic. I'm starved now, ya know."

She stared at him with a hopeful expression and then began fidgeting with a stray wisp of hair that bothered her cheek.

"Never at a loss for words, either, I see," he said with a half smile. "But it is shocking how you were brought into the life. That I will grant you."

"It was fucking unrighteous!" she said, slapping the table.

"Mademoiselle, your mouth is way too beautiful to be filled with profanities, might I suggest—"

"What? That I suck your dick? Give me a break." She tossed her hair over her shoulder and then fidgeted with a black rubber band that was on her wrist, snatching her long tresses up into a lopsided ponytail that oddly suited her.

He had to smile. "No, I wouldn't allow that until you've learned to control your fangs. Darling, they are showing—in public."

"Can I get a drink at least, then?" she snapped, clearly peeved. "It doesn't matter. Regular people wear them all the time. They have shops that sell the real McCoy, porcelain ones... you can get vamp type, demon type, werewolf, whatever. People aren't scared of us showing a little fang. So what?"

"What do you drink?" he asked, taking in her words. What she said was true. There wasn't the shock and rarely the awe of anything that seemed supernatural these days. It was all so clichéd that it had become boring. That was part of his disenchantment with the era, if he were to be honest with himself.

"A vodka martini, under these circumstances."

He nodded and called over a waitress, placing the order before dismissing her and noticing how the young woman before him cringed.

"Hungry?" He stared at his new companion.

She nodded, tears filling her eyes. "Yeah. I already told you that. But every time I try to eat, I throw up."

"He didn't feed you, either, I take it? Not even a sustaining suckle?"

She shook her head no and bit her lip.

"Well, you said you woke up at one of those ghastly human entertainment establishments... I'm sure the wait staff or the—"

"No!" She covered her face with her hands as a few people looked around and briefly stared at them. "I didn't want to do to somebody else what had been done to me."

"Oh, for crying out loud—a vampire with a conscious." Christian let out another weary breath and pushed his merlot across the table toward her, watching her snatch the glass, almost spilling the contents as she greedily consumed what was left it.

"And you don't have a conscious?" she asked, panting as she wiped her mouth with the back of her wrist.

"Hardly, *mon cheri*. I am an equal opportunity feeder."

"Bull shit. I bet you wouldn't have just made someone and then left them without teaching them anything.... Would you?" She stared at him, her eyes seeking answers he wasn't sure he had.

"*Non*," he finally said. "I do not feed on the very young ones or the ones who have a life... family. I pick from the human leave-behinds, this way, no one's life is impacted very much... and I don't let mine wake up. To make one of us is an honor; to be one of us is a privilege. Some have forgotten the old ways, in their famine, I suppose."

"That's how I thought it was supposed to be," she said quietly. "A code of honor... like a little chivalry, as corny as that sounds. So, when we went into the bathroom together, I knew we weren't going to have sex... I knew what he was, could tell—read everything about vampires, ya know. I was so excited. I had seen him there night after night, and he'd seen me... and we had danced and talked and I thought I was something special to him. And when I figured out what he really was, could sorta tell, you know... when he asked me to go with him, I did. I wasn't scared." She shrugged and let out a huff of breath. "My life was shit, anyway... and then, he dumped me, just like a real asshole. Maybe he thought I was dead and was gonna do me like a *leave behind*."

She shivered and rubbed her upper arms as though staving off an internal chill. It saddened him to see her beautiful eyes moisten. From out of nowhere his voice spoke words that had not been sanctioned by his mind.

"You are not a leave behind. Never consider yourself that. You are young and vital and should have been allowed to flourish in your human state."

Her martini came and he covered her hand, waiting until the server had left their table. He took the glass and quietly slit his wrist with a fingernail, allowing his blood to darken her drink. "So you won't get sick, *cheri*."

"See… that bastard never told me any of that, or how to fly, or how to disappear, or any of the cool stuff. He just didn't care."

"How old are you?" he asked, becoming more upset than was warranted. She was just a stay, an abandoned *made* that was left to her own devices and certainly not his problem.

"I was… well, I guess I'm still eighteen? Will be that forever, now," she said with a sad smile. "Last night was my birthday. So do I refer to myself in the past tense or present tense, since I guess I'm really dead?"

Aghast, he sat back and watched her slurp her drink. "Might I examine your bite wound?" he asked carefully, unspent rage kindling. He wanted to know who'd done this within his territory—what aristocratic bastard had been so sloppy.

She shrugged. "It disappeared when I woke up. I couldn't see myself in a mirror to tell, but I couldn't feel it. So I think it's gone."

"I can see it," he said quietly. "The humans can't; we older members of the society can look beneath the illusion when we want to. Don't worry, you're lovely on the surface," he added as she self-consciously covered her neck with a palm.

When she relaxed, he leaned in, carefully assessing everything about her, drinking in impressions of her more than was necessary for the routine information he'd requested.

She smelled of French milled soap, and her clothes were freshly laundered. She didn't smell like a bathroom stall in the least, nor was there evidence of vomit on her clothing or breath. He lingered at her throat, truly understanding his competitor's dilemma… but, still, he wouldn't have made her. Sexed her, yes. Fed from her, probably. Killed her? Most assuredly not. Turned her into the undead, no.

"I know your maker," he said in a low, sensual murmur. "I will speak to Guillaume about this affront. His behavior toward you was unnecessary and inappropriate."

"So, you'll kick his ass?" A rush of anticipation filled her eyes and tugged on his groin.

"Hardly, Mademoiselle. We will discuss it like gentlemen."

"You seem like you could kick his ass if you wanted to," she said brightly, polishing off her drink with flourish.

Something irrational and completely male now tugged at his reason. "I could."

"See, I knew it," she said, sitting back with a smile.

For the first time since she'd sat, he noticed she had on red panties. The wide-legged stride about the chair left nothing to the imagination.

"How old are you, really?" she asked, toying with her empty glass.

"Old enough to mind my own affairs, *cheri*—and this dispute you have with Guillaume is truly none of my business... but I can inquire about his motives. Perhaps he'd, in his haste, meant to leave you for dead."

"Oh, nice," she said, eyes now blazing greener.

For some odd reason, he didn't want her wrath, and much preferred her awe.

"I bet that's why your sorry ass is sitting in a bar all alone!"

He stared at her for a moment, watching her jugular raise to the surface of her porcelain skin as she fumed.

"Once you've seen a couple of centuries pass, you'll pick your battles more wisely, *cheri*—trust me on this."

Outrage became instant awe. "A couple of *centuries*? Wow..."

Her whisper felt like a purr petting his shaft.

"Then you really could kick that guy's ass, couldn't you? I mean, like, in vampire oldest-equals-stronger terms, right?"

He nodded. It had been a very long time since he'd encountered a newfoundling, much less one so pretty that had been horribly abandoned. Based upon Ducal rights within his territory, in any event, he could claim her. But what was he thinking? Commitments for him had died out with several mates being staked. He didn't engage in such fantasies any longer. It was bad for the heart.

He watched her lace her pretty fingers together under her chin as she stared at him. "What do you want from me?" he finally asked in earnest.

"Everything," she said calmly. "I got this immortality and it would literally suck to just hang out alone. Like, I wanna learn what's possible."

He closed his eyes and groaned. "I do *not* need a disciple... even one who smells as lovely as you do."

"I bathed!" she said, taking offense and then sniffing her underarms to be sure. "I stole new clothes from the store and hid in a hotel, and used all their soaps and creams. I won't keep smelling like I did when I died, will

I?" she asked seeming horrified. New tears brimmed and then fell down her cheeks when he didn't immediately answer. "I brushed my teeth and—"

"Shush, shush, calm yourself, *cheri*. I meant it as a compliment. You smell divine, and your skin is magnificent," he said, allowing a thumb to brush her cheek, taking mascara stain across it. Then he showed her his thumb to make her smile.

"I must look like a raccoon."

He nodded and leaned forward and kissed the tip of her nose. "I can fix that. We have to be each other's mirrors until we learn the magic of being our own."

She nodded. "Then how did you manage to look so good—or is it the same way in death as in life—guys just have to take a shower, finger comb their hair, and that's it?"

Another half smile pulled at his cheek. "It's been so long since I've seen myself that I guess I never gave it much thought."

"You've got dark, shoulder-length brown hair… the clearest blue eyes I've seen in my life… good jaw, strong nose. You were killed in your prime, dude—that I can tell… like twenty-five-ish, right?"

"I was considered at mid-life in that era," he said, inwardly pleased that she liked his appearance.

"Well you're also tall… great shoulders and fab body," she said, openly appraising him. "Not my style of clothes, though—the silk shirt and designer pants…or the leather slip-ons—too Beverly Hills rich-boy, but it's a look."

"*Merci*, I think," he said, chuckling. "We will agree to disagree about styles, then. But without clothes, does that matter?"

It was her turn to smile. "So, you do wanna be my boyfriend, then?"

"Let us take one step at a time."

"Oh, I get it, you wanna screw but not commit? That's cool—as long as it's out in the open."

He wrinkled his nose. "Mademoiselle, why *must* you always make things sound so… so—"

"Real?"

"I was searching for a word but not sure that was the one I was looking for."

"I'm just honest."

He nodded and then leaned forward to wipe the black lipstick from her mouth with a white linen napkin. "And that's perhaps the most refreshing thing I've encountered this evening."

"Why'd you do that?" she said quietly as he continued to clean her smudged makeup off her face.

"Because you're beautiful and don't have to hide behind garish makeup."

"It's a style," she said, slapping away his hand in protest.

"Someone will miss you," he said sadly, changing the subject, but continuing to wipe away the offending makeup. "Who did you leave behind in the living world?"

"A Mom strung out on meth, who doesn't know me or even who the hell she is half the time, and a dad I never knew… a trailer park of so-called friends and neighbors. Nobody will miss me." She let out a sad laugh. "I came down here from Memphis because of what I'd heard about Mardi Gras, and look what happened. If anybody cares, which they don't, they'll just list me as a runaway, since that was my thing before… always running away, guaranteed once a year."

He stood, needing to move before a section of his heart collapsed for her. "Then you are lucky, fortunate," he said, extending his elbow to her as he rounded the table. "I left many who wept, and spying on them until they each perished from the human condition takes a lot out of you, trust me."

"Where are we going?" she asked in a low, trusting murmur, standing and then taking his elbow to allow him to escort her out of the bar.

He flung a hundred dollar bill onto the waitress's tray and waved her away as she asked if he needed change.

"We are going to where you can feed in private… and then maybe somewhere we can enjoy the rest of the evening."

"Your place?" she said, looking up to him with innocence.

"No, since you wanted to be out in the open," he said teasing her.

"I meant up front, you know, straight, about what this was," she said, scowling.

He knew what she'd meant and delighted in attempting to broaden her horizons to the use of word games, double intendre, and subtlety that was an old vampire trait.

"I thought you might like to go out for your first encounter with the new world, seeing it all through your new eyes. Therefore, Mademoiselle, I thought you might enjoy a small park that is gorgeous under the skirt of the full moon… replete with a hundred year old carousel, albeit most of the humans have gone for the evening."

"So you aren't gonna make me pay you back for the thing you did with your wrist?" She stopped walking and stared up at him.

"Your body is beautiful, but after the way you were made, you deserve to decide, at least, when you want to share that and with whom. I am not in the habit of making a woman a blood prostitute."

Her quizzical look haunted him as they resumed walking.

"A woman who would sleep with me because I can feed her. That is like having a pet, a dog. I don't want that around me any longer."

"You had them before, though."

He looked away and sent his gaze ahead of them, sweeping for potential food prospects. "I was young and impetuous, like Guillaume, then. This is why I won't exterminate him, but will chide him regarding his excesses."

"Oh," she murmured, leaning against him. "I don't want to kill people… but don't want to end up like LeStat—eating rats."

He chuckled. "LeStat, and his impoverished end in the human bowery, is fiction."

She stopped walking, ignoring the pedestrians that passed them. "Noooo freakin' way!"

"Born of the creative genius of Anne Rice."

"Seriously? I thought he was like an urban legend—like she had channeled that!"

He bit the insides of his cheeks to keep from laughing. "*Non.* Pure fiction. But I will show you some really *cool*, as you say, *stuff*, to keep you from harming humans. You can feed on those willing, and not turn them… they wake up feeling like they've had the flu on the first morning after, but then that evening, they experience an unparalleled high after that. We have willing donors within our human vampire community. There is an underground, you must become privy to… and when we must feed, there are different levels of bites. You do not have to murder or turn a source to eat well…blast Guillaume; there is so much to teach that he is responsible for!"

Stopping by a bench deep within the park, he bade her to sit beside him. He looked up at the moon and then released a sad sigh. The werewolves would be out in full hunt, and the slayers would be turning over graves, but this woman-child beside him had to feed. He could feel hunger still clawing at her insides, even though she wasn't his. It was the waif look in her eyes that did him in, seeming as though she might not have ever really had a satisfying or decent meal in her entire short life.

Threading his fingers through her silky hair he studied her face and her wide, pretty eyes. "I want you to break the skin at the jugular and take until you feel the burn begin to subside, then pull back. It is a sensual act to let another have your throat… but I do not feel you deserve to be treated as an underling, given all that you've endured. Thus, I will allow this, and not feed you from my wrist. But when you're done, I will teach you protocols, *oui*?"

"Okay," she whispered, her gaze searching his. "But, I'm scared." She bit her lip as her fangs lowered quickly, the anticipation making her entire body tremble. "Drinking a little blood from a glass was one thing, but biting somebody…"

"Will be the most sensual act of feeding you will ever experience. The method of taking sustenance, in and unto itself, is addictive."

"I ran from the club, past all the people, to where I felt a presence—I can't explain it. I thought you were the guy who bit me, but I'm so glad you weren't."

"You were homing to one of us. An older one of us. Natural instinct of the newly made… like the survival instinct of a baby that knows to cry to be fed. With all the slayers about, we try to find our own for the first feeding."

"Does that mean I'm yours?" she asked, wetting her lips and closing her eyes.

It did, but he couldn't answer. It had been so long since he'd had a first feeder that passion strangled the words in his throat. With a gallant shrug, he made his hair cascade over his shoulder, exposing his neck, and then held his breath as her dainty face neared his.

Her bite was so swift and so savage that he groaned out loud. Fully embracing her to appear to passers-by as enamored lovers, he tried not to arch beneath her siphon. But each pull of her suckle not only dredged his vein but also pulled pleasure up his shaft and through his sac until he had to force her away, panting.

"*Cheri*, I—"

She took his mouth and climbed onto his lap, moving forcefully as she bit him again and began drinking. He didn't care that they were out on a park bench or that humans might see. *Shit*, this was New Orleans, and it had been so long since he'd felt so free… so alive.

"I don't even know your name and this feels so damned good," she gasped, unzipping his pants as she found his jugular vein again.

Public displays of affection had never been his thing, as a gentleman, and here this newfoundling was taxing every bit of his aristocratic reserve. The creamy globes of her ass were in his hands beneath her short skirt. People, humans, strolled by with a smirk… her panties were a thin crimson line easily pushed aside, and the things she was doing to his throat…

"Christian," he managed to choke out between thrusts.

"You're a Christian?" she said on a heavy exhale and then stopped moving. "Oh, shit, my bad!"

He shook his head no, and then bit her, causing her to cry out as a hard orgasm made her clench her teeth. "No. That's my name," he murmured more calmly, and then chuckled. "I haven't been one of those in a lot of years."

"Deep," she said gasping.

He obliged her.

"No. I meant, deep as in *profound*," she said laughing through puffs of breath. "But that did feel really, *really* good."

Winded, they both laughed.

"We are going to have to work on our communication. Tell me your name, *cheri*."

"Deb… and my screen name is Batgirl, but I like *cheri* better."

"Batgirl?" All he could do was stare at her. What the hell sort of name…

She laughed and kissed him quickly, extricating herself from him with a moan and making him gasp. "That was *totally* awesome. Have you ever cum that hard before?"

"A gentleman never kisses and tells," he said, zippering his pants and buckling his belt before sheepishly glancing around. Truthfully it had been since forever, but she didn't need to know that. "Suffice to say that there are many things from our realms that I can teach you that you might find *cool*."

Oddly, he felt expectant and hopeful that she'd want to be his companion at least for a little while. He was looking forward to teaching her things, going exploring with her, using her newfound excitement as a way to crack the jaded seal that had been blinding his era-dulled eyes. The night was glorious and she was radiant.

"I have a lot of things I could teach you, too, ya know." Her smile was infectious. "So, am I your girlfriend, or what? Just because we did it, I don't want you to think I'm some kinda blood ho. I'm not. I really like you. In fact, even without the blood, I really wanna do it again… if you want to."

He smiled back at her and took her mouth slowly, wondering how to get her corset off in public without arrest, and having no doubt that she might just be the one to help him make his peace with the twenty-first century.

But now that she'd drained him, he had to eat.

"There is an establishment we can go to, not far from here," he said, avoiding her question. "They have excellent music, premixed merlots, and a wonderful variety of entertainment."

"Like on a date?" Her smile widened as she plopped next to him on the bench.

"An outing, of sorts… would you like that?"

Her smile contained a level of warmth that his nights of pure debauchery never seemed to offer.

"Well, yeah," she said and then began picking at her fishnet gloves. "I'd like to go check it out, if you wanna."

"I say we shall," he murmured, kissing the place on her neck that he'd bitten to staunch the slow ooze of blood.

But as he stood, the hair on the back of his neck bristled, and she got to her feet slowly.

"What is it?" she whispered, glancing around nervously.

Within seconds he pulled her into the nothingness and then back out again as a huge wolf parted the shrubbery with a snarl.

"It's the full moon," he said flatly. "We should go to Delilah's Den for the evening and allow this fellow his hunting grounds. The last thing I want to encounter while out with a lady is a brawl with one of those beasts."

She just stared for a moment at the stalking creature, hang-jawed. "Get *out*... an *actual* frickin' werewolf?"

"*Oui*," he said, pulling her into a vaporous escape and landing her in the parking lot of the establishment that was five miles away.

"Whoa!" She spun around laughing and patting down her body. "How *cool* was *that*! Sweet!"

"You have no idea what those terrible beasts can do, *cheri*. They can rip off your face, tear off a limb—"

"—But we can regenerate, right?"

Christian let out a weary sigh. "*Oui*. But you must endure the pain, be sure that you have the strength to crawl to darkness where you will not be discovered during daylight hours, and hope that you can feed yourself or that one of your own with mercy will find you and feed you well so that you can heal... and for territorial males, being left so vulnerable is an invitation to a coup. It is not a trivial matter, *cheri*."

"Wow," she said, hugging herself. "I never thought of all of that... and, yeah, I could see how some low life dude might try to take you out while you were already in bad shape. That's really foul."

He smiled, loving her possessive stance. "It is the way of the vampire— absolute power corrupts absolutely."

"Well, *I've* got your back."

For a moment he just stared at her, knowing that she'd truly meant what she'd said with all her heart.

"Then maybe before we go inside, I should teach you the first lesson in the art of escape and detection."

She glanced around at the patrons coming and going and the surrounding trees and shrubbery.

"Don't worry," he said, amused. "No werewolf would dare come within a quarter mile of this establishment filled with old members of the society… and with human bouncers possessing sawed-off shot guns loaded with silver shells. Not even on a full moon, *cheri*."

"Okay, I'm impressed," she said with a wide smile, visibly relaxing.

"*Tres bon*." He disappeared and watched her spin around searching for him. "Follow my voice," he said as a ruse, throwing his voice in one direction while he alighted on a high tree branch behind her.

Making a little tsking noise of displeasure, he finally allowed himself be seen, smiling as she whirled around.

"You threw your voice!"

"But of course I did. My objective was to beguile you regarding my whereabouts. Yet you should have still detected me."

"How?"

"You can see like a bat, in three hundred and sixty degrees, true?"

She opened her mouth and then closed it as he came out of the tree to materialize from the mist before her.

"You aren't letting go of the human habits. Open yourself to the night, let it run through your hair, through your veins, and just *think* about what you want to do. Train your mind to be still for a moment, focus, then become."

"No fair. You still would have been invisible," she argued, crossing her arms over her chest. "How would I have seen you?"

"*Oui*, but the branch and the leaves that my body disturbed still would have moved. That was your point of detection."

She allowed her arms to fall by her sides, captivated. "Now that is awesome."

Pleased, he inclined his head. "Try it once. Close your eyes and feel yourself drifting as though mist, and then will yourself to become nothingness. You should pass over those fallen leaves as silently as the night breeze."

He waited, watching, mesmerized as she began to slowly fade and drift off from him by a few feet. When she opened her eyes he clapped.

"Bravo!" he exclaimed, feeling a rare rush of excitement.

"Did I disappear? Did I do it?"

"Yes, *cheri*! *Oui, tres bon, tres, tres bon*!" he said, laughing and grabbing her up to swing her around for a moment. "Now do it with your eyes open."

"Kinky like, huh?" She offered him a sexy pout and then laughed.

"Absolutely the way I like it," he said with a low chuckle.

"Now you're making it hard to concentrate."

It was a high compliment that she'd offered him and he cherished it for the jewel that it was. "You will become a student of physical science as we try new things, and over time, you'll learn how to master the elements around you. Then—"

Slow applause interrupted his lesson. Annoyed, he spun on the intruder, losing his battle to hold back his fangs. Guillaume emerged from the mist, and Christian quickly grabbed his young charge's arm to keep her from foolishly lunging at her maker.

"You asshole!" she shouted. "How could you just do that to a person and—"

"Shut up, bitch, you were just dinner."

"Guillaume, why so foul to such a lovely young lady? Was that necessary?" Christian's gaze narrowed on his blond, younger adversary as he retracted his fangs. He gave Deb a hard look to stay put and then advanced calmly.

"So, now that you've exploited your ducal rights with her, I can take over from here."

"I'm not going anywhere with you, you bastard!"

Christian held up a hand to deflect the black charge that would have knocked Deb off her feet, and then gently moved her to stand behind him. It was a protective stance, but an instinctive one that he couldn't have resisted if he'd wanted to… and at the moment, he didn't want to.

"*Mon ami*, why so violent a temper tonight? This young woman was left for dead on a *bathroom floor* at a rave—surely you didn't expect her to wake up happy about her circumstances, no?"

"I was high," Guillaume said in a petulant tone. "What can I say?"

"You should apologize," Christian murmured too coolly and too calmly, making the younger vampire bristle. His tone was a thinly veiled threat, a command, akin to a growl in less refined species.

"It's always about control—a display of power with you, isn't it, Christian?"

"*Non.* It is about what is right. You have made her, you should have been responsible for her welfare."

"Oh, and like you haven't done this?" The younger vampire smirked as Christian's gaze raked his biker outfit.

"*Non…* not like this. I cannot say that I have been in an opium daze, or whatever you ingested, and have left a young female on a urine and vomit drenched bathroom floor. I have left the young and willing in many impassioned circumstances in my time, *mon ami*, but not lying in piss, to be sure."

"I thought you said I didn't reek?" Deb said quietly, the shame in her voice making Christian angrier.

"When I bit you, *cheri*, the circumstances of your life and subsequent death became known to me... as they *should have* become known to Guillaume. You smell lovely, as I told you." He'd addressed her question, but had kept a hard gaze on Guillaume. "You do not deserve her."

Guillaume laughed. "Oh, so now, in addition to being the feudal lord of this province, you've now become like the ASPCA, taking in abused animals and stays from their owners who cannot keep them on a leash? Are you so bored, Christian, that this is the best way you can manage your time?"

"Do not provoke me tonight, Guillaume. I awakened this evening in a very foul humor. I should not like to have an ongoing row with you that might end in devastating consequences."

"You *threaten me* over this piece of easy ass? He has thrown down the gauntlet in a so-called lady's defense! How long has it been, man, since you've made one of good breeding?" Guillaume sniffed and laughed, wiping his nose with the back of his hand. "Are you really that old that you can't tell the difference between good stock and not?"

Christian snarled. He would not dignify the charge—it had no bearing on the discussion. Outraged, he was about to walk away to allow his narcotic-compromised coven brother live to experience another night, when a sudden loss of presence made him stiffen. The air bit into his back; the vacancy he felt there was real. He knew she'd left him, had focused on disappearing, but only hoped that she wasn't as insane as she might be. Rage was a dangerous thing in a woman. The loud crack and immediate yell by Guillaume, however, told him all he needed to know. He impassively watched a fallen tree branch instantly enter Guillaume's back, cracking ribs and vertebra as it pierced his heart, and exited through the center of his chest while Guillaume slowly fell forward, eyes wide.

"I got your *dog*, asshole," she spat, and then released a loud scream of rage. "Good stock? Ha! I'm not some trailer park trash! I'm a person! You left me for dead in one of the shittiest places a person could die—so you die in a fucked up way and see how you like it, okaaay!"

Perplexed and deeply pleased, all he could do for a moment was to watch Guillaume's body slowly age, then become a maggoty mass before disintegrating into dust.

"Not many newfoundlings can release themselves from the bonds of their masters," he said with quiet awe. "You were very fortunate, young lady, that

Guillaume was high out of his mind and his reflexes were dulled, or… but rights and code, I would not have been able to save you from whatever fate he elected. An attempted assassination of one's maker is highly frowned upon by polite society."

"Yeah, well," she said, spitting on Guillaume's ashes as they blew away. "He didn't teach me that, so I didn't know."

Christian smiled. "As in the human world, ignorance is no defense. The law is the law."

"What's that old saying, about women and scorn and fury?"

"Touché." Christian extended his elbow and she threaded her palm through it as they leisurely strolled toward the club entrance. "But you'll have to tell me where you learned how to fight like that—upon such brief instruction." He stopped walking and stared at her.

She laughed. "I watch *everything* on TV… Charmed, Buffy—"

"You are *actually* a fan of the aggrandizement of a slayer?"

"She rocks, dude. She kicks ass—I love Buffy."

It was a stalemate. Christian let out a weary sigh as they resumed walking. "Why don't we keep that tantalizing bit of information between us, shall we… especially in here."

Deb giggled. "Like a boyfriend-girlfriend secret?"

He stiffened but kept their pace.

"I suppose."

"So, like, now that I got rid of Guillaume, am I like your girlfriend? I told you I could watch your back, since you like the kickass types."

He had to smile; there was nothing else to do with this delicious trollop of a girl. "You sensed that about me during our… exchange?"

"Yep… and I know your favorite color, and what your fav food was before, and…"

He listened without listening, her voice trailing off as he allowed it to blend into the night. Who in hundreds of years had cared about the most infinitesimal trivialities of his life?

"So?" she said, coming to stand before him and making him abruptly halt. "Am I special to you or what? Like, why is it so hard to get a straight answer?"

"Because the nature of a vampire is to be oblique."

"You like me, tell the truth."

He nodded. "Very much."

"So before we go in here and guys might ask me to dance or something, I don't wanna piss you off… I just want to know where we stand, because I really like you, too."

That she was asking permission, trying to find boundaries, wanted to be sure not to offend, was one of the sweetest acts of honesty he'd encountered in one so young from the modern age. A soft kiss on her mouth was his initial reply, and then he realized that this woman-child who'd hungered for love all her life was willing to give her all in that pursuit. For eternity. It wasn't for power or special access to wealth that she'd lusted, but for love, someone to care for her… a craving larger than the hole she'd left in Guillaume's chest.

"You are my girlfriend," Christian said quietly. "If you'll have me, I will care for you for a very long time."

A high pitched squeal, a leap, and she had jumped into his arms, her legs a vice around his waist, causing him to stumble backwards. The more reserved patrons looked on with a sniff of disdain and the bouncers, as usual, saw nothing. He had to laugh as he caught his balance and she pelted his neck with kisses.

What a wonderfully unsettling night it had been after all. Definitely a night to bring out the dead. A slayer fan… an on-line computer-phile… a Goth girl… an outrage, was now his mate? How did all of that come to be when he was supposedly the older and wiser of the two? Their worlds were so different, so impossibly far away from each other, but there was a single point of reference… the need to be cared for in the smallest of demonstrations by another being. A man was exterminated; there'd be an inquiry and underground buzz, roiling gossip. So much had transpired all too quickly and he had no rational explanation in the least.

Perhaps that was the subtle beauty of it all—it defied explanation and the entire encounter was just utterly insane.

The Company You Keep

by P. N. Elrod

St. Paul, February, 1938

G ABRIEL "Whitey" Kroun drove himself to St. Paul because it wasn't Chicago. In a new town chances were good no one would know his face and thus his reputation. The reputation belonged to the part of him with the nickname, but Whitey was gone and Gabe was now in charge.

He was still getting used to it.

Gabe had few memories of being Whitey Kroun, but counted it to be a good thing. Whitey had been bad company, a real bastard. Gabriel, however, was a nearly blank slate, thanks to the bullet still lodged in his head. He needed to figure out what to do about himself, so he drove to St. Paul, found a hotel, and paid for a week's worth of thinking time.

One full evening of staring at the walls gave him cabin fever, not insight.

On the second night he asked the desk clerk about local distractions, preferably noisy ones that closed late. He'd noticed a bowling alley farther up the street. He didn't know if he could bowl, but the option to find out was there. He might like it. Instead, the clerk recommended a nightclub close to the hotel called the Royal Arms—which turned out to be in a *cave*.

Well, that sounded interesting.

Local lore had that the place was originally used to grow mushrooms until the owner found more money was to be made in the booze business. A later entrepreneur fancied up the entry to look like a castle, complete with crenellations and fake drawbridge, which was nuts, but the gimmick worked. Business boomed even through Prohibition, and had attracted dubious types like Dillinger and Baby Face Nelson.

Gabe thought he'd fit in unnoticed.

Inside, away from the snow-laced wind, he decided the place would appeal to anyone looking for something different. The natural cave had been improved on, carved more deeply into the side of a massive hill. The barrel-vaulted stone ceiling about ten feet overhead flowed seamlessly down into rounded walls. Except for tables, chairs, and the bar, there wasn't a corner or sharp angle in sight. It looked like a giant worm had burrowed out a huge cavity for itself, then unaccountably left.

He decided not to check his hat and coat, unsure of how long he'd stay. His shoulders kept trying to crowd his ears, as though reacting to the press of surrounding stone. The room was huge and a heartening number of electric lights made up for the lack of windows, but what if the power failed? However excellent his night vision had become, he didn't like the dark, which was ironic, but there it was.

For all the Royal Arms being under the insulating ground, it was gratifyingly loud. The stone walls threw the band music back, forth, and inside out if you counted the echoes. People trying to talk over it added another layer to the din. He liked the distraction.

He pointed toward a table where he could sit with his back to the wall. A cheerful waitress who didn't see anything odd about that led him over. He ordered coffee.

"What do you want in it?" she asked.

"Sugar," he said with a smile, giving her fifty cents. "Keep the change, cutey."

She flashed a bigger smile back and bounced away. He liked the view. Maybe he just needed company, female company. That was a possibility— if this was the kind of place where one could arrange such a transaction. He checked things over, appraising the crowd.

The band was small: a piano player, drummer, and a guy who switched between a horn and a clarinet, depending on the tune. The three played as though it was the first time they'd ever worked together. It'd be embarrassing if anyone paid them attention. The few couples in the room weren't dancing, being absorbed by their own concerns. Other drinkers had the bored air of long-time regulars who had nowhere else to go. Most glanced his way when he came in, but that's how it always was when a newcomer shows up.

He spotted some familiar-looking mugs, but only because their type was to be found in every town. The odds were that he didn't know them personally, but Gabe kept an eye open for the subtle and not-so-subtle signs of recognition.

Like the ones coming from the guy over there in the corner with *his* back to the wall. He was in shadow, which would otherwise have made him invisible to anyone else. Gabriel let him keep his illusion and pretended not to notice how the man's face tightened, making his eyes go hard and narrow.

Two things *could* happen: the guy would leave him alone or he'd come over. If he came over he'd either pay his respects or cautiously ask if there was a problem. Gabe would assure him there was no problem and not be believed.

Cripes, I should have gone bowling.

The waitress brought him a cup of coffee and a sugar bowl.

"Can you take a load off for a few minutes?" he asked. "I don't like drinking alone." In his quiet room he found the acid from his newly-formed and inexperienced conscience had an easier time of etching holes in his brain, which was very annoying. The bad stuff had been Whitey's doing, after all. He wanted some practice being Gabriel, whoever the hell he might turn out to be. Getting out and about with strangers would help.

She glanced around and slipped onto the chair across from him. "I guess so, it's slow tonight."

"One of these guys your boss?"

"He keeps to his office, doesn't like the band we got in this week."

"I've heard better." Gabe pushed the coffee toward her. "Here, I don't want it after all."

He knew he must have drunk coffee in the life he'd had before waking up dead and craving something entirely different, but now it smelled like cigar ashes. She said she couldn't, but he mentioned it'd be a shame to let it go to waste.

"If you're sure…" She spooned in three sugars, sipped, and apparently liked the result. He wondered if that much sugar would sweeten her own taste, should he get the opportunity.

He could easily make that happen. All it took was a little hypnosis, one of the advantages of being a vampire. Fix her with a focused look, whisper a few words, and she'd do anything for him. He could lead her outside into dark and freezing shadows and drain her dry. She wouldn't be aware of any of it. When he was done, he'd leave the body in a drift to let the flying snow blanket her from view. They wouldn't find her for weeks. That'd be funny.

Gabe's muscles twitched as though from electric shock, and he had to fight to keep the revulsion from showing. Such sickening ideas were nightmare remnants of the dead and unmourned Whitey. As a human he'd been monster enough, God help the world if he survived as a vampire.

That's not me. I'm not like him.

Gabe was better than that.

He wanted to be, anyway. He'd decided that much about his second chance at life.

Gabe got the young woman's name—Inga—how long she'd worked at the Royal Arms, and when she expected to go home tonight. She shared a flat with another, she added.

"That's lucky," he said, noting that she left out whether her flat mate was friend or sweetheart. "No chance to get lonely. You've got someone to talk to."

"I guess I do," she agreed. "But maybe I'd like talking with someone else for a change."

She didn't get huffy when he mentioned his hotel room might be a good place to have a conversation. He took it as being only fair when she mentioned she'd like more than a forty-cent tip. They settled on a sum and a time to meet so he could walk her over, then she asked if he wanted another cup of coffee. Inga had finished his.

"A glass of water is fine." He gave her a dollar tip for that one, and she seemed to glow a little brighter. If things went well, they'd both have a fine evening ahead.

He smiled fondly after, enjoying the view all over again as she went back to the bar. Inga had dark hair, which was a contrast to her name. He thought she must have some Swede in her, but weren't they all blond? Were they different from dark-haired girls once the lights were out? He'd not had opportunity to look into it. That had to do with his future, one of the things he'd come here to think over, though he now had a chance to talk it out instead.

He hoped—afterwards, of course—that Inga would be a good listener. He could always pay her extra. Didn't crazy people give head-doctors lots of money to talk about their troubles? Gabe didn't want a doctor who would take notes and give advice, he wanted a pretty girl who would lend a sympathetic ear for an hour or two. What she heard wouldn't matter; he'd make sure she forgot everything before she left. Using hypnosis always gave him a headache, but he needed only a few seconds, well worth the risk. She wouldn't even wonder about the marks on her throat.

His improved mood was spoiled when the man from the shadows came over. He looked down at Gabe for a moment, then sat as though invited. He seemed not to notice when Inga came up with the glass of water. She shot Gabe a nervous look, which told him just what kind of man was across from him. Gabe gave her a brief smile and quick, subtle wink. He had everything—whatever it was—well in hand.

"Yeah?" he said to the man, just to get things rolling.

"I know who you are. Whitey Kroun."

Gabe no longer thought of himself by that name. The bastard was dead and good riddance.

"I'm Harry Ziemer," the stranger announced. He seemed to expect some kind of reaction to that fact. He was solidly built, just starting to go bald. His mud-brown eyes had that soulless cast some guys get when they've killed one man too many or hadn't killed nearly enough. Not a face one would forget, but still unfamiliar.

Gabe had learned early on that the best way to compensate for a memory that didn't exist was to not respond and let the other guy do the explaining. "Oh, yeah?" It was a useful phrase he'd picked up in Chicago.

"Things are gonna stay friendly and quiet here, no need for you to trouble yourself."

"Uh-huh."

"My friends and I are gonna do our deal."

"Uh-huh."

"We got an understanding?"

"Whatever you say, Harry Ziemer."

"Thanks. Whitey."

Gabe felt a shifting inside him, like the throwing of a switch.

He'd just found out something new about his reborn self: he hated that name, but it was still his and he'd not given this bozo permission to use it. He didn't like the accompanying smirk. He didn't like the man throwing his weight around as though he owned the world. If he'd shown even an illusion of respect Gabe would have let it go, but he hadn't.

And, since to some people he was still Whitey Kroun, he couldn't ignore it.

Ziemer left the table, returning to his three friends. It was no surprise that they were the mugs Gabe had spotted earlier. Of course they'd be armed like their boss. Ziemer's shoulder rig was blatantly visible through his suit.

Gabriel was also armed, having a revolver in his overcoat pocket. Six shots. If it came to it he could miss twice or—more likely—have two bullets left over.

He had to only look at a target to hit it square; you couldn't learn that particular talent. You were born with it. Whitey Kroun had been born with it; when he died and Gabriel Kroun emerged, the talent had carried over.

This is nuts. I was imagining it. He wasn't...

Ziemer looked right at him, smirk firmly in place. He murmured to the mugs. They chuckled and looked as well, smiling as though they'd put something over on Gabe so slick that he hadn't yet caught on.

His long fingers went around the base of his water glass to pick it up. He let it slip, and water slopped over the table. He grimaced and waved to Inga, pointing at the mess. She hurried up with a towel.

"I'll get you more," she said.

"Never mind that, cutey. Who's Harry Ziemer and why is he here? No, don't look at him, just do what you're doing and smile at me."

"He wants to be a big shot. He's been moving in on things, takes 'em over. Garages, taverns. He's been loafing here for a week. There's rumors we're next."

"How's he operate?"

"He talks the owner into signing over the deed."

"At gun point?"

"I wouldn't know about that. The owners always get out of town right after. Leastways no one sees 'em again. If Harry Ziemer's got a beef against you, you should maybe leave, too."

"You'd think so. Relax, cutey, we've got a date." He winked again, but her walk wasn't as bouncy when she returned to the bar. Couldn't blame her. Any time now she could have a new boss or be out of a job or worse. With guys like Ziemer there was always a worse.

Ziemer and his cronies were gone from their table. The last of them was just walking into some kind of passage off the main room. Maybe it was the call of nature. One way to find out.

The hall was wide and low, the ceiling and walls rounded. A wire with bare bulbs every ten feet hung from hooks in the ceiling. Their glow, all fifteen watts of it, wasn't much help against the darkness, not that Gabe was worried. It was plenty bright to his eyes.

Maybe this was where they raised the mushrooms once upon a time. The size of the place surprised him. Wasn't it easier to build walls than carve out a hole? Had to be. People were nuts.

I should know.

He sniffed the air, for the first time picking up the kind of dank scent associated with caves…or tombs.

Now why the hell did I think that?

If only that smirking idiot had called him "Mr. Kroun" and not the too-familiar "Whitey."

I should be out in the main room charming the socks off Inga, not doing this.

The racket from the inept band faded with distance and a turn.

A few yards along, he came to a branching. One way was absolutely black, even to him, and the source of the dank air. It must have led to the outside; he picked up the scent of snow, dead leaves, and moldy earth. Something dead and rotting was there as well, but the stink of decay was so faint that a human would not have noticed.

The other branch had light, a weak glow far down where the hall turned again. Gabe could see it, but only because of his supernatural edge. The bare bulbs on their wire had been shattered in this whole section, making a powerful discouragement to anyone without a flashlight.

He went that way, drawn by voices echoing off the stone. Glass was underfoot. He kept to the one side, wincing when he couldn't avoid stepping on the shards. The crunching sounded very loud to him.

No one can hear me, they're too busy talking.

The hall had shrunk in width and was more like a tunnel. His shoulders hunched up again. He forced them down.

He reached the turn, took it, and came even with what seemed to be the boss's lair. It wasn't a room in the sense of having a door and a chamber beyond, but an especially large and deep alcove cut into the side of the tunnel. It had a big desk, chairs, file cabinets, and plenty of light, which was cheering.

On the floor almost at his feet was a wide scatter of desk clutter, pencils and other junk, including a stone paperweight the same pale color as the walls. The name *Lars Pargreave* had been carved into one side. It was too small to be a cemetery marker, but the image crossed Gabe's mind regardless. He could picture Ziemer swaggering in and knocking things from the desk as a way of getting the owner's attention.

A blond man—most likely Pargreave—sat behind the desk that faced toward the tunnel. His doughy face was sheeted with flop sweat. Even at ten feet Gabe picked up on air made thick and sour by the man's fear.

He had a right to it. Harry Ziemer, smiling, leaned over him with a gun muzzle pressed hard against his head. The smile had reached Ziemer's dead eyes, animating them. He clearly liked his work.

The other three were ranged loosely around the desk with their backs to Gabe. Like Ziemer, they were too focused on their prey, hyenas who'd not yet noticed the lion walking up.

There was a long piece of paper on the desk that had the look of a legal document. The blond man was trying to hold a fountain pen in his shaking hand. It had to be hard to concentrate while four guys with their guns hanging out stared at you like that.

Gabe came fully around the corner. "Harry!" he cheerfully called. "How you doing?"

All five men jumped. Gratifying.

Ziemer snapped around. He lost his smile. "We had a deal."

"Of course we did. I came to watch." Gabe bent and picked up the paperweight, hefting it idly.

"Watch?"

"Yeah, it was this or bowling." He swung the stone experimentally like a bowling ball to demonstrate, then put it on the desk. The men were looking at it and not noticing his other hand, which was in his coat pocket holding the revolver. "Doing a little taking-over?"

"Whitey…" but Ziemer didn't seem to know how to finish. Must have been a new kind of situation for him.

Gabe drummed his fingers on the stone, gauging distances. He could bean the guy at the end, grab Ziemer and toss him over the desk at the other two, but one of them could still get a shot off. He didn't want noise. "The band out there stinks. I hope you'll be hiring better talent."

"I'll make money, don't worry," Ziemer said. "Whitey…"

"Hm? Oh, don't let me stop you. Go on with what you were doing. Act like I'm not here."

That had to be impossible, but Ziemer finally gathered himself and turned his attention back to the sweating man. "Sign it, Pargreave. Now."

The hapless Pargreave somehow managed to hold the pen long enough to scratch his signature on the paper. He shrank, visibly shrank, inside his ample skin. He was nothing to Gabe. For all he knew the man might be worse than Ziemer, but Gabe wasn't here to defend any side but his own.

I should just leave. These guys aren't worth the trouble.

Ziemer had the smile back. His eyes were bright and alive as he put a couple steps between himself and the moaning Pargreave, sighting down one extended arm.

Gabe recognized that look, and thought he knew what it felt like. Some black ghost of a memory scuttled out from a corner of his mind, grinned, then darted from sight again.

Whitey Kroun used to look like Ziemer—or so Gabe imagined. Whitey put himself forward to do jobs like this so he could feel the kind of thing Ziemer was now feeling.

That's wrong. Gabe had a conscience, just not much of one yet. It still managed to give him a twinge. It wanted him to do…something.

"Harry?" Gabe spoke loud enough to disrupt the headlong rush to bring death in.

Ziemer flinched, irritated. "What?"

"There's witnesses out front."

"They won't know. This far in you can fire a cannon and they'd never hear it."

"Really?" That was interesting. "What about the cops? Won't they wonder about this guy turning up dead?"

"Cops won't do squat. We keep our business under the table, don't bother them, and they leave us alone."

Gabe had heard about St. Paul's infamous deal with the gangsters. The pact between law and disorder was an uneasy one, but mostly worked so long as the town got its share of the take. "Glad that's covered, but come on, Harry—think about the mess. You'll get blood and brains all over your nice bill of sale or whatever that is."

Ziemer was sufficiently distracted now. He looked fully at Gabe, not Pargreave. "What?"

"Scrag him if you have to, but not here. Take it from one who knows. Blood soaks right into stone like this, you'll never get it out."

"What do you want?"

"Nothing. I'm just saying you can do this better someplace else. You'll have this guy's leavings all over what's going to be your desk. Instead, you ought to be sitting behind it from the first minute, laying down the rules like a big shot should."

One of the mugs who had the wit to move clear of Ziemer's line of fire nodded. "He's got a point, boss."

"You don't want to get that stuff on your suit," Gabe added. "Any of you guys in a mood for lugging a body around and mopping up afterwards?"

A silent exchange of looks between the three of them resulted in a unanimous shaking of heads and murmurs against such lowly labor.

"I'm getting rid of him," stated Ziemer, teeth on edge.

"Well, of course you have to, just not here is all I'm saying." Gabe stared indifferently down at the terrified Pargreave and thought of that branching into blackness and its stink of decay. "I bet *you've* got a place where you do that kind of business. Somewhere here in these caves? Yeah, I thought so."

Pargreave, shivering now, hadn't given an answer. Ziemer and his pals saw what they wanted to see in the man's gray face.

"What do you think, Harry? Let's make him take us to where he buries his bodies."

"Why do you wanna know? What do you care?"

Gabe gave a shrug. "I help you out and maybe down the road you do me a small favor. It's how the business runs, you know that. Think about it: what'll it do for your reputation when it gets out that you got backing from Whitey Kroun himself?"

"How small a favor?"

"I was thinking free drinks from your new bar."

They gave a short laugh. Pargreave didn't, but they talked over him.

"You don't want a cut of the take?" Ziemer was reasonably suspicious.

"The take from a joint like this is peanuts to me. I'm just here 'cause I'm bored. Like I said: it was this or bowling."

They laughed again, and he could see his death in their eyes.

I could be wrong. But killing an interloper is what I'd have done a few months back.

He wasn't that man anymore, but some piece of him lurked within. Gabe couldn't recall Whitey, not exactly, but could judge him by the company he'd kept. Much of it had been scum like these.

That's why I understand them so well.

Ziemer got an idea. "You've heard of me. That's why you came to St. Paul. You heard what I'm doing."

Gabe sobered and slowly nodded, approving. "Good…you figured it out. Word gets around."

"So what's your real angle?"

"Harry, I'm here to size you up for the big boys, see if you're someone we can work with. How you handle this—" he indicated Pargreave, "—with kid gloves or a wrecking ball, tells us what we need to know. I'll give you a hint: use the kid gloves, and we'll cut you in on *our* take."

Ziemer looked as though he had the number on what they were talking about. Hell if Gabe knew. He was making it up as he went.

Ziemer's smirk was back, and he relaxed by a whole inch. "You're all right, Whitey. I heard stories about you, but they—"

With unnatural speed Gabe pulled his revolver free and shot four times. The noise was deafening in the confining space.

He braced for return fire, but none came.

He blinked against the smoke and ascertained there were four bodies on the floor, none of them getting up again. They had that look.

Under the tang of gunpowder, the heavy perfume of their blood suddenly bloomed in the alcove. It seemed to fill his head. He made his normally dormant lungs take in a full measure of the scent, but not for a moment did he consider feeding. Those mugs were garbage, and you got rid of garbage.

Gabe glanced at Pargreave, who looked like he'd swallowed his own tongue.

"You gonna be a problem and remember *any* of this?" Gabe asked.

Pargreave struggled past his shock, shaking his head. "No, sir," he finally whispered.

"Can you make them disappear?"

"Y-yes, sir."

Gabe didn't trust him, though, and put him under anyway to make him forget. He washed himself from Pargreave's memory, put the revolver in his hand, and told him it was self-defense, then walked quickly back down the tunnel before the man woke up.

Gabriel returned to his table in the club's main room, noticing that nothing had changed. The music from the amateurish band continued uninterrupted. His nerves settled, and the tightness inside his skull abruptly eased and vanished.

Inga came over, face solemn. "You okay? Something wrong?"

He found himself smiling warmly at her. "Nah. It's copasetic."

"What's going on with Ziemer?"

"Just wanted a card game is all. I'd have joined in, but you and I have a date."

"I should get them drinks."

"Leave 'em. They'll come out when they're thirsty."

Inga was doubtful, looking at the hallway opening.

"Hey." He reached out, gently taking one of her hands. "Lemme ask you something…"

Her attention shifted to him.

"Do you think if I slipped the bartender a couple of bucks that he'd let you off early tonight?"

She brightened again. "I'm pretty sure he would."

"Go find out for me, would you?"

Inga bounced away, and Gabriel's gaze swept the room again. Nothing. Absolutely nothing. Not one hint of what had happened and just as well.

But four men dead. Just like that.

For the two seconds it took for him to draw and fire and put them down Gabe had been a machine. He'd had no thoughts, no feelings, he'd simply functioned and had been coldly efficient.

Gabe didn't like being a machine. He suspected that if he let it run one time too many it might open a door in his mind that would allow Whitey to return. That would be bad.

He had faults and flaws and on the really tough nights only a tenuous hold on sanity. He thought insanity had to do with loss of control, though. And back there he'd been very much in control, of himself, of the situation. He'd gone in, eyes open, knowing—

Four men dead.

He couldn't feel remorse for them, though.

But shouldn't I feel something?

He looked for, but didn't find anything more than a sense of letdown. Then it occurred to him that he'd *not* felt the unholy joy he'd seen in Ziemer. Whitey had been like him once upon a time, but not the reborn Gabriel.

That had to make a difference. Maybe that's what it was about.

Or not. Or…

Nuts. He'd think about that crap later. Inga was returning, pulling a coat on, her face bright with a big smile.

She was much better company.

Damphire

by Bill Messner Loebs

I DON'T like Transylvania. I know how that sounds, but it's not the easiest place to earn a living. For one thing they make a fetish out of impalement; you tip a cow over and the next thing you know you're two feet taller with the most uncomfortable piece of pine imaginable kissing your fundament. For another, they really know their vampires. I mean every jot and tittle. On the other hand, Ruritania hugs the eastern frontier of Transylvania, they share a common language, religion, a traditional cuisine that is truly delicious, the women are equally scrumptious and in Ruritania they only hang you. No comparison, really.

The coach had crossed the border into Ruritania about ten minutes before and I was feeling fine. The sky seemed bluer, the air smelt sweetly of hay and corn pudding and there was a beautiful woman in the wooden seat across from mine. Our knees were nearly touching. I straightened the lace at my sleeve and cleared my throat.

"The weather has gotten so much better these last few days..." I began, but she cut me off impatiently.

"Please don't try to be witty. You haven't the brains for it."

"I haven't?"

"You haven't. You got on at Luchengardt, didn't you? And Luchengardt is full of Jews and Gypsies. And garlic merchants. All three are stupid. And they smell bad." She wrinkled her adorable nose in distaste. I attempted to be tolerant. She did have a point about the garlic merchants.

"As it happens I was only visiting. But I'm sure there are many fine..."

"There aren't. We aren't in Austria and we especially are not in Vienna, so there isn't anything "fine" about for several hundred miles. You may take my word for it. I was raised in a very good family, and brought up to appreciate fine things. I am affianced to the Burgomaster of Tresstrassa, the wealthiest and most cultured town in this horrid little country, and so when I tell you your clothes are out of fashion, your manner is offensive, your accent is lower class, you are likely a garlic merchant and everything about you is so completely déclassé, you can certainly believe it. I really have lowered myself even in addressing you." She sniffed in the most delightful way imaginable. "Please be so good as to not bother me further." She contrived to stare out the window, while her sweet little foot stamped defiantly on the floor. She certainly had the right not to be offended by my association. I, on the other hand, had an hour to kill.

"Actually, I'm not a garlic merchant. I am a Mesmerist and Alienist, specializing in weight reduction, and other self-improvement techniques. Dr. Wilhelm Varny at your service. Not that Fraulein needs any weight reduction." This was very true. Everything tucked into her charming frock was slender, shapely and quite spectacular. Not that any of that would matter. She held out for five minutes, regarding me shyly out of the corner of her eye. Her beautiful clear brown eye.

"Weight reduction, you say?" We came to an immediate understanding; I would put her into a trance and make it impossible for her to gain weight. She would sneer at me.

"Please don't be disappointed when everything you try comes to naught. My will is much too strong for me ever to be mesmerized." Two minutes later she was honking like a goose. Now you are probably thinking this would have been the ideal moment to suggest she loosen her garments, which were in the very height of fashion, and allow me to kneed her like bread dough. Well, for one thing, though she was entirely at my mercy, I am no cad. For another this was business. I proceeded to suck on her neck.

We arrived at Tresstrassa, which was as advertised a lovely little town, shot through with gingerbread and gables, its boxy second stories overhanging the first. Every building had tiny panes set in windows surrounded by vast shutters, and massive doors decorated with heavy gargoyle knockers. Every house was clean and tastefully painted, every hedge clipped, every gate whitewashed, each wagon horse brushed to within an inch of its life. The place smelled like money.

There was a small contingent of local officials waiting for us; more fairly for her, the fair affianced. We all disembarked. Maria (for her name was one of the things I had discovered about her) introduced me to everyone. I made a swift though not rude exit. The two lovebirds were eager to impress one another. I was eager to suss out the town. But before I left the Burgomaster shook my hand. "It is good to meet you, Herr Doktor," he smiled. "We are always pleased to have professional people visit our fair city."

"Thank you, I'm looking forward to it."

"Have you made reservations for a place to stay?" He was pleasant enough, shortish, plump, pink, exquisitely dressed, with silky black side-whiskers and very shrew hazel eyes.

"No, I thought I'd stroll a bit, compare prices, check out ..."

"The better sort of people all stay at the Green Dragon Inn."

"Well, sometimes I like to find a quiet, picturesque little place where the common people stay..." Did I mention I was broke?

"Everyone stays at the Green Dragon Inn. Everyone but riffraff and criminals." His eyes became ever so subtly sharp. "I'm sure you wouldn't want people to think you were that sort of person."

"Or a gypsy or a garlic merchant?" This from Maria, who was smirking. Her husband-to-be obviously suited her very well.

"We have a God-Fearing little community here. Even visitors find it very pleasant to fit in; to be the Right Sort. Are you the right sort, Doktor?"

"The very rightest. The Green Dragon Inn it is." And off I went.

As expected, the Green Dragon was pleasant, almost clean, and steeply over-priced. The fellow behind the front desk was smiling and looked very like the Burgomaster, save the side-whiskers were light brown and a tiny mustache was in evidence. He had that sweaty strain of someone trying too hard. "Ah, my dear cousin," he beamed. "He does take care of us. And of course, of our guests. It would be a shame if they ended up in some run-down, unpleasant little place." I smiled and signed in, being sure to add my title and occupation. "And did my cousin mention we prefer that our honored guest pay two days in advance?"

"But I may not be staying two days."

"Oh, you will. Everyone does." I was willing to bet they did. That would pretty much exhaust my purse. As I put my money down I noted the manager was wearing a girdle of some kind.

"May I say, Herr, how pleasant it is to see a fine figure of a man, like yourself, in a public position like this? In my profession I see so many, so-called fashionable fellows who look like scrawny sticks." He preened, but also looked at my signature.

"Your profession as a mesmerist?"

"I specialize in the elimination of various bad habits. And in weight-reduction." There followed an interested pause.

"Weight-reduction, you say?" Once he was under, I re-pocketed my money, then gave him several extremely useful suggestions. Once out on the street again I checked my pocket watch. It was still two hours or so before dear Maria would allow the pretty scarf she was wearing about her neck to be removed.

"Herr Doktor? May I have moment, Herr Doktor?" He was a very tall younger man, dressed in the scarlet and braid, epaulets and cap, gilded belt, dress sword, gloves and cape of someone desperate to pretend he had been in a war. He had no side-whiskers and his mustaches were long and pointed, but there was still something very familiar about him. "I am Captain Kreegar of the Imperial Town Police. I was just visiting my Uncle Fritz at the Green Dragon Inn and I couldn't help noticing he forgot to ask you to pay two days in advance." I sighed. This town certainly kept track of you. There were too many people on the street to risk weight reduction. I handed back the money. He looked sadly dutiful. "There is also a ten penny fee for hotel collections."

"Of course there is." As I went on my way I reflected on just how hard it might be to make an honest living in this village. My next stop was the barber, who looked blessedly nothing like the Burgomaster. He was however thinning a bit on top. As he shaved me, I let slip that my mesmerizing talents extended to growing hair. He was interested. A bald barber can look forward to nothing but grief. Once he was under I gave him the usual commands, including the one that made him forget he had ever been mesmerized. At the stables I expressed an interest in horse breeding. The stable master was somewhat overweight, but not the sort to care. I did find out that he owned a couple unfoaled mares. You can never know that in advance and it can make the whole plan so much more difficult if you have send away for them. I then convinced him he had a sty in his eye and needed a treatment which involved a small spinning mirror. Before I left I made sure he forgot he had ever met me.

My last stop was a tavern. I had sausages and a beer. I also flirted a bit with the maid and offered to help her lug the washwater out back. There, away from prying eyes, I gave her a treatment in weight reduction and a couple of deep red suck-bruises along her pulsing artery. Then I gave her a very pretty scarf and her marching orders. Feeling pleased with myself, I wandered back through the town, poking into this store and that, playing with the occasional dog, wandering through the local cemetery, dozing in the setting sun next to a couple of ancient fellows in wicker chairs. In short, doing absolutely nothing suspicious. I didn't know where the Burgomaster lived and I had no desire to spark inquiry by asking around. Maria would have had an intolerable desire for a nap after her long trip and when she woke up … the scream tolled through the town like a church bell calling the faithful to Mass.

Like the rest of the residents I wandered into the town square to see what was about. Maria was lurching in little drunken circles in her undershift, clutching the scar to her throat. She seemed distraught. The Burgomaster was trying to quiet her. "It's all right, my dear. Please don't scream. What could possibly be wrong?"

"My throat! My throat! Someone … some*thing* has bitten me!" They managed to corral her and remove the scarf from her neck. The crowd gaped. There, swollen and red, were two round areas just along the pale arch of her beautiful throat. Everyone was appalled. Now in stories there is always a healthy skepticism about these things. The commonsense everyday people simply refuse to believe the more esoteric, supernatural explanations until escalating events and some authority figure has beaten it into them.

"Vampire!"

"Vampires!"

"The walking dead!"

"Rampaging blood beasts!"

"Vampires are everywhere!"

"The Vampires will eat us in our beds!"

"Vampires!!"

However, in my observations people prefer the supernatural explanation. It's easier, doesn't require study and it breaks up their day.

Fortunately the Burgomaster was made of sterner stuff. He raised his hands. "People, please. We mustn't yield to fear. We must not give in to heedless childish terror. There is some rational explanation to all this. Your village officials have this situation under control. After all this is a single incident, not some kind of epidemic …" There was a second scream, a second round of gasps. We all looked. My little tavern wench was standing in the middle of the street, horrified, her brand new scarf blowing away, regarding herself in a store window. People had surrounded her and were moaning, gasping, screaming. As well they might, for on her neck, plain as anything, were scarlet marks that might very well resemble the bite of a vampire. Chaos ensued.

I don't know about you but I enjoy a good riot, with people running here and there, sharpening stakes, throwing garlic about, repeating the Lord's prayer and checking everyone else for bite marks. Gradually however these activities came to a halt as people realized they hadn't a clue what they were doing. There was silence. And into that silence came a single clear voice of reason, belonging as it happened to the stable master.

"If only we had a real vampire hunter in town. Someone who could recognize the beast and knew how to find them!"

The Innkeeper, and as we remember, the Burgomaster's cousin, then stepped forward. "Yes, a great specialist like Wilhelm Varney who is known throughout Europe and the Orient." At this the tavern maid spoke up.

"Do you mean Wilhelm Varney who ended the plague of Vampires in Groesbeck?"

"The very same. And he battled the mad Blooodsucker of Minsk!" This from the Barber.

"That's true. He is a legend. Why, the Czar himself once hired him to clear out an infestation of ghouls from the royal palace." At this point other voices in the crowd spoke up.

"Yes, I've heard of that!"

"Why, yes, Wilhelm Varney. Wasn't he called in to exorcize the Ghost Cattle over at Marlebadden?"

"Wilhelm Varney. He stopped the postmistress of Orn from turning into a werewolf."

"And there was a mummy in the Abbey on the other side of Hidden Wood. I think he had something to do with that!"

"Wilhelm Varney."

"Wilhelm Varney!"

"Yes, Wilhelm Varney is the one we need!"

"Wilhelm Varney!"

"Wilhelm Varney!"

"But Wilhelm Varney must be far away."

"He must be. Where ever can we find Wilhelm Varney?" At this juncture I stepped modestly forward.

"My friends, I am Wilhelm Varney."

The innkeeper spoke up. "He is! He is Wilhelm Varney. Doktor Wilhelm Varney. I checked him in today myself." Well, you can imagine the effect. Everyone crowded in, wanting to know where I'd come from, what I could do for them, how I'd become the marvelous person I was. The Burgomaster was looking a little sour and Captain Kreeger seemed rather ungenerously suspicious, but I smiled cheerfully nonetheless.

"I would like very much to help you. I've fought these terrible beasts from Paris to Ravenna. But there's nothing to do until morning …

"But how is it you can fight these things when the rest of us cannot?"

"Because I can *find* them! My friend I am a Damphire, a hunter of these Children of the Night. When my sainted mother had me in her womb she was attacked by one of them. She survived, but by the nature of the attack a window was opened for me into the nature of the Vampire. I can sense a Vampire. I can smell a Vampire and by dint of many years of study, I know what to do to destroy them." This made everyone very excited.

"Where is the beast now? Let's kill it now!" There was a general mutter of approval with many knit brows and snarling lips. I struck a thoughtful pose.

"Well, right now it's out there somewhere in the deep velvety night," I said gesturing into the deep velvety night. Everyone gathered a bit more closely to me. "We could go out right now while he is ravening and tearing through the countryside, and I'm sure a majority of us will survive…" The fierce expressions around me began to fade. "I mean lurking in the shadows as he doubtless is, he can pull down stragglers and the unwary, ripping open their throats and clawing their soft flesh into ribbons of gore…" People were crowding so closely now it was difficult to speak. "But that will make it that much easier to see it, and to bury it beneath our weight of numbers. I imagine it will only take a half hour or so to incapacitate it, as it exhausts itself trying to claw free." Enthusiasm for that option was draining away. "Or we could retire to the local tavern, have a touch of medicinal ale, make our plans and get a good nights sleep…" I was nearly extinguished in the stampede.

There was no way to diplomatically refuse the numerous ales that were forced on me during the next few hours. Nor once the information was pried out of me was there a way to keep the citizens from demanding I be given free room and board. "But how will I sleep in peace, with that thing out there?" sweetly complained Maria.

"Simply lay a thick trail of salt around the bed. Vampires cannot cross it. Added to the usual garlic wreaths at the windows, that should keep you safe." I smiled. "I'm sure we can find a garlic merchant somewhere about."

"It seems impossible that something as simple as salt can repel so terrible a threat."

"As impossible as the actual fact of the *walking dead*?" I thought, but didn't say. Once Maria and the tavern girl were bundled off I sat down and examined the stakes piled on the counter in front of us. I sighed.

"Maple, Oak, pine, teak…What pray tell are these for?"

"Why, Herr Doktor, they are for piercing the heart of the Vampire!"

"But they won't work. We need stakes carved from ash and yew, the trees upon which Our Lord was crucified. They must be soaked in holy water and dried beneath a mat made of hair shirts and Nuns' habits." The crowd crooned at my obvious knowledge.

"Really? But where can we get such stakes in time?" I smiled.

"As it happens in my second traveling case I have a selection of such stakes." Everyone began smiling, the worried looks upon their faces melting away. "And while I would love to simply give away those stakes, I am alas a poor man…" Very quickly everyone had bought at least one stake – and some had three. Things were looking up. I also sold them several crucifixes, vials of holy water, sacred medallions, mistletoe, garlic oil and the rest. It's a wonderful world when a few pennies worth of tin and condiments can be spun into gold.

"Now we are protected, but where will we find this horrid vampire?"

"Well, the first place to look is in your local cemetery. I find that often an inadequately shriven corpse, or one who died with some terrible guilt often becomes a nocturnal bloodsucker." They were of course appalled.

"Our dearest relatives are in that cemetery and they all led blameless lives. You must be mistaken."

"I must be. If you can't think of any moment when those beloved dead were mean or greedy, or lied or engaged in usury, or gossiped or in some other way transgressed against the commandments before they died, then I suppose we will just have to look elsewhere…" A pause followed, while the moral traits of the late beloveds were weighed.

"Well, it couldn't hurt just to check." By this time dawn was starting to break. We adjourned to the burial ground. The place was rather overgrown, as I had noticed yesterday, and bulging at the seams with markers and gravestones. People began to digest just how many graves there were to explore. "How are we ever to find where that creature is sleeping?" I looked thoughtful.

"The first thing to do is find a beautiful virgin, and strip her naked."

"What?"

"You see, purity cannot coexist with these loathsome supernatural creatures. So if a beautiful young virgin rides upon an unfoaled mare she will not be able to pass over a grave where a vampire sleeps."

"And she has to be naked?"

"Oh, yes. Virgins are much purer when they're naked." The stableman perked up.

"I have three unfoaled mares."

"Excellent. Then we just need the virgins." In a surprisingly short period of time the virgins were found, stripped and seated on the unfoaled mares, Maria first among them. She showed some reluctance, but could hardly refuse. It was a lovely sight. As those sweet, pure creatures bounced upon the backs of their equally pure mounts, their blushes suffused not only their faces, but almost, well, everywhere one chose to look. I was very pleased, not only because naked women on horseback is a thing I enjoy, but because I could look ahead to a least a couple of weeks of vampire-hunting; weeks filled with profitable exchanges, many more naked women and the subservience of the populace. There were many places in town a vampire might lurk and I planned to explore each one in exhaustive detail. It was at this point I saw the Burgomaster running towards us, waving papers in his pudgy hands. He was quite flushed himself, but not any more attractive.

"Herr Doktor, I have just received replies to my telegrams sent to the many various villages you have claimed you have freed from vampire epidemics." Have I mentioned how much I dislike the telegraph? "Not one has ever been troubled by vampires, but they all remember a wandering mendicant, selling fake nostrums and implausible cures to imaginary diseases, a liar named Wilhelm Varny!" Within moments I was seized by many hands, bound with heavy ropes and strung by my feet to a nearby lamppost. And then kicked by a couple of the naked virgins, who seemed especially unforgiving. Their weeping parents had thrown themselves on suddenly embarrassed girls with bulky coverlets and the other citizens were as horrified now as they had been fascinated by the spectacle a moment before. The Burgomaster was in his element.

"My friends — fellow citizens and patriots of Tresstrassa, this – this criminal, this mountebank, this *foreigner* has tried to make fools of us, has attempted to besmirch the happiness and goodness of our fair city. But we have fooled him! Our native common sense has found him out. And now our bountiful Christian charity will judge him. Prepare the tar and feathers!" Heated tar has a particularly noxious aspect when combined with self-righteous indignation and hysteria. The town was distracted ripping apart pillows and mattresses, all the while rehearsing my various shortcoming, and the sins of all the other foreigners and mountebanks who had previously besmirched Tresstrassa. From the drift of the conversation I was apparently to pay for them all. Fortunately I keep a keen blade strapped to my forearm against just this sort of occasion. Five strokes and I fell free. I climbed out of the dust and ran for the hills, stopping at a cart to stuff apples down my shirt against the night's hunger.

There were actually hills to run to. Outside Tresstrassa were the beginnings of a mountain chain called *The Devil's Fingerbowl*. Surprisingly steep crags arose from gloomy glades and dells, through which mockingly burbled crystal rills. I climbed all day until my shoes were torn and my clothes ragged. I had seen the flicker of torchlight back in the village and sought the higher elevations to discourage pursuit. I was pretty low. As many fine dreams as I had had, now the miseries of everyday life seemed ever more depressing. I missed the little familiar keepsakes in my luggage, the books and toiletries, the pens and pencils, the counterfeit marks sewn into the lining, all things I would probably never see again. I drank at a stream and longed for wine; I ate my last apple and pined for steak. I tried to think of this as a lovely hike. I might be bruised and blistered, but it was all context. I would cheerfully put myself through more effort than this were I on vacation. Alas I was not on vacation, and the hardest person to fool is yourself.

It became dusk. I could not but reflect how changed were events since last dusk. How hopeful I had been, how joyful, how innocent. I came upon a deep cavern. This would be the best and safest place to find tonight's cold rest. There were obscure Latin words carved over the cave mouth. I don't read Latin, but I decided they said: "Welcome poor traveler." I wandered from one vast chamber to the next. I couldn't help but notice the grade went evermore downward, and that there must have been hidden vents to the outside. The light never entirely faded. At last I found a small antechamber with more Latinized gibberish carved about the entrance. I figured I was deep enough and the connecting chambers were high and wide enough that I could risk a fire. I had passed various dry twigs and rats' nests to use as fodder; soon I had an armful. Once I arranged my fire, I needed a couple larger branches to last the night. As it happened my luck held. At the rear of this cave was a stout ash stake, thick as my wrist and long as my leg, thrust deeply into the earth, amidst some scattered bones. Yes, yes, I know. Ash stake, bones, Latin, etc, etc. But I was tired and cold, and not thinking clearly. The ash wood was much too tough to break. I laid it across my small fire and put myself down next to it, hoping for it to catch. I wondered what I was going to do.

Not every dinkwater town had a telegraph yet, but things were moving that way. There had to be a way to make this aggravating instant communication work for me. I cudgeled my poor, exhausted brains but nothing occurred. At last I just lay back and watched the spider. There was a small black spider spinning its shining web in the back corner. Through some whim it began to slip down its silken thread. What was I thinking? "Pretty web. Pretty spider." That was all. Would I have done something if I had realized what was happening? Doubtful. I was sunken in so deep a brown study, so powerful a lassitude had seized me that my limbs were like stone. The spider reached the cave floor and touched the bones. There was a small spark, a puff of smoke. "Interesting," I thought. "The spider made a fire too." But that was the last calm thought I had, for the dry bones began to shift and draw together.

Imagine a large wax candle in the shape of a bundle of bones. Imagine it melting, but instead of melting down in to a puddle of wax, it was melting up, gaining form and substance. Crumbling bones went from dark brown to white, becoming strong and being lashed together with tendons and muscle. Organs grew in place, skin covered organs and things that looked like dusty raisons swelled into eyes and ears, tongue and toes. Bright red hair grew over pale white skin. The eyes, by the way, were a pale green. If you are an Englisher, you've probably been told that Vampires are a dark, swarthy crew; here in the Slavic countries we believe they are very pale. Those of us who believe in them at all.

The tall, scrawny figure leaned clumsily against a wall. He looked dazed and nervously licked his inch-long needle sharp fangs. "God," he muttered in English. "I'm so hungry!" Then he looked down at himself. "And I'm naked. And I'm still a vampire. Damn." Did I mention I was terrified? Of course I was. I had staggered back while all this was happening and was poised to flee for my life. However the vampire seemed more confused than dangerous. "I can't see much at all, " he remarked, groping about. "I hope those vicious idiots didn't steal my glasses." I felt about in the dirt and twigs under his feet and came up with wire-bound lenses of an antique design. I wiped them off and handed them to him. He squinted through them. "Thank you. Thank you very much. It's good to meet an honest man. You're shaking." He noticed the fire for the first time. "Was that the stake you pulled out of me?" He snapped the ash pole in half, then put the pieces together and broke them again. Vampires are very strong. He took one chunk in his slender, bookish hands and twisted in opposite directions. The wood shredded into, well, shreds. Those immediately caught fire and soon we had a cheerful blaze going. We sat side by side, warming ourselves. He extended a hand. "My name is Timothy Morton-Johnson and I'm afraid you're meeting me on the worst day of my life." I was thinking very quickly by now and was glad he was carrying the conversation. He scratched the back of his hand.

"I was born a miller's son and my two great loves have always been history and theology. Thus I read a lot about the early church. I developed a great love of St Francis of Assisi and early resolved to emulate him as a mendicant friar, doing good, begging for alms and speaking to the birds and beasts. I would go about in a single sack cloth garment, preaching to the poor and knowing joy and happiness all the time."

He scratched his other hand. "I think I'm allergic to something around here. Probably the grass. I've always been allergic to grass. Anyway, I had resolved to walk to Italy, give away all my money and clothes and preach to the poor. Well, hardly had I gotten more than ten miles from home when the poor stole all my money and clothes, beat me and left me for dead."

"So things were working out?"

"You would think so, yet the process was less satisfying than you would imagine."

"It's hard to give things away when people keep taking them."

"Very true. I had to return home to get more money and clothes, and a gun to protect them until I could give them away. This time I got nearly to Italy when I was shipwrecked and taken captive by pirates. Most of whom were poor, by the way. I escaped and managed to reach what I thought was Italy, but what turned out to be Rumania. I was captured by a tribe of gypsies who used me as a mule to carry dung."

"And none of *this* was the worst day of your life?"

"No. One day a pack of wolves attacked the gypsies and drove them away, leaving me to be devoured by the pack. I had just finished praying to God for courage and salvation, when a miracle happened. The great wolf who was the leader transformed into a Vampire. He immediately bit me, infecting me with the dread curse and left me for dead. Which of course I was."

"You had had some experience in that by now."

"Yes. Once I had fully transformed into a vampire I discovered there were advantages. I could become a wolf, a bat, a flood of rats or even a mystical creature like a Chimaera. I had strength, I could fly, I could control people at a distance." He sighed.

"But it was not quite the uplifting spiritual life I had longed for. For about a week I rampaged about the countryside, but to bite people and suck their blood... well, you have to bite them and suck their blood. "He shuddered. "Finally I surrendered to the local priest. I tried to explain this was just a horrible misunderstanding, and perhaps he might shrive me and return me to human. Or perhaps I might be hired as a guard, to guard villages from other vampires. I thought negotiations were going well, when suddenly a mob with torches appeared, doused me with holy water and dragged me down here. The last thing I saw was the sharpened stake heading for my heart." He poked sadly at the fire, scratching at his neck. "I'm sure it's the grass." I shook my head.

"We must be half a mile from any grass. It's probably the rat dung."

"What?"

"I've heard of people who were allergic to it, especially when its in a gritty powder and worked into the pores of your skin..."

"Aiiee!"

"Or bat dung. "

"Aiiieeee!" He began to brush vigorously at the nonexistent dust on his skin.

"We are in a cave after all. Or mummified snake skin. Or sand fleas. Or spiderwebs; after all there's one right over there..."

"AAAAIIIEEEEE!" He seemed to be awfully touchy for a Vampire. After a bit he calmed down. "I've got to get out of here, find a scientist who can cure this damned infection".

"You keep calling it an infection, but that's not what it is. Probably. The best authorities say when a man dies and his soul goes away, well, a hell demon takes residence, even taking on the memories and personality of the late human..."

"So I could be a demon and not even know it?"

"Yes."

"Aiieeeee!!" He was fumbling in the dust and came up with a small tarnished silver crucifix. He slipped it over his head. "At least I can still glorify...Ouchhhh!" Immediately his skin where the holy item touched began to smoke and burn. I watched as he danced around the cave floor, leaving a trail of smoke and raising clouds of bat dust. Finally I pulled off the trinket and wrapped it in a bit of my linen shirt. Then I put it back on.

"Thank you." He wiped his glasses then scratched at his shoulder blade. "This is dreadful. How am I to emulate St. Francis when I haven't even my own soul to save? How can I even go home and look my dear old parents in the face?"

"I doubt that'll be a problem. What year do you think it is?"

"Why, the Year of our Lord 1762."

"Actually, it's September 1874." I held up a hand. "Please don't scream."
He bit his lip.

"So all my friends and relations are dead? And the world I knew has
been wiped away like the morning mist?"

"I really don't see the problem. Most of us would pay good money for
such an opportunity. "

"An opportunity to be hunted and hated, to starve and live a life of utter
loneliness and depravity? I can't even show my face among honest, decent
men!"

"Actually, you can. I have a proposal for you…"

The next day dawned bright and clear. It was the day of the wedding
between Maria and the Burgomaster, who as it turned out rejoiced in the
name Rolf. Rosy tinted hues painted the skies above the lovely church of
St. Matthew of the Vale, and nearly the whole town had turned out to see
this ceremony run its course. There were many happy faces and colorful
costumes; a scrumptious lunch had been laid out on long tables in the street
before the church, and everyone was very, very happy. Of course I was
watching all this from outside, with a noose about my neck, waiting to hung,
but I tried not to let this prejudice my enjoyment of the occasion. I had to
admit I was largely to blame for this awkward position. An hour before I had
strolled into the church as things were just getting set up, kissed Maria on
the cheek, shook Rolf's manly hand (a bit sweaty I noticed) and announced
my willingness to let bygones be bygones. I explained that at least one or
two vampires were still rampaging around the countryside and I couldn't
allow our small misunderstanding to put them in such danger. As it turned
out feelings were still pretty raw.

I was seized, run through a ten-minute trial and sentenced to be the post-
wedding entertainment. There was some loose talk of nose-slitting, and of
disemboweling me and burning my entrails before my eyes, but I think that
was largely for effect. People hate to be embarrassed, and I was sure that once
everyone calmed down in a couple of weeks they would regret whatever it
was they finally decided to do to me. I would be beyond caring of course, but
they would regret it. Captain Kreeger prodded me with his dress sword.

"It's a lovely ceremony, isn't it? They make a beautiful couple. The
town has been so looking forward to this marriage." His giant white stallion
snickered in what I viewed as an unfriendly way.

"Lovely. I don't suppose with the general celebration going on that
people will be inclined to forgive me?"

"I shouldn't think so. You frightened us and disrupted the whole peaceful life of the village. Pretending to have religious powers, not to mention fraud and theft, really are capital crimes. You are a worthless, parasitic sort. You have to admit that." He prodded me again. I've noticed that no matter how grotesquely people punish you, what they really want is for you to agree with them. Then they punish you some more. I was starting to worry. The plan I had improvised last night was sound, but it all revolved around Timothy doing his part, I really hate being at people's mercy. "After all you chose the life of a mountebank and liar. And thief," continued Kreeger, belaboring the point to death.

We were distracted at this point by the sound of bells, as the wedding party spilled out of the church and swirled happily down the street. The Burgomaster decided to make a little speech. "My friends, and you are my friends, this is the happiest day of my life. I stand before you with the love of my life…" He seized Maria's hand and they stared at one another with the sort of unconditional love you only see in ballads, and pet stores. "And my heart is bursting. I feel the need to share this love with all of you, and with the Universal Judge of all of us, the Creator of all Love and all Peace. It's time for a hanging!"

As they gathered around me, checking and rechecking the noose, I wondered poignantly where my erstwhile conspirator was? A bit late it occurred to me that my entire future depended on the reliability of a fellow who, to be fair, hadn't even had the brains or the talent to *give* money away. And I was starting to imagine what it would feel like to die.

The rest of the world was going on as though nothing important was happening. A stolid man was herding his… well, herd of pigs down the street. A woman was driving a wagon in the other direction. She had three barrels of tar in the wagon. I can't imagine why. At the Burgomaster's declaration many of the guests gathered around, to see how entertainingly I would choke. Others spread down the tables groaning with food. They couldn't be bothered; I wasn't even important enough to see die. Frankly in their place I would have ignored me too. I realized I was hungry. I wanted a sandwich.

Then, far down the street I saw a small reddish-blond bat flutter unnoticed to the paving stones and turn into a slender young man, wearing the clothes I had stolen for him very early that morning. He looked about him in a confused way, then stepped forward and sank his fangs into the throat of the first person he met; it happened to be the barber. For long moments he sucked, then released that worthy, who reeled drunkenly down the street and collapsed. He next grabbed a plumpish dame, and when he released her she wobbled over to the drinking trough and slid down to a dazed sitting position. A third and forth person followed. He was under strict orders not to kill anyone by draining their blood. The last thing we needed was competition. Still his attacks were unnoticed; lost in the general excitement and street bustle. Someone tightened the rope around my neck. I was going to die at the moment of my greatest triumph. Damn.

Someone screamed. People were milling, starting to run. Panic spread through the crowd in turgid waves. I saw the terrified, screaming mob come towards us; it was as beautiful as a sunrise after a cold and rainy night. The Burgomaster had gone horribly pale. He grabbed Maria and pushed her forward towards the tall, red-haired nemesis who was approaching us. "Take her! Eat her!" he cried. "Not me! I'm important! Take her!!" You know what I love about people? They are so predictable. Maria was trying to climb over him, and finally dove into the wedding cake. This was going to make the wedding night deuced awkward.

Kreeger touched spurs to the flanks of his mighty steed and drawing his blade with a hearty huzzah hurtled down the street toward the foe, who was currently snacking upon a councilman. "There!" said our noble Burgomaster. "Now we'll see that creature taken care of! It's probably just a wandering madman. He'll fair badly against honed steel!" With surprising speed and competence Timothy dodged the blow, seized Kreeger with one hand and the horse with the other. First his teeth closed on the neck of the man, who frankly screamed like a girl; then still with one arm lifted the huge, snorting terrified beast over his head and sank his mouth into the glossy neck. When he released it, the steed was weak as a kitten and could only manage to stagger half a dozen steps before collapsing beside his weeping master. I had anticipated heroics by Captain Kreeger, and I had suggested tossing him like a bean bag, impaling both him and his horse on the church steeple, but Timothy wouldn't hear of it. Horsies were apparently inviolate.

"It's a nightmare, an hallucination!" Rolf was getting his courage back. "It has to be! Stand firm everyone. We can face down this ... thing!" The priest agreed. A stately, florid type he approached the vampire reading the sacrament of exorcism. Slowly the creature began to shift and change, turning into a pillar of smoke, a wolf and finally a flood of hundreds of rats. The priest fainted. Everyone else ran. Well, everyone but me who was still tied to the improvised gallows.

"Pretty solid hallucination," I remarked. By this time Timothy had reformed twenty yards down the street and was lovingly feasting on the swineherd and his swine. Not all of this was theatrics. He had had a century long fast and we'd only been able to find a lizard and a couple of squirrels to experiment on. The poor boy was terribly hungry. Also, he was tugged between his gentle human morality, and his crazed (and frankly more interesting) vampiric lusts. As it turned out animal blood would feed a vampire just fine. At this point several of the braver souls turned a tar barrel over on Timothy and set it alight. Instantly there was fire everywhere, including the swine who hated being set aflame. They fled squealing in every direction, including the nearby buildings and suddenly half the town was burning. Smoke was everywhere. People were beset by flaming hogs and found their clothes on fire. Everyone was screaming. At the center of this chaos Timothy shrugged off the burning tar like an old coat and walked totally naked and untouched into the center of town. Maria stopped beating Rolf with her bridal bouquet to turn and goggle at him. Slowly he stared about the town with his blazing eyes, and the flames flickered and died out, leaving only smoldering wreckage. It was a moment when a hero should step forward.

"Hey!" said one of the virgins. "If that's really a vampire… then Dr. Varny can probably really fight him!" At last! I had been loath to suggest it myself. The crowd turned as one and set me free, with many pleas for forgiveness and tears of relief. Then as everyone stood and watched I wandered over to one of the overturned tables and made myself a sandwich. Ham and beef. With egg salad and touch of dill. Then I began walking towards the vampire.

This was the great test. All would be for naught if we didn't make this impressive. Timothy had begun to change again. A great cloud of flies rose around him. He became taller and bulkier, hair sprouted all over him, great leathern wings came out of his back. He grew the head of a lion, the body of a goat and the tail of a serpent. This was apparently the chimera. He was suddenly larger than an elephant and looking over the gaping jaws into the narrow, blazing, nearsighted eyes, I sincerely hoped he still remembered me in this current shape.

I spoke several very joyfully confused and nearly religious incantations, all the while pulling a sharpened stake from the sheath in the small of my back. The creature caught me about the middle and lifted me to its dripping maw. I thrust the stake deep in its breast. It screamed and windows shattered. Men rolled deaf in the street. For a moment the whirlwind blew and the sky was as black as night. The beast swelled up to cover nearly all the town. I was thrown free, and fell on my back, and stunned, watched as it fell to pieces, turned to mist and vanished utterly from the sight of humankind. The sky was blue again. The stake had fallen beside me; I scooped it up and slid it under my shirt before anyone could examine it too closely. The day I can't carve a retracting stake out of a tree limb, I won't deserve to be called "Doctor." The rest of the day was a triumph. People came running to congratulate me. I had another sandwich and I was brought more ale. Would the doctor need anything? Well, I modestly requested my old room at the Green Dragon Inn, and my luggage of course. Much nodding followed. Nothing would be easier. Timidly the Burgomaster wondered if the vampire was truly dead.

"Perhaps so." I struck a thoughtful pose. "Of course, once I … left yesterday, you continued to explore the cemetery and checked all possible candidates for signs of life in death?" There was much shuffling and clearing of throats. No one would meet my gaze. "I see." I was not too stern with them. After all, we had all made mistakes. "Our first task should be searching the town. There may be more than one vampire, perhaps of different types and different conditions." The virgins began to disrobe without even being asked. I love an obedient child.

Very much later that night I reeled through my door at the Green Dragon Inn, pleasantly exhausted from honest labor. Under my blankets I encountered Maria, quite naked. We made the usual motions, created the usual noises, produced the usual fluids. Afterward she shook the sweat out of her hair, slipped back into her dress and paused with her hand on the doorknob.

"Well, that was disgusting," she remarked. "At least now you know I am no longer suited to be stripped naked and forced to amble through graveyards. " Then she was gone. I felt so used.

After a bit Timothy slithered out from under the bed. Fortunately no one had remembered that vampires can turn to mist as a general thing. "I've been watching from the window. Those unfoaled mares stopped at several graves, indicating a possessed corpse. And yet no vampire was found." I stretched.

"Yet. I still have hope. It is amazing how reluctant horses are to cross a grave once it's had red pepper scattered on it." We thought our own thoughts.

Timothy scratched his chest. "You know there are elements to this situation, as well as everything has turned out, that don't seem strictly… moral." I yawned.

"On the surface. But you may after all be possessed by a demon. That could be impeding your moral sense."

"I guess. I hear people talking. They want to have *you* appointed Burgomaster."

"I've heard that." I shuddered. "All that paperwork. Heaven forefend! I think we'll let Rolf stew and crawl for a few days, then save his job." There was a knock at the door.

"Herr Doctor? It is I, Fritz, the manager…"

"Yes, Fritz? I remember you."

"There are several messages for you from neighboring villages, even as far away as Berlin and Paris."

"Really?"

"Word of what happened today has spread everywhere. They all want you to come to their cities and search for bloodsuckers. And werewolves. And mummies." A great joy began to bubble through me. I smiled at Timothy. He smiled back. Did I ever mention I love the telegraph?

Man Bites Dog

by Paul Kupperberg

FIRST thing you've got to know is, everything we publish is true.
The names may be changed to protect the innocent (or, more likely, to protect *against* the litigious), but it's all true. From the boy-bat hybrid found living in a West Virginia coal mine to the Department of Homeland Security using psychics to recruit reincarnated Wild West gunfighters to patrol the border with Mexico.

I'll never forget the first time I got close to some second undersecretary of the D.O.D. as a newbie reporter, still stringing for *Weekly World News* from college in Arizona, and demanded to know the truth about Area 51. The guy just laughed and said, "Sure, what'd you want to know?"

He not only handed me a stack of photographs of the aliens from four different races currently residing as guests at the infamous Nevada military installation, but provided me with images of their spacecraft as well, *and* offered to set up a guided tour and a meet-and-greet with the aliens, complete with photo op.

Needless to say, I was excited. I called my editor. He told me not to bother. He had "Area 51 shit" running out his ears. "Try and dig up something new, willya?" he said to me, like I was the idiot of the century for wasting his time with a legitimate scoop on the existence of extraterrestrial life.

Turns out, I was.

See, the government had learned a long time ago that the best way to keep a secret was to tell it to everyone.

Building an atomic bomb in a super-duper top military secret project? Make it the stuff of science fiction magazines and comic books and no one will believe it could actually be happening in real life at the same time.

Answer anyone who asks about E.T.s with absolute, one hundred percent honesty. Hold back nothing.

Know why?

(And this is the brilliant part, really!)

Because only the nutjobs are ever going to ask in the first place!

Think about it. Unless he's doing a prime time special during sweeps week, what're the odds of Brian Williams opening the *Nightly News* with a hard-hitting investigative piece on E.T.s and Area 51? Anything out of the realm of the natural, carbon-based, terra-born has been relegated to the lunatic fringe where it can harmlessly percolate amongst the choir with World Trade Center Conspiracy Theories (all false) and the belief that the first shots of man on the moon were produced in a movie studio (true, but not for the reasons you think). They've made it so anyone who asks anything about everything from ESP to aliens is a wacko.

Or, as we like to call them, "our readers."

And if you happen to be of that small, elite group, my byline will not be unfamiliar to you. My name is Strange. Terrence Strange.

If, however, you were a neighbor when I was growing up in the Canarsie section of Brooklyn, or a resident and/or transient guest of the Saint Stanislaw Hotel on West 27th Street where I currently reside, you would know me as Leo Persky. What can I tell you? 'Persky' lacks the *umph* and authority you're going for as an investigative reporter of the weird and the unusual. The strange, if you will. Believe me, at five foot seven, one hundred and forty-two pounds, glasses, and a spreading bald spot that's got me to wearing hats, no one ever calls me Strange. "Asshole," sure. Strange, not so much.

You can call me Leo.

Nightshift editor Rob Berger called me both, as in, "Leo, you asshole, ever hear of answering your phone?"

"Sorry, boss," I said, dropping into the guest chair in front of his desk. "I was out in Pennsylvania ... *somewhere*, with no sign of Bigfoot to be found, by the way. I finally remember to bring my cell phone charger with me," I said, pulling the tangled wad of cord from my trench coat pocket. "See? All I needed was an outlet to plug it in and a cell tower within a hundred miles of me and I would've been happy to talk to you."

"No one's ever happy talking to me," he growled. Berger was a big man, handsome, bearded, fit, and, of particular importance to the work of filling pages with news, intimidating.

"That's because you're an unpleasant excuse for a human being," I said. Unfortunately, intimidation only works until you fail to follow through and kill the intimidatee. That I was still upright, mobile, and in possession of all my teeth, limbs, and testicles was proof that Berger was lots of bark, very little bite. The only thing keeping me in line was my (forever unspoken) respect and admiration for his skills as an editor and writer. Otherwise, I'd really bust his chops.

"Who ever said I was human?" he muttered, digging through the mess on his desk.

"I'll issue a retraction immediately."

"Don't bother." He found what he was looking for. A ticket folder. "You won't be here long enough. What'd you know about West Virginia?"

"Uhm, coal mines, hillbillies, moonshine. Did I miss anything?"

"Only the four o'clock Greyhound to Morgantown if you don't move your ass."

"*Greyhound*? Rob...!"

"What?" He glanced up at me from under dark, knitted brows. I suddenly remembered what about him I used to find intimidating.

"I hate you," I said. I snatched the ticket from him. "So what's in West Virginia, except misery, despair and a ten-hour bus ride with the dregs of humanity?"

"We got us a biter," he said, flipping a file folder my way.

I just stared at him and let the folder bounce off my chest. "First the bus, now vampires. You know I hate freakin' vampires, man. After that thing in Skokie, my name's not exactly at the top of any of their invitation lists."

Berger smiled. It was the smile of a well-fed carnivore sated on his own kill. "Oh. Was that *you*?" he said, "It completely slipped my mind." His smile widened; he was tasting something he liked. My misery.

"Fine," I snapped. "Great. But keep this in mind, boss man. I get bit, first thing I do is come back here and turn *you* into one of the undead."

"What makes you think I'm not already one of them?" His grin was the broadest I had ever seen it, revealing canines that did seem extraordinarily...

"Bite me, Berger," I said and was out of my seat and through his door.

"Better hope I don't," he shouted and laughed.

I needed a new line of work.

The bus ride was everything I dreaded and worse. Long, hot, crowded, smelly, and unsettling. Highway rest stops and fast food. Too much bad coffee in giant-sized containers because, God forbid, you should go a hundred miles without a four dollar cup in your mitt. Heartburn. Headache. And cell phones.

That little piece of technology that declared "drop dead!" to whatever shreds of civility were left in the world. It's like the device *forces* people to bleat their boring lives out loud for the rest of us to listen in on. I got news for you, Sparky, I wouldn't give a crap about your life even if it was interesting. Shut up!

But the worst is how it just trampled to death the notion of privacy. All of a sudden, you're supposed to be instantly accessible to everyone, everywhere, twenty-four/seven. Or get screamed at if you're not.

I'm not.

I get screamed at a lot. I turn off the cell as soon as there's no one around who might want me to have it on, like bosses, creditors, and ex-wives, and blame my lack of accessibility on bad service or low battery. I usually don't even carry it, leaving it at home, hotel, or in the car. On top of it being intrusive, who needs the N.S.A., D.H.S., F.B.I., and A.T.&T. tracking my every move like they do everyone else's through the phone's built-in GPS function?

And yet, by time the bus driver wheeled us into the curbside Greyhound station in Morgantown, West Virginia, I would have traded the one screaming baby who plagued us all with six straight hours of shrill, slobbering crying — accompanied by its mothers only attempt to quiet the child, a ceaseless, sibilant "Shhh! Shhh! Shhh!" that quickly became even more annoying than the crying – for a battalion of cell phone users, all discussing their relationships with their mothers, spouses or bosses or trying to impress the rest of us with their big shot business dealings.

I stumbled from the bus, gasping for air, pining for silence, praying for a drink.

The grime crusted neon of *McSweeney's Tavern* winked at me from across the street. The rear end of an ancient air conditioning unit, wheezing and dripping water the color of tobacco juice onto the sidewalk stuck out of the facade, under black painted windows.

Cool, quiet, and alcohol, all in one convenient location.

Is it any wonder I sighed with contentment as I passed through the doorway, moving from bright sun-lit streets to standard-issue tavern-dim? I didn't even bother to let my vision adjust to the gloom or turn my trained journalist's eye on the details and faces around me. I just stumbled to the bar and said, "The biggest glass of whatever you got on tap."

I was working on sending the second beer down to rescue the first before I stopped to smell the roses or, in the case of *McSweeney's*, the stale beer, tobacco and pine-scented puke. It might, for all I knew, be *the* in-spot of Morgantown but I hoped not. There was a bar, half a dozen booths along the wall opposite it, and a scattering of tables in the rear arranged in a semi-circle before the jukebox. I couldn't see the restrooms but I was betting if I followed my nose I'd be able to find them in no time. Seven men, all of them older, all of them looking like Clint Eastwood's older, craggier brothers, were scattered around the place.

"Yo, chief," I said, crooking a finger in the direction of the bartender, another of Clint's relatives.

"Get you another one?" he asked.

"Naw, this one's still good." To prove it, I took a good swallow. "I was just wondering if you guys'd heard anything about vampires?"

You know those old western movies, where the hero walks into a loud, crowded bar, asks about the bad guy and suddenly the whole joint goes dead quiet? Well this was just like that ... even though no one was making any noise to begin with. It just got quieter somehow, and everybody was looking at me like I was the turd in the swimming pool.

"Ain't no such things," he said, too quickly, his hand going involuntarily to his neck. Most people think it's all Bela Lugosi and Frank Langella. But not these guys.

"C'mon, boys," I said. "It's just me."

Clint, Jr. whisked my half finished beer from in front of me and dumped it in the sink.

"And you were just leavin'," he said in a 'make my day' voice that sent shivers up my spine.

"I'll take that fresh beer now."

"You'll take a hike," he said, same gruff tone as above.

"Okay, now you're just making banter," I said. "Look, I'm a reporter for *Weekly World News*. We got a couple of tips that there's been some vampire activity in these parts."

"Maybe it's them aliens you're always writing about," one of the other Clints quipped to a wave of hearty, manly chuckling.

"No, *these* guys are sucking blood. Aliens give you anal probes."

Looking back in review, I'd say it was the use of the word "anal" that triggered the violence. At any rate, that's when they started beating the living crap out of me.

There's an old chestnut I'm always seeing in mystery novels where the P.I. stirs the pot by charging around like a bull in a china shop and, when someone tries to kill him or beats him up to warn him off, he's happy, figuring it means he's getting close to cracking the case.

I might've been close.

Or maybe I'm just an obnoxious prick most people naturally want to pound on. Either way, I got my nose bloodied, one eye blackened, a lip split, a couple of ribs that felt like they were rattling around loose in there, plus a swell assortment of bruises, abrasions and contusions. And arrested.

On the upside, my knuckles were unmarked. I never got in a shot.

I was booked, photographed, fingerprinted, then given ten minutes with a wad of paper towels and a sink to clean myself up before being planted in the interrogation room, i.e. a table and two chairs in the corner of a file room.

Much as I was ready to stereotype him as a small town hick lawman, Lieutenant Ward Baker of the Morgantown P.D. was anything but a Sheriff Hogg-type. He was well-spoken, immaculate in his pressed uniform, and polite. He offered to send me to the hospital if I wanted medical attention (I declined), then listened patiently to my side of the story.

"You said 'anal probe' to those guys?" he asked, not bothering to hide his grin.

"Yeah, well, in retrospect..."

"Look, Mr. Persky, you don't strike me as a naïve man," he said, the local Appalachian twang still in his voice, just buried, like the coal in the nearby mountains under an Eastern education and a few years living someplace else. "You start poking around in this sort of nonsense, you're not going to make any friends around here."

"Lieutenant Baker," I said with a smile that caused me to wince from my split lip. "I'm not really interested in making friends here or anywhere else. I'm funny that way. All I want to do is get my story and get the hell out of Dodge, so let me spell it out:

"You have yet to indicate in any way, shape or form that you think I'm a lunatic or a fool from a fake-news supermarket tabloid looking to shake up some bullshit for the sake of a story. Well, okay, I *am*, except for the 'fake news' part ... *but*, unless you happen to *know* that vampires, Bigfoot and/or aliens are real, your first reaction's going to be that I'm some crazy conspiracy theory nut. I'm not naïve, you're right, and I know what people think when they talk to me.

"Take you, for instance. You're looking me straight in the eye and treating me like I'm a rational human being. Know why? Wait, that's rhetorical. Because you know I *am*.

"So, what'd you want to tell me about the vampires?"

Baker leaned back in his chair and folded his arms across his chest, spending the next few moments chewing on the inside of his cheek and looking at me. I didn't interrupt his revelry.

"By rights," he said, "I should toss your ass in the can for a few days or boot it out of town."

"Haven't you read the Patriotic Act? We don't have any rights left."

He shook his head and said, "Shit."

I smiled.

"Shit" always meant they'd caved.

He said, "Come on."

The morgue was in the basement of the hospital Baker had earlier offered to take me to for treatment. It was a big block of a building, up on a hill, about halfway to a bulge in a few miles of road called Grafton, and it stood dark and cold against the evening sky.

Morgue. Basement. Where else? The short of it was, soon me and Baker were standing with the coroner, who doubled as the hospital's chief pathologist, or vice versa, along with a trio of bodies, covered by nice, clean white sheets in a vestibule outside the doc's cutting room. His name was Dr. Sanhar Muthupalaniappan, "but you may call me Sandy." No, I couldn't. He wasn't a Sandy. Sandys were happy-go-lucky brown-haired dudes who played tennis and watched golf on TV. I don't know what a Muthupalaniappan was supposed to be, but just in case it was "alumnus of one of my own autopsies," I stuck with calling him Dr. Muthupalaniappan.

"We've had four cases, all involving exsanguinations via dentally induced puncture wounds," he said in a pleasant sing-song voice that belonged more to PeeWee Herman than Uncle Fester. "The forensic evidence indicates in each case the bodies were found where they were killed, but the volume of blood *in situ* did not add up by one third."

"So someone's taking the blood," I said.

"Doesn't mean they're drinking it," Baker said.

"No, of course not. It's just that no one's yet invented anything better than *teeth* to puncture human flesh in order to get to the blood contained therein."

"Cult killings *mimicking* vampyric behavior are not out of the realm of possibility," Doc Dr. Muthupalaniappan interjected with a happy grin.

"Yeah, they are, statistically," Baker corrected. "According to the FBI, there's never been a documented cult killing in this country."

I snorted. "You sleep better believing that, my friend."

Baker stared, pop-eyed. "Just because there *might* be something to this vampire stuff doesn't mean I'm buying into the rest of that garbage you print."

"We're getting off the rails here. The topic's vampires. You got any of the vics on file, doc?"

"Of course, yes. The lieutenant called me you were coming." He took a step to his left and whipped back the sheet of the nearest gurney. I gave him extra points for style. "May I present Miss Wanda Olivia McMartin, age twenty-three, T.O.D.," he said, glancing at his wristwatch, "two days and little more than eighteen hours ago."

Like a vampire myself I went straight for the neck but Muthupalaniappan stopped me, pointing to the south end of the gurney. I indicating her mid-section, then her thighs, getting a negative head shake both times. The young lady had once been attractive enough, but near three days dead from massive blood loss had left her dry and ghostly white. The twin puncture wounds stood out like two pink *Good & Plenty* (were the pink ones the good or the plenty?) in the middle of a bowl of white ones.

On her ankle.

"What've we got here? A sucker with a foot fetish?" I mumbled. I leaned in for a closer look. It took me only a second to know that what I was looking at wasn't right.

"This isn't a human bite," I said to Dr. Muthupalaniappan.

"Of course not. What human would do such a thing? I thought you suspected a vampire."

"Yeah, but they *start* as human. They still are, just undead ones who subsist on blood, so fangs aside, the dentations should be human."

The good doctor grabbed a magnifying glass from an instrument tray and shouldered me aside. He hummed a single note as he poked, probed, and examined the wounds.

"Where were the others bitten?" I said.

"Two neck, one femoral artery, one ankle," said Dr. Muthupalaniappan. "I assumed there would be some non-human deformation for vampire bites. I have, as you might imagine, scant experience with this manner of homicide. But ... if not vampire, this is some manner of dog bite."

Baker looked at me, the poster boy for miserable. "A dog bite?"

"*Some manner of*, yes," Muthupalaniappan said, "but the canines are in a strange formation." He popped a collapsible metal pointer from white lab coat, extended the tip and inserted it into one of the bites. He pressed it in, then marking the depth with his thumbnail, pulled it out. It sounded wet. My stomach fluttered.

"Two inches deep. That is one heck of a dog, yessiree."

"But it's not a dog, is it?" Baker said.

"Two-thirds of her blood missing?" I said. "*Not* a dog."

It takes a fair amount of rationalization and an incredibly open mind to accept that compared to what really goes on in the dark places, your average summer horror blockbuster film is pretty tame stuff.

Lt. Baker was trying, really he was. He could look at a crime scene and intuit what went down from the evidence. As long as the evidence made sense.

"Sense" being the operative word. The trouble he was having was that I had just come along and changed the definition. I had to hand it to the man, though. He worked his own process and at the end of it all, he'd got to where he needed to be.

"So what's the deal?" he asked, sitting in his car in the parking lot of the 4 Corners Restaurant at the junction of U.S. 50 and 119 in Grafton (population 5,489 and birthplace of Mother's Day, according to the sign at the junction), drinking some of the best coffee I'd ever tasted out of paper cups. Baker was smoking. An ex-smoker myself, I was happy for the semi-pacifying effects of his second-hand smoke.

"It's vampires," I said.

He nodded. His eyes didn't flicker.

"You're okay with that?"

"No, but I'm willing to believe it."

My turn to nod.

"So, what's next? Garlic? Stake through the heart?"

"Sure, you want to get that close. Me, not so much. I'm not exactly on the best of terms with the vampire community."

He didn't nod.

"Community." Silence. "I'm really *trying* here."

"You're doing fine," I said. "Look, like I said, vampires are just people. Just undead, blood-sucking people who want the same bullshit as us live ones. Friends, lovers, yada yada yada "

"Yada yada yada?"

"So they form communities. They give me the willies, all of 'em, but ninety-five percent of biters are okay. They get their blood without killing, from blood banks or butchers. Or volunteers. They can't reproduce the old-fashioned way, but you'd be surprised. There're plenty of folks willing to be turned in exchange for a few good feedings."

"Okay, now I'm nauseous."

"Tell me about it. Anyway, like I say, most of them are harmless. It's the loners you've got to worry about. Maybe they were freaks *before* they got turned, but some of them get off on the chase and the power. They like being blood-sucking killer scumbags."

"Charming. But I repeat: what's next?"

"Depends on the biters. Let's review, shall we?" With me looking on, creepy ol' Doc Muthupalaniappan had gone back to take another look at the three bodies still on hand. The fourth, actually the first victim, had been a fifteen year old named Wally Hudkins. His parents had buried him within days of his death. Still, the autopsy photos were enough to show me that *his* bite, at least, was inflicted by human jaws. The other three, not. They were animal bites, and three different animals at that, plain and simple.

I said, "The first attack was two weeks ago, and there's been one every three or four nights since, right?"

"Right. Tonight's night three since Wanda McMartin. All four attacks were after midnight, all within about half mile of the old schoolhouse hill."

"The sheriff and his two deputies are staking out the area. I'm supposed to play roving back-up and coordinate. These guys don't get many homicides, so Morgantown usually take the lead when it's got one. Or four."

"You check out the old schoolhouse?"

"We made sure it was still boarded up tight, yeah."

"That wasn't the question."

"The place's full of asbestos and god knows what kinds of mold and carcinogens. It's off-limits until the town can afford to have it taken down properly."

"Vampires are already dead. They don't sweat cancer. They don't sweat, period."

"Shit," he said.

I shook my head.

"Shit" also meant they'd realized they better start listening to me.

He handed me his coffee cup and twisted the key in the ignition. "Come on," he said.

We raced down two-lane Blueville Drive and screeched up and down a few dark country roads before finding the one that climbed the hill the back way to the schoolhouse. The front way was by foot and featured, according to my host who had attended said school several decades earlier, ninety-two steps to the top. How quaint. Drive, I said!

It was almost midnight.

Baker got the Grafton sheriff on the radio and filled them in on the situation, just short of the vampire parts. He told them to move in on the schoolhouse but stay out of sight and quiet.

"They got crosses?" I asked.

"Around these parts?" Baker said, and keyed the mike again. "Sheriff, you and the boys, keep your crucifixes handy, you copy that?"

"Uh ... say again, Ward."

"You're gonna want to have the Lord on hand, Bob, trust me. Just keep it handy and make sure you shove it in the face of *anyone* comes within spitting distance, got it?"

"Uhm. Roger that, you're the boss."

"What've you got in the truck?" I asked.

"Spare tire, a jack, can of gas, shotgun, tear gas canisters, roadside flares, emergency kit, couple of blankets, a..."

"Yeah, that's good." I looked at my watch. "How close can we get before they see us?"

"Without headlights and in neutral, I can roll us in to fifteen yards, quiet as can please."

I exhaled, loud and hard. "I hate biters."

"So I gathered."

"They're scary, Baker. No bullshit. If you're lucky, they kill you. Otherwise, gobble-gobble, you're one of them."

"I've seen the movies."

"I'm just warning you, that's all. Be afraid, be *very* afraid and be *very, very* careful."

Baker smiled. "You're worried about me."

"Look, just be careful, willya?"

Baker did something on the steering wheel and our headlights flicked off, plunging us into a deep back country road darkness. "You like me and you're worried."

"Jesus," I said, both to him and about the pitch blackness around us.

"So you've met vampires?"

"Uh-huh."

"What about werewolves?"

"Those too,"

"How about the Mummy? Or the Creature from the Black Lagoon?"

"This isn't Monster Thriller Horror Theater, okay?"

Baker began to slow, peering through the windshield.

"You sure you know where you're going?"

"Relax, Leo," he said. "I grew up in Grafton. Been wandering these parts since I was knee-high to a grasshopper."

"You never were."

"Swear to god I was," he said and right around there we ran out of nervous chatter.

He found what he was searching for in the foliage stippled darkness and made a gentle, wide turn into it. It was too dark to see where we were, but I heard branches and leaves whispering along both sides of the car as we bumped along, so I figured it was some overblown footpath. As soon as the nose of the car started to dip, Baker stopped, switched off the ignition, then shifted into neutral. He lifted his foot off the brake and we began to roll down a gentle incline. Baker eased us down the slope, riding the brake the whole way.

"Used to bring my dates up here," he said softly.

"Chicks around here dig the whole asbestos scene?"

"It was fine. We used protection."

For some reason that made me laugh. I tried holding onto that feeling as long as I could.

We bounced onto level ground and he came to a full stop and shifted into park. "Last stop," he said. "School's right beyond the tree line here."

"Okay, flares, blanket, gasoline," I said.

"Huh? Oh ... Christ. Fire?"

"Fire's a sure thing. It's either that or get in close for some stake-work. You volunteering?"

"Not me, man. I spent four years in the marines. Never volunteer."

"I hope you saw action," I said.

He threw what I assumed was his badass cop look, totally wasted on me in the dark, and said, "I can take care of myself."

"Semper fi. I'll go inside, make sure school's in session, and you'll wait out here to spark the flames."

He grabbed my arm. "I'm the cop. I should go in."

"You're just saying that to sound all macho and get in my pants, right? What'd you do if you run into one of 'em?"

I heard him draw a breath to respond, then pause before saying, "Let me sketch you a floor plan..."

There was no sense trying to bullshit vampires. Undead they might be, but biters had animal-sharp senses of smell and hearing and they were going to smell me long before I got to the door. Especially since I'd splashed some gasoline on my pant legs before making my way around to the front of the old schoolhouse through the woods.

"Hello," I called. "Anybody home?"

The schoolhouse gave dilapidation a bad name—its old clapboards, those that chose to still cling to the sagging frame, dripping long curls of once-white, no doubt lead-tainted, mold-mutated paint, windows boarded up, doors barred, and its bell tower sitting at a disturbing angle. Big yellow signs pasted to the door and all the boarded windows warned of hazards to be found inside. They didn't know the half of it.

According to Baker, it was a four room schoolhouse, two on the east side, two on the west; the common area between them serving as lunchroom, gymnasium, and auditorium, as needed. Electricity and water had long been cut off, but that wouldn't bother a vampire.

I walked up to the door and pounded on it. "Yo, wakey-wake! Hello?"

The door swung open under my fist.

I've seen this movie.

But I went inside anyway. I'd tied a handkerchief over my mouth and nose to minimize the carcinogens I'd be sucking in up with every breath inside the old deathtrap, but it wasn't enough to block the stench. It smelled like twenty years of mold and rot, topped by six years of rotting flesh, unwashed ass, and animal crap. It was toxic, forget the asbestos, and it was dark.

And things scurried in the darkness.

Don't they freakin' *always*!

I'd brought Baker's big six-cell cop flashlight and was holding it like a club. Just, you know, in case. Now I reluctantly turned it to use as a source of illumination to see the source of the scurrying.

Which was a squirrel.

Sitting there, in the circle of light, staring at me like the proverbial deer in the clichéd headlights. It didn't seem to want to do anything but stare, so I started to sweep the room with the light.

More squirrels. I came looking for vampires and I find squirrels. Oh, wait, and some chipmunks. And a few rabbits ... and raccoons ... cats ... dogs ... possum...

And bones, stark white, sticking out through what remained of the hides of the stacks of deer, dog, and god only knew what else carcasses stacked and shoved against the north wall.

And the cast of every other Disney cartoon ever made?

They were everywhere. The larger dogs and raccoons were between me and the door, while dozens more cute, furry little critters with their whiskers and crinkly little noses and blood matting their fur and dripping from little mouths wide with gleaming, razor-sharp fangs encircled me.

"Animal bites," I whispered.

Then one of the little bastards pushed the door closed behind me.

The squirrels came at me first. I've always hated them, nothing but rats with good P.R. I didn't even want to think about the consequences of getting bitten by a vampire squirrel. I didn't have time to think, just to scream like a school girl and start swinging my flashlight.

I caught the first one square on the side of the head, sending what little brains it had and much of its blood spraying the room. I stomped on a second, hearing its ribs snap and crumble under my heel. Others were swatted, batted, stomped and kicked, and all the time it was all I could do not to turn and just run away in terror. They were mindless and hungry and purely instinctual and everywhere.

I was breathing hard, hyperventilating, pretty near running on instinct myself. I'm no hero – no, wait, let me rephrase that: I'm a freakin' *coward*. Shit like this scares the living hell out of me. The only reason I go looking for it in the first place is so I'll know *where* it is to stay *away* from those places. And things don't *usually* get ugly. Journalists *usually* don't get involved in their stories, just report them.

Except at times like this, when, without even realizing it, I would start *doing* something instead of just observing. That screwed me every single time. Just not usually with vampire possum.

I watched in the wildly swinging light as Pogo's left eye went flying from its head with a solid shot from the flashlight, but he just kept coming. Garfield had jumped onto my leg and was clawing at me through my Dockers, trying to get to an artery and bite. I kicked at a salvia dripping standard poodle, snapping its spine while I tried fending off a raccoon with one hand around its throat.

Didn't matter though.

Plenty more where they came from, dead little eyes watching, snarling, growling, screeching, scampering in place, almost too excited to wait their turn. But they did wait. This group had hunted together before. A lot.

A squirrel started squirming up my pants.

Oh shit oh shit oh shit!

"Baker!" I screamed.

That was our fancy-schamcy signal to light the fire. There were nasties in the house, don't know if it was all of them, but it was plenty enough for me and the fire might just distract them long enough for me to break free and get out. Maybe even kill them. If I didn't, I'd fry with them. Either way, I was meat.

I broke the front legs of a golden retriever that, in life, had probably been a pussycat. Now, frothing blood at his lips, this snarling carnivore kept coming at me, shoving itself along the floor with its hind legs.

Fur and flesh, blood and gore, and I was screaming Baker's name but wasn't being rewarded with any answering fire or smoke. Stupid dumbshit hick asshole cop all he had to do was throw a goddamned match on the gasoline we'd splashed on the back and side walls before I went inside. What's it got to take? Two seconds, tops!

The animals were all over me. It was a miracle I hadn't taken a bite yet but it was coming. Especially when a German shepherd hurled itself at me and knocked the flashlight from my hand. It went spinning, light and dark dizzyingly across flashes of blood red eyes, dead white teeth and bristling fur. It landed, rotating as in a mad game of spin-the-bottle and didn't stop until a foot stomped down next to it.

Not Baker's foot, though. That would have been too easy. Whoever it was, he grunted, and suddenly, the animals retreated from me, scampering off into the darkness. But not too far. I could hear them, just close enough claws skittering, jaws snapping, but no breathing. The dead don't breath.

"Hey, what the...?" I started to ask, but he said, "Shh!" so I shh'ed. If Doctor Doolittle was leader of the pack, I wanted to stay on his good side. So I waited while he leaned down slowly, lifting the flashlight and rose, letting the light wash slowly over him.

"Jesus," I whispered.

"Forget that," he said in the voice of a kid. "Forget all that, okay?"

"Relax," I said, trying not to let my voice crack as much as the one I'd just heard. "I gave up on it a long time ago. How old are you?"

He didn't let the light reach his face. But I saw he was holding onto something, a bundle of rags dragging behind him on the floor.

"Doesn't matter, right? I'm as old as I'm ever gonna get."

"You're a kid." I took a step forward but was stopped by a growl from the darkness behind me. "Yeah, it sucks, I know, no pun intended. Look, I want to help. This is ... this ... Christ, I dunno *what* this is, but it's got to stop, kid."

He rustled, his face hidden by darkness.

"I know. I, I'm sorry."

"What's your name?"

"What difference does it make?"

"Because I don't want to have to call you 'hey, you" all night."

He shrugged and his bundle of rags moved and moaned. I focused in on it and it suddenly took shape, becoming Baker.

"I don't think you got all night," he said. "I'm sorry."

It hit me then, who this had to be. Wally Hudkins, fifteen, the only one in the morgue with a human bite.

Who'd then been buried. In his native soil yet.

Yet another good reason a reporter shouldn't get involved in his stories. He spends all that time running around and not enough putting the pieces together.

"Wally, right?"

He shrugged. "So?" Even undead, a fifteen year old can stuff a whole lot of snot and attitude into one lousy syllable. I wanted to smack it right out of him.

"Hey!" I snapped, causing a chorus of growls and snarls to erupt around me. I tried, really tried, to ignore them. "I don't need your lip, kid."

"What're you...?" he took at a step back at my tone. I was supposed to be afraid. Instead, I was acting just like another asshole grown-up.

Baker's head thudded on the floor and he moaned again. I couldn't tell if he was out, dazed, playing possum – a *live* one only *pretending* to play dead, I mean – or what. I had to assume I was on my own ... not exactly my first choice for back-up.

"I'm just a reporter, okay? Terrence Strange, *Weekly World News*, and I..."

"No shit?" he said and suddenly his entire demeanor changed. "*You're* Terrence Strange?"

"You read the *News*? Good, so you know I don't want to hurt you. All I want..."

"You're gonna write a story about me," Wally said, his voice quivering. "So my folks and friends and everybody'll know what I've become."

"It doesn't have to be that way, kid. We can help you..."

"No you can't!" he screamed and the menagerie howled and screamed with him. The next thing I know, he whipped the beam of his flashlight at his head ... correction, at what was *left* of his head, which was about sixty-five percent of it. The top right part of his skull was gone, the eye hanging where his cheek ought to have been, gray matter glistening in the gaping wound and the white of his jaw visible through his torn cheek. Petrification had set in around the wounds.

"He bit me," he raged and there would have been tears if the dead could cry. "Made me into a monster and said I'm sorry doin' it and ran away and when I woke up I was buried and I had to dig my way out for days and days and I was so hungry but I didn't wanna hurt no one!

"I, I knew I wanted blood, tried getting it from Mr. Tumley's cows but he shot me with his twelve-gauge, took off half my head so I ran away, tried getting what I needed from the animals in the woods but then they wouldn't stay dead and started biting the others..."

He was raging now, swinging Baker around like a rag doll.

"I didn't mean for nobody to get hurt," he screamed, a bloody froth spraying everything in its path. He opened and closed his mouth several times and moaned. "I gotta kill you, Mr. Strange. I'm so hungry, all the time, animal blood don't do it, y'know?"

He opened his hand and let Baker drop.

"Just this once," he said and he sounded so sorry as he took the first of three steps that would have brought him to my neck. I stepped back but a solid wall of furry animal flesh blocked any retreat.

"Shit," Baker said.

And I smiled.

"Shit" *also* meant that what they were about to do was *so* thoroughly gross, but they were going to do it anyway.

Baker rose behind the kid and with a scream that sounded like a nauseated samurai, he plunged a bright red road flare into Wally Hudkins' gaping skull, gave it a good twist to make sure it was properly seated, then did whatever the hell you do with them to ignite it.

I'm glad I didn't have a camera with me because I would have taken the shot and Berger would have printed it and then I'd never get the vision of half a human head suddenly erupting in chemical magnesium fire out of my brain.

The brain started to bubble and fizzle almost immediately and he screamed with more surprise than pain, but when he raised his hands to his head and they started burning, *something* hit him. Could've been pain... some biters told me they no longer felt pain. Others that the agony never stopped.

Either way, Wally's would be over in a few seconds.

The animals reverted instantly to instinct and as flames from the screaming, wildly gyrating kid flew around, igniting dead, dried carcasses and rotting old timbers, they flew into mindless panic, forgetting all about us.

And me, being an idiot, just stood there, transfixed by Wally Hudkins' final, macabre dance of undead death. Baker, obviously not a patron of the arts, knew enough to grab me and get us both out the front door, which he slammed behind us, before there was a gigantic, deafening sound like the air exploding and the old schoolhouse became the biggest bonfire Taylor County had ever seen.

The old building was only still standing out of luck and, maybe, some fluke of gravity. The moment the flames hit the roof, the leaning bell tower finished its westward sway and collapsed and I could have sworn I heard Wally crying and screaming for his mother.

Baker insists I imagined it. Said he didn't hear a thing.

Whatever.

Being on top of a hill in the middle of town, the blaze brought people running fast, but not fast enough to stop a building's worth of rotten timbers and dried old wallboard and filled with corpses from being reduced to a couple of dumpster's worth of ashes and charred sticks and bones.

The local cops and fire fighters found only animal remains in what was left. We had decided to keep Wally's name out of the official report. People could read it in the *News*; they wouldn't believe it there, but for his parents' sake and sanity, we opted to leave him, for the record at least, dead.

What there was of the vampire-puddycats and other critters were too charred to produce any analyzable organic information. Creepy ol' Doc Muthupalaniappan theorized that just as bird or pig influenzaviruses sometimes mutate into a form that can migrate from animals or birds to humans and cause illness, Wally Hudkins was some sort of genetic crossover or gateway. Whatever his body did to whatever it is that passes vampyrsm from person to person enabled it to leap to animals in a form capable of spreading among the non-human population.

"Imagine," the doctor whispered in a low, campfire story-telling voice, "assuming vampires *do* exist, if the spread of this zoological vampyrsm had not been curbed!"

"But it has," said Baker. He squinted at me. "Right?"

I shrugged. "How the hell'm I supposed to know? I didn't get to take a head count."

"Oh, Leo, for crying out loud..."

"What do you want from me?"

He stared at me, his eyes wide. "What if there's more of them out there?"

"Baker, I *don't* know. I can give you the names of some experts, have them check it out."

"How much is that going to cost?"

"Uhm, less than being attacked by a vampire Bambi?"

"Christ, Leo…"

And suddenly, the pending endless, hideous Greyhound Bus ride home was starting to look almost attractive. If my luck held, I'd wind up with *two* screaming babies.

Ebb Tide

by Elaine Bergstrom

July 1955

PICKING up the morning papers, Lettie began to leave the Tilton grocery when the owner grabbed her arm. "If yer looking for a fourth at yer place, I'm available," he said.

His hair was stringy, his white shirt sweat stained and he smelled like he hadn't bathed in a week, hard to do when you live right by the beach. He works to be a slob, Lettie thought, as she jerked her arm away. There was a wet patch on it from his sweat, and she pulled a tissue from the box on the counter and wiped her arm, dropping the tissue beside to box for the owner to pick up. As the screen door slammed behind her, the owner yelled, "Police been asking about you three, jail bait. Be careful, nigger!"

Lettie kept walking. Damn no count! She'd come north hoping to get away from white trash like him.

But even no counts could mean trouble so she'd ask Dawnie to come for the papers tomorrow. It wouldn't be worth it to suggest that Charles get them himself. He always slept until late afternoon. "One of those night people," he called himself. Well, if that was what night people were like, maybe she'd been missing something. Herself, she was a morning person by nature.

They'd met Charles a week ago. It had been after midnight and she and Dawn had been finishing off their last bottle of Catawba red. As they sat at the tacky oilcloth-covered table, they tried to be serious long enough to decide whether they should pool their remaining funds and rent the beach cottage on Lake Erie another week or move on to look for work.

When they heard a car drive up and park beside it, they blew out the lantern and crouched behind the screen door. Soon fear gave way to choked back laughter, as in the revealing moonlight, they watched a man strip off all his clothes and walk into the water, not bothered one bit by the high waves rolling around him.

Looking at him, Lettie felt like her heart was beating a whole lot lower in her body. Dawnie must have felt the same way, because she did something awfully strange for her. She snuck out of the cabin, went down to the beach and moved his clothes back a good twenty feet to a patch of moonlight just outside their door. Inside, between giggles, she said, "Sharp stuff. Now we'll get a better look when he comes back."

So they'd crouched behind the screen door and waited, and waited some more. About the time they'd begun to worry that he must have drowned, he was back; half swimming, half crawling. When he reached the beach, he lay face down at the edge of the shoreline, one hand stretched forward clawing the sand. The moonlight flickered on the drops of water clinging to his dark curly hair, his pale muscular body.

Lettie and Dawn stood inside their cabin door. "Do you think he's hurt," Lettie asked.

"Maybe," Dawn replied and they both stared out the door wondering what they should do.

When another few minutes passed and he still hadn't moved, Dawn got the blanket from their bed and they walked to the beach and stood above him, looking down at his body – long limbed and muscular. Dawn touched him, then shook him and said she was pretty sure he was still alive. A wave broke over their feet, covering the man's back nearly to his shoulders.

"Maybe we should pull him further up the beach?" Lettie suggested.

Dawn looked at the pile of sharp stones just above the water line and had a sudden silly thought, which along with her uneasiness and the wine made her break into giggles. "If we do, he's going to be awfully sore."

Lettie thought this a little smutty but laughed too. "We'll just have to turn him over and let his behind take the beating. If we leave him here and he doesn't drown by morning, someone will call the law in for sure.

They bent over him, then jumped back in surprise when the man began to laugh. Before they could run, he'd grabbed them by the ankles, pulling them down into the waves. "Steal my clothes, will you!"

Dawn squealed as a wave drenched her completely. "I didn't, I just moved them a little."

"Really? And why did you do that?" When she didn't reply, he held her down and a wave broke over her face.

She sputtered, a little frightened. "So we could see you better," she confessed.

He turned to Lettie. "And you? Were you going to watch, too?"

Lettie grinned. "Sure. This is our beach. We can watch."

"Well, in that case, I suggest you thieves or voyeurs or whatever you are, invite me into your cabin to dry off."

"If you promise to behave," Dawn warned.

"I promise." He held up his hand like a Boy Scout. "I promise to be as civilized as I possibly can." Then, naked as a newborn and just as unconcerned, he took their hands and walked past his clothes and into their cabin.

It might have been the wine, or it might have been him (Lettie didn't know and didn't care) but the next morning the three of them were all tangled in the sheets of the one double bed. And the girls decided that the last thing they wanted was to see him go. And that turned out better than they'd expected. He was loaded and didn't mind spending. Their money worries were over.

Soon things settled into what Dawn, who sometimes read smutty novels, called a menage a trois, a term Charles changed to menagerie. He looked at them lying there: Dawn, short and buxom and fair; her, tall and thin and quadroon chocolate; and him, pale with dark soft curly hair. "A menagerie, a most peculiar zoo," he said, not unkindly. The term stuck.

Life was smooth, except that Lettie knew that Charles was crazy. Late in the morning after he'd arrived, Dawn and Lettie had fussed over him, fixing him the last of their eggs and bacon, toast and canned fruit salad. He watched them, looking amused until they put the plate in front of him. He'd pushed it away and pumped a glass of well water, watching them eat. Lettie had stood next to him, her fists on her hips, about to demand, like his mother, that he had to eat something. Before she could say a word, he looked up at her and said, "I only eat when the sun goes down."

His expression had been lewd as he ran his hand up the inside of her bare thigh, his fingers curling around the elastic on her cotton panties, so she wasn't sure what he meant.

She was bothered, too, by the odd way he sometimes looked at her, as if he's forgotten her name. Always, before she could ask him what was wrong, he'd say something reassuring and things would be fine for awhile. With Dawn he was even more distant. Except for sex, he sometimes didn't say anything to her for days. Charles' odd behavior might have frightened Lettie had she not been used to it. In his last year, her daddy had been a champion fader. Never touched a drop of whiskey in his life, but he died like a drunk anyway, poisoned by his own blood.

One night, Charles brought home an artist's sketch book and some pastels and sat drawing in the dark. Dawn had missed his body between them and, half asleep, rolled over and put her arms around Lettie, her full breasts pressed against Lettie's back. Instinctively, Lettie had slapped her arm and pushed her away. There were times when touching was proper, but certainly not when Charles was missing. As she fell asleep, she heard the sound of chalk rubbing on paper. It reminded her of mice scurrying inside walls and she did not sleep well.

Lettie was awakened before sunrise by the grating of the cover on the little pot belly stove that heated the cabin. She padded softly to the table and, in the bleak morning light, stared down at magnificent visions, terrible visions, nightmares and the portrait of a woman of unearthly beauty. She shook her head no, no, but did nothing to stop him as he fed each drawing to the flames. Later that morning, he'd drawn the three of the. Her as a dark gazelle. Dawn, as a golden plump lion. Himself as a strange animal, powerful and ugly. "What is it?" Lettie had asked.

"Some beast, sloucert headerhing off," he'd replied. That afternoon, he'd handed Lettie a thousand dollars and disappeared for three days. When he came back, he began asking for newspapers from Cleveland and Sandusky.

Charles and Dawn were asleep when Lettie returned with the morning news. They lay close, his dark curls tangled with her blond ones, his face nuzzling the back of her neck. The day was already hot and getting hotter. Moving softly, Lettie undressed, pulled on her swimsuit and walked down to the lake.

A little after noon, dry but still cool, Lettie heard Dawn scream. Rushing through the screen door, she saw Charles, one hand pressing hard against the small of Dawn's back while he poured a glass of ice water over her bare buttocks. "You rotten pig!" she yelled. "Darn creep!" But by then, she sounded like she enjoyed how it felt.

Well, Lettie, she heard someone whisper in her mind. *Are you going to stand there like some demented voyeur or are you going to join us?*

And let Dawn have all the fun, hell no! Lettie had taken only two steps toward the bed when Charles pounced like a cat, grabbing her and dousing her with the rest of the water.

"I thought you didn't do that until the sun went down," Lettie said to Charles later.

"Lunch," he replied, his dark eyes dancing. He kissed her open mouth and as she returned it, his sharp teeth bit her tongue.

Later, while the girls napped, Charles sat down to skim his papers. When he'd arrived, he'd had a different idea of how the night would end. He'd waited patiently, letting his still form lure them forward. But they had been so much like mischievous overgrown children that he'd been unable to strike. And what a night it had turned out to be! Lettie, virginal but enthusiastic.

Dawn, too experienced for her age, full of sad secrets he struggled to ignore. He had found it a challenge to make her respond, but then ...

Well, soon the happy vacation would be over. Its end would be a relief. Too many weeks here and even this lighthearted pair would not be able to hold back the dark memories groping for his soul. His sanity smirked slyly, waxing and waning like a Cheshire cat. Before it vanished completely, he had to die. The police would find the body he had left for them soon, decipher the note he had left near it and come for him. Before they did, he'd give Lettie the keys to his car and the key to his safe deposit boxes in New York. He pictured their expressions when they opened them and found out that they were rich.

But the vacation would end sooner than Charles expected, because in a small town in Kentucky, Sam T. "Doc" Martin sobered up and decided that he missed his little girl.

The first thing everybody noticed about Doc Martin was his hands. They were short and wide and pale with coarse hairs covering the first digit. They looked weak and piglike in a man who had a body much taller, leaner and far more powerful than those fingers deserved. If the person noticing his hands was a stranger, he might ask what the "Doc" stood for. If Doc was drunk enough and the stranger looked friendly enough, Doc might say and the stranger would likely look down at those pudgy hands and say to themselves "it figures." The men who hung around Doc's favorite tavern were distant but friendly because they sometimes needed him. The women never spoke to him at all, but Doc didn't care. He had his little girl. He's raised Dawnie alone, he had, since her ma died in '49.

The day of the funeral, Dawnie had stood dry-eyed and brave while friends and the few family members who had traveled in for the funeral took turns covering her ma's casket. Than father and daughter had gone home; she to her room, he to his bottle. That was the way life went on for nearly a year until the night Sarah was so real that Doc could almost touch her. He'd started to sob and Dawn heard him and came out of her room, put her arms around him and cried along. He'd looked at her then, at her round cheeks, pink like a Kentucky mountain sunrise, her blue eyes with the pale brown lashes to match the sprinkle of freckles, the soft blond curls which were Sarah's curls. Then held her too tight, not like a father ought to hold a daughter at all. And she let him because she was almost old enough to understand.

Her comfort hadn't helped. The bottle did and soon Doc Martin found he had no practice left except for the kind that was outside the law. And somewhere in the bottle, he found a sort of bitterness to replace the sorrow, and black moments of forgetfulness which were just as well. There were a lot of things Doc wouldn't have wanted to know about.

Dawn had run off a year later, but she was too young to get far and the sheriff had brought her back. Doc had taken a switch to her, then locked her in her room until the marks didn't show. It was the first time he remembered beating the girl, but she had to be taught.

And now she was gone again, this time with that pale colored bitch who used to wait on tables over at the diner. And the two had the money he'd been stashing away in his cash box. He'd kept the box locked, of course. He bet it was that damn Lettie who suggested that they just walk off with the whole thing.

Well, when he found them, he'd make them both pay. Maybe if her Pa had thrashed her good when she was younger, Lettie would have stayed down in New Orleans where she belonged instead of coming up here and getting his little girl in so much trouble.

When Doc realized that his drinking wasn't making it any easier to find Dawn, he sobered up, put on clean clothes and stormed into the sheriff's office to demand action. Ron Parker, being young Jim's uncle, was not likely to want to cooperate but Doc figured he had to make do. Parker ran his fingers through his short and thinning hair and scratched a mosquito bite on his neck. In a thick slow drawl that was the perfect accompaniment to a slow but honest mind, he said, "Girls ev been gone more than six weeks. Kinda late to start lookin. And Dawnie 'ell be of legal age soon. Hand to hold onto then."

Doc slammed his fist on Parker's desk. "Damn it, find my little girl before she gets into more trouble."

Parker was amazed Doc has the gall to show up there and remind him of family history, so to speak. Jim had told him some unsettling stories about Doc. Parker suspected they were true. "You sure you want her back? She can give you a lot of trouble if she starts talking."

"She stole over $700 from my cash box. I'll take every penny out on her hide!"

That was more serious, assuming that Doc was telling the truth.

Doc started to cry. "It's why I waited so long. I didn't want her in any trouble with the law and I figured that once the money ran out, she'd come home. But she hasn't so she might try something stupid again." Doc sank into one of the wood armchairs. "I'll offer a reward, too. $200 to anyone who finds her and a match to the lawman who brings her back."

Parker stood and leaned over his desk. "I don't want your damned money but I'll find your little girl. And when I do, she and I are gonna have a nice long talk and she'd better have nothing but nice things to say about you."

It was pure luck Parker got a reply so soon. A woman at a convenience store near Tilton noticed a young colored girl buying groceries and paying for them with a fifty dollar bill. It looked suspicious enough that the woman mentioned it to the sheriff. Eight days later, when he read Parker's bulletin, he remembered the girl and decided to do a little talking. It didn't take him long to track Lettie down. The store owner had plenty to say about her and her blond friend and the strange rich guy no one saw. A pimp and two pros, though he admitted he'd never seen them solicit.

Still, the missing money and reward made them worth looking into, so two days after the owner had sneered his warning to Lettie, Sheriff Panetti had done just that.

Dawn had gone to the outhouse and Charles was still asleep, so Panetti saw only Lettie sitting on the cabin's porch looking a little frightened — understandably, he thought — by his arrival. He walked up and gave her a friendly, "Hello."

As she stood, Lettie glimpsed Dawn round the side of the cabin, see the sheriff's car, slowly back off and crouch down. Probably going to hide, Lettie thought, deciding this was one of those times that you didn't level with the law.

"Your name Lettie James?"

"Yessir." She couldn't deny it. It was the name on the cabin rental certificate because no one would be looking for her.

"Dawn Martin here?"

"Nossir, she left."

"Do you know where she was headed?"

"Nossir, didn't say."

"You here alone?" Panetti started up the steps.

Since their only resemblance was in their dark hair, Lettie prayed that Charles was still asleep, wrapped in a sheet and facing the wall. "Nossir, my brother is staying with me for a few weeks. He's still asleep, little too much to drink last night. Want to come in and look around?"

Panetti did, but only for a minute. There was no place for the Martin girl to hide inside, too many outside. He decided it would be most productive to just act casual and keep an eye on the place.

As he left, Lettie screwed up enough courage to ask, "Did Dawn do something wrong?"

"We have a warrant for her arrest. Seems she stole a lot of money in Kentucky. There a $200 reward, too. You see her, you turn her in. It'll be worth your while."

Lettie gave him a look she hoped was greed. "I'll do that, sir."

The girl was lying, of course, and as soon as Panetti got back to the station, he phoned Parker who gave Doc the news. "Want me to drive up and bring her in?"

"Naw, I got a letter call from her aunt up in Charlottesburg. She showed up there. I'll go pick her up in day or two. I guess we can just forget the whole thing."

"And the money?"

"I'll take that out on her hide." Doc laughed and hung up the phone.

Then he packed his trunk with some clothes, a gallon jug of cane corn and a loaded shotgun. He put a hunting knife in his glove box. As he took one last look around the house before locking up, he glanced at the calendar. August 10. The 25th was Dawnie's birthday. Well, he had a surprise for her alright, and when it was over and that colored bitch was dead, his little girl would never cross him again.

As soon as Panetti left, Charles rolled over, flung his arms wide and exclaimed, "I can pass!"

"This isn't funny," Lettie reminded him. "We're in trouble. He didn't believe a thing I told him."

"Dawn's in trouble," he said and walked outside and peered under the porch floor at Dawn who cowered in the shadows. She flinched, then realized who it was and relaxed.

"He's gone," Charles said and held out his hand. She crawled out, brushed the sand off her knees and rushed inside.

"Someone wants you bad enough to lie big," Lettie told her.

"I know, I heard." Dawn's voice revealed a provocative mix of fear and hopelessness. Charles had no desire to know anything about the girls and in their presence that darker side of him slept. Now, sniffing Dawn's emotions, it woke and focused its powerful senses on the girl. He prodded, but barely a ripple marred the surface of her thoughts. There was only a face, a word, a beginning ...

"Dawnie," Charles whined in a voice that made Dawn stare at him to assure herself this was not the feared other.

She shook her head and backed toward the door. "Don't call me that," she whispered.

"Dawnie," he repeated and an ugly smile did terrible things to his handsome face. She might have run but her feet seemed frozen to the floor as she struggled not to remember all the things she had vowed so recently to forget.

Lettie's eyes darted from one face to the other, not sure what was happening, only knowing from Dawn's expression that Charles was playing some horrible game. − Get out! − Charles ordered, though his lips did not move.

Lettie ran. As the door slammed shut, she heard Charles continue, his voice obscene with drink and desire, "Dawnie, come over here and give your daddy ..."

No! Dawn broke his mental hold on her and lunged for the door. Charles was faster. He grabbed her arm and though she kicked and wanted to bite, she couldn't harm him any more than she ever could her pa.

"Dawnie." Though he still used her pa's nickname, it was his own voice now. "Dawnie, what is it you're hiding?"

"I won't say! Nobody believed me the last time and I don't wasn't to tell it to anyone again!" Her voice was wild, pleading, all that Charles had expected. He knew her story already, but he wanted more than that. He wanted her to feel.

He pushed her down on the edge of the bed. She clutched the sheet. "You don't have to say a word, just think about it one last time."

She scuttled over the mattress to the far corner, her back pressed against the knotty pine wall, her knees against her chest as if by guarding her body she could also protect her mind. "Stay away from me! I'll scream if you touch me now." Her voice was desperate. If she started screaming, she thought she might never stop.

Such abundant fear was too powerful a temptation to Charles' dark addiction. He crawled slowly over the bed toward her, a predator closing in on its wounded prey. When she thought that she would scream, his hand covered her mouth. With no will to fight on, she retreated to her own private place, allowing him to unbend her knees and roll her sideways to press against him. Only then did he lower his hand and his eyes, insistent as Doc's fresh scalpels, slashed through her will. − Now, Dawnie. Remember. −

And she did. From the nameless uneasiness to the helpless defiance, the pain, the ever-present self hate to that last year, the worst year of all, the year that she, in love, had lost the last barrier of innocence and was open to Doc as well.

This was all he'd expected, and more. He began to feed, to devour this sad banquet. As he took it all, he anticipated how much he would relish the slow destruction of his next victim.

After, he held her and stared at the planked ceiling, the dusty lantern, the curled ribbon of old flypaper handing from it. He waited, knowing the memory would return as always returned. Eternal. Inevitable. His mind moved down its own sad paths ...

... He paces, one corner to the next to next, welcoming her screams, for when she is silent her hate pounds against him like a full moon tide ... one corner. Another. Another, just like any father and she like any woman and this birth not also a wake. The nurses come, holding cuffs in their hands.

"Tie her down? What do you mean?"

She pulls out the tubes, they say. She must have blood. They are apologetic. It's not uncommon. The pain maddens, you see.

He remembers what they are. I will hold her for you. She will not struggle with me. They lace the heavy fabric to her wrists and tie her to the metal bed. Ah, Claudia! So weak. Weaker even than one of them. But I am here and I will be strong for you.

"Her feet? What are you doing? No, she'll have the babies here! Here, do you understand. You can't cut her. But, yes, she'll kick if you don't tie them. Stirrups? Yes, I understand. Here, let me."

Claudia! You promised me. You promised me you would not die! ...

Lettie was sitting at the water's edge, toes digging into the wet sand when Charles stalked out of the cabin and, without a word or even a nod toward her, went and opened the trunk of his car. She watched him unload a strange wooden bow and some short arrows and head for the woods. She went to the cabin and looked inside at Dawn lying on the bed, eyes closed, pale and still. Instead of waking her, she followed Charles. She'd gone a hundred yards or so into the trees when something whizzed past her shoulder and stuck on the trunk of a tree. Four more whizzes, so close together they might have been fired at the same time, and now there were five short spikes sticking out of the tree trunk in one straight line, each separated from the next by less than an inch.

"Hey!" she yelled more in irritation than fear. "You might have hit me!"

"I'm an excellent shot," he said, and followed that with a peal of high-pitched laughter, which only made her more angry. "This is no time to be fooling around. What will we do if the sheriff comes back?"

"Nobody is going to take Dawn away."

"But what about the money?"

"We know it's a lie. Her father wants her back, but it's too late for him." He sent five more arrows flying, reloading and shooting so fast she could not see his hands move. When he went to retrieve them, his feet made no sound, as if they were not quite touching the ground. "These bows were the ultimate weapon in their day, until those using them realized they were too slow," he said.

"Too slow?"

"For human hands, but not for mine. No, Dawnie will never have to run anyplace again."

Only her stubborn streak kept Lettie from bolting from the woods. Instead she asked Charles if he knew what was bothering her friend. He didn't reply right away, but then he sat beside her and told her about Dawn and Doc. Lettie's stomach grew queasy and her eyes watered but she didn't cry. Instead, she said with firm practicality, "We got to get out of here."

Charles' eyes seemed sad as he shook his head. "We aren't going anywhere. He'll come to us."

"We can't kill him."

"No, Lettie. *We* won't have to."

If he meant to be reassuring, it didn't work. She wished he'd give her the car keys and some money and tell them both to get out of here. She didn't want to go without him, but she wanted even less to stay. He didn't make the offer. In the game he played with fate, Lettie and Dawn were no more than pawns.

Doc drove into Tilton two days later. He parked his car off the main street and sauntered around the corner to the town's only tavern. Spreading a little money down the bar paid off and, after an hour or so, he knew exactly where to find his little girl. She was holed up with Lettie and some guy. A couple of niggers, the talk went. Well, talk would change fast. Some time later, he took a quick drive over to it, parking some distance away and casing the place. He liked the way it sat at the edge of the others in the rundown resort, made private on three sides by wood and brush.

He stayed only a few minutes before heading back to town. He'd come back after dark and catch them unawares.

A few hours after dark, feeling the false confidence of numerous shots and beers, he returned and parked at a picnic area at the edge of the cabins. He pulled his knife from the glovebox but left the shotgun in the trunk. This was a private matter and shotguns had a way of making things public.

Grabbing his flashlight, he circled through the woods and approached the cabin by way of the beach. The waves were high. They would stifle any noise. Charles, aware of Doc's arrival from the time he'd parked the car, agreed.

Doc's powerful legs slipped quietly over the smooth sand and up the two rickety steps to the porch. The door was unlocked and he entered. Inside, he was greeted by night and silence. No snores. Not even any breathing. He was alone.

As he began to switch on the flashlight, something grabbed it from his hand. He heard it hit something and shatter. He tried for his lighter and an open hand slapped hisso hard his fingers numbed. He waited, listening and hearing nothing, then reached into his other pocket for some matches, but something clamped down on his wrist so tightly he thought the bones would crush, so quickly that, when he slashed down with his knife, it landed on air. "Hold still, damn it!" Doc growled then, realizing he had no advantage here, added, "I want to talk to you about my Dawnie."

He expected some reply but there was only silence. Doc was alone, yet not alone. With that realization, the fear began and the thing in the cabin with him responded.

This was the second night Lettie and Dawn had slept in Charles' car with the doors locked and the windows cracked for air. Charles had said Doc would come soon and Lettie had the feeling "soon" meant tonight. She peeked out from time to time and was rewarded by the sight of a dark shadow moving up their porch stairs. "Dawn!" she whispered and shook her friend. "Dawn, wake up."

It took Dawn awhile to stretch and sit up. She'd been sleeping on and off for two days now, not sick but not well either. She didn't seem to care about Doc or the police, either. Strange behavior given how terrified she'd been. Lettie had no way of knowing that Dawn's fear had been so much a part of her that, with them gone, little of Dawn remained.

"I think I saw someone coming up the beach. I think he had a knife." Dawn just shrugged a reply.

Lettie had met Doc a few times. He had at least three inches and a good fifty pounds on Charles. Though it was hard to imagine anyone as quick as Charles losing a fight, Lettie worried anyway. Doc was mean and had a reputation as a dirty fighter and that strange box, ready and hung close to the door, would be next to useless in the dark. If Doc got a good grip on Charles, there was no telling how the night would end. Maybe Charles needed help. Jesus! He needed her help. If she didn't give it and ...

She grabbed the small kitchen knife she'd brought along for protection and groped on the car's floor until she saw the flashlight. Rolling down the window, she climbed out and crept up to the cabin's side window. She tried to see inside but it was so dark she might have had her eyes closed. She listened but all she could hear was the insistent roll of the waves, the rustle of impatient falling leaves.

Was anyone inside at all? Could it be over without any noise at all? Could they have killed each other. She refused to believe any of it. She hadn't seen anything. Nobody killed anybody. Everything was fine. She repeated these three thoughts until she almost believed them, then worked her way slowly to the front porch. She breathed in slow nervous puffs as she searched for the courage to turn on the flashlight and open the screen door.

The few minutes Doc had stood in the dark cabin had sobered him up like ours of sleep and a quart of black coffee. With his confidence in a disorderly retreat, Doc gripped the knive and began an indirect backwards shuffle aimed at getting him close enough to the door to make a quick bolt to freedom.

Two yards shy of the door, his feet refused to move though Doc's mind barked orders for them to continue. When his destruction began, he did not need pair or words to know it. Fear made him pant like a woman in childbirth as something seemed to grab his brains, squeezing out memories like dirty water from a sponge ... the moans, the occasional screams, the fighters who sometimes had to be restrained. Dawnie had been a fighter, he remembered, but not out of cowardice. No, he'd tricked her, never letting on he knew she was pregnant until the night he drugged her and she's come to strapped to his table, her legs tied to the stirrups. She was his little girl and he's done what was right for her, oblivious to her screams that she did not want him to take her baby. She'd unnerved him, and he'd grabbed his bottle for relief. Hours later, he woke up on the floor and looked up at her bare spread legs, the blood dripping down, her eyes dry with hate. He saw that she'd been further along than he'd thought and before he freed her, he'd gotten some old rage and cleaned up the mess so only would know that if it had lived it would have been a girl.

He heard a long hiss, something sucking in its breath, and the words formed in his mind, – I won't touch you. Even don't want the poison you have to give. –

In that instant, the door behind Doc swung open and a flashlight burned Doc's useless eyes. With his knife held out, he lunged and, as it penetrated, something flung him back to strike the wall and fall stunned to the floor. The flashlight outlined Lettie's slim form just long enough for Doc to see her before darkness returned.

Charles caught her before she hit the floor. Lifting her gently, he laid her on the bed the gave her the sheet and showed her how to press to hold back the bleeding. She had come to defend him – the brave fool! – and though he knew the wound was mortal, he hoped she would live until he was through with Doc. He had a use for her, especially now, though inside he howled at the loss of her. Behind him, Doc struggled to his feet and, for the first time Charles spoke, "I think this might be murder."

Doc thought his oddly accented voice too cold for its owner to have been Lettie's lover. If the man was trying to make Doc feel remorse, he'd have to try a hell of a lot harder. He raised his knife. "That was an accident," he growled. "But you'll be justified homicide."

The answer began with laughter. "It won't be homicide at all." Charles pulled a kitchen match from the box on the stove, struck it, and held the flame to his face and grinned. "See," he said, then lit the lamp.

Not waiting to get a good look at his opponent, Doc charged. Charles, smooth as running water, stepped out of his way and Doc stumbled past him, catching his balance just in time to keep from landing on Lettie. She lay, mercilessly conscious, looking past him at Charles.

Something in her expression made Doc turn and for the first time, he saw the face of his attacker. He took a step back, another, until he reached the dresser beside the bed.

Doc thought of the night birds of prey, of the bats that used to brush his face in the caves he'd explored as a boy, of the huge-eyed demons that haunted his intoxicated dreams, He slid down the wall, dropping the knife as the creature walked toward him and knelt beside him. He heard music as it spoke. "You died before you ever walked into this place. I chose you, you who hold the knife while I am unarmed. Can you doubt your end for even a moment."

Doc shook his head, never moving his eyes from that taut, inhuman face. Fear held the rest of him motionless.

"No, I won't touch you. Not until I milk all the venom you have to give."

Doc recognized his earlier memories, but these came from a different, more hidden, place. He lowered his head and pressed it between his hands, his body shaking with dry sobs. "Dawnie, Dawnie," he moaned because it was Dawn he saw in his mind, Dawn watching him, hating him for how he touched her, what he did to her, and what he saw, and had done, he had never known until now. "My child," he sobbed. "I killed my own child."

The being before him did not speak, but in his mind Doc heard an assent. With a final display of dignity, Doc lifted his knife and, never moving his eyes away from the face of his attacker, he plunged it down.

After Lettie had gone, Dawn slipped back into a fitful sleep, only to wake with a start, uncertain how much time had passed. She missed Lettie; she wanted Charles. Walking as if still asleep, she went to the cabin and opened the door. Just inside, she stopped, immobilized by the horror of Lettie, unconscious now, her blood soaking the mattress, and the presence of her father, the agony distorting his familiar face. Charles, his back to her as he knelt beside Doc, she barely saw at all.

− He will never hurt you again. −

Not her father, Dean thought with misplaced despair.

"Dawnie," she heard him call and moved toward him until some force pushed her back. When she reached the wall, she stopped and watched the strange, silent battle continue.

Dawn did not wonder who had wounded Lettie nor remember what Doc had done to her. Charles had stolen the worse memories of her past, so she thought only of her childhood – Sarah and Doc and her in the good times too long ago. Her hand rose to grasp the crossbow, bring it down, level it and wait.

As her father raised the knife, she screamed, "Daddy, stop!" and fired the weapon at Charles and almost missed. He whirled and leapt. She never had a chance to struggle, just as Charles, trapped by instinct, could not control his attack.

After, there was silence, broken only by Lettie's labored breaths and the soft drips from the dead, the wounded, the dying. Charles sat beside Lettie and brushed away the damp hair clinging to her forehead. He willed her to wake.

Lettie opened her eyes, surprised to find there was no pain. "Is Dawn all right?" He lied and nodded. "But I'm going to die?"

"Yes," he said, thinking of the kitchen knife. So brave, and paying such a terrible price.

"It's too soon..." She struggled to breathe and her voice was so soft even he had difficulty hearing her words. "I wanted to get away. ... I wanted..." She couldn't go on.

– Show it to me. –

Lettie obeyed, and he saw fragments of her life. The poverty. The first understanding of hate-filled slurs. The struggle to save and, finally, to leave for some glorious unknown future as if someplace north was her Emerald City and happiness and riches were something you only had to work for and, with persistence, claim.

The he saw himself, the climax of her seventeen short years, and a broken ugly cry crashed into the night to drown in the waves. Pressing his lips to her wound, he began to feed, to hear her confession and absolve her of others' sins and leave her to face eternity with grace.

After death had claimed its enormous debt, Charles sat among the bodies, thinking of his people, his brother, his one slim hope. He washed and changed his clothes. Then, gathering up all evidence of his presence here, he overturned the table and watched the lamp fall, the kerosene spread and the bright flames follow.

As he turned to leave, he glimpsed the drawing of the menagerie tacked to the door. Ripping it down, he held it to his chest, bent forward, sucked his lips between his teeth and bit hard. When control returned, he straightened and threw the paper across the room, another piece of his life condemned to the flames. The fire had already reached the bedding, and the last thing he saw before he left the cabin was Lettie's hand, a dark still silhouette against the rising hungry light.

Dead Ringers

by Dan Wickline

THE 1974 Ford Maverick whined its way up the drive towards the main office. Bradley wondered for a second that if the car died here, would they let him bury it. The sickly yellow four-door popped and sputtered, but kept rolling forward towards the main office in the distance. This was just one of the many reasons that Bradley decided to take the night shift at the cemetery over mornings and weekends at the Book Palace. He needed a new car, he wanted a better apartment and he was tired of eating noodles five nights a week. The cemetery job paid three times what the Book Palace offered him and to do what? Walk around in the dark? Chase off some kids? It sounded like a job where he could mindlessly make it through his shift without having to deal with the living.

Bradley parked his car, and it thanked him for ending its torture by popping and banging for about thirty seconds after he got out. He headed up to the front door. The main building looked more like a small house than a place of business. Before he could open the door, a young blond woman ran out past him like the building was on fire. She bumped into Bradley on the way by, but kept moving towards the cars.

"Sorry… got to go. It's getting dark." The woman called back.

"Where would I find David Witzig?" Bradley called after her.

"He should be out in just a second," the woman said as she closed her car door and sped off.

Bradley yelled out 'thanks' towards the speeding car, but she was already way out of earshot. He turned back towards the house to see a small, somewhat round man bolting out the door. The man came to a screeching halt when he realized that Bradley was in front of him. It had to be Mr. Witzig.

"Uh… what? Who are you?" Witzig asked.

"I'm Bradley Ford, your new night man, Bradley said, adding a smile to the end to make a good first impression.

"Welcome aboard, Bradley; I think you're going to do just fine." With that, Witzig pointed Bradley towards the groundskeeper's shed up on the hill. "You'll find your supervisor up there. Just do what he says and we'll talk in the morning." Witzig turned and practically dove into his car, kicked it over and sped off. His new boss had some quirks; Bradley could accept that. Hell, you'd have to have a few quirks to work at a cemetery. Since he now worked in one, Bradley wondered about his own quirks as he started the long trek up the hill. He had left Los Angeles, land of eternal sunshine and tan lines, for the bayou. His friends figured he was going for Mardi Gras; that would mean New Orleans and Bourbon Street, but Bradley wasn't there for the all night parties or women flashing for a set of plastic beads. Bradley had woken up one morning knowing it was time for a change and where he was supposed to go.

Walking through the cemeteries in New Orleans was nothing like the ones he had seen back home. There it was nothing but little headstones or markers lined up in almost perfect symmetry, like being dead was neat and organized. But in New Orleans the water level was too high to bury the dead in the ground. One good rainstorm and you could have bodies floating through the city, so instead everyone was buried in a cement tomb or mausoleum. The more money you had, the better looking the slab. If you really had the cash, you could throw a statue of an angel on the top; one last final way of saying "Maybe I can't take it with me, but everyone will damn sure know I had it when I was here." The side effect of this was that the cemetery looked like a scale model of the chaos theory. There was no straight path to get anywhere. Often times loved ones are given directions by way of other departed souls. "Okay, you go down the path till you get to Avery Johnson then make a sharp left, about three angel statues down you will see Paul Chambers, make a 45 degree turn to your right and…."

Bradley reached the groundskeepers shack just as the sun dipped down over the horizon. The shack looked ancient and weathered like it had seen far too many hurricanes in it's time. If it were more than 8 feet squared, Bradley would have been surprised. He tapped on the old wooden door and was startled by the response. "Bout damn time you got here, boy. Get your ass inside." Bradley stepped into the broken down shack and looked around the single room. In one corner there was an old recliner that must have come right off of the Archie Bunker set. Next to it sat a TV that still had the two big knobs, and Bradley was almost certain that the movie it was showing wasn't meant to be in black and white. In the other corner was an ice chest, a hot plate and shelves filled with canned food such as corned beef and Spam. On the wall above the hot plate was a Playboy calendar page from 1972; even without the year printed on the page Bradley could guess the age due to the 'wildness' of the woman's personal grooming habits.

But most of Bradley's attention was drawn to the center of the room, where a man sat with his back to the door. "Well, stop staring and close da damn door, ya fool." Bradley did as he was told. "Now sit down, I've gots lots ta tell ya and no time ta do it." Bradley quickly moved across the room and into the recliner. As he sat he could feel the sharp poke of a loose spring dig into his thigh, but he was too riveted on his host to react. The man looked old. Not Bill Clinton at the end of his term old; more like if you stretch saran wrap over a skeleton. His pale skin appeared nearly translucent and you could almost see his blood moving through his veins. The only hair on his head was sickly white and formed a semi-circle around the back of his head in line with his ears. The hair itself looked brittle and came to an end at his shirt collar where Bradley was sure it snapped off rather than having been cut. The man was sitting on a bucket, and to Bradley's disbelief, he was sharpening the edge of his shovel like a knight tending to his sword before a battle.

"Dey call me Digga", the man said, never once taking his attention away from his shovel.

"Your name is Digger, really? Were your parents hippies or something?" Bradley joked, hoping to get a smile or some sign of hope that his new boss wasn't going to be a nightmare.

"No, you fool. I say dey *call* me Digga, you don be needing my name ta do what we gotta do. Now tell me boy, have you ever heard of da vampires?"

Bradley had read Stoker's Dracula in school and had seen all the Universal and Hammer films. He had even read some recent comic books about them. But to him, vampires were the stuff of horror movies and Halloween costumes. Why would this old man want to talk about vampires? Bradley figured it must be like hazing in college; scare the new guy, tell him monsters haunt the cemetery. Having the old creepy guy sharpening the shovel is a very nice touch. Bradley decided the best thing to do would be to play along, if for nothing else it could be good for a laugh.

"Yeah, I know all about vampires."

Digger turned to face Bradley for the first time. There was an intensity in Digger's eyes that literally sent a chill down Bradley's spine.

"Good, den you wont be pissing your pants when dey get out of da tombs tonight."

Digger stood up and grabbed his coat from behind the door. It was a shabby old army jacket with the name Thierry scrawled above the left pocket. He then put on a beat up old brown fedora and pulled the brim down to just above his eyes. The back of the fedora lined up just right with the ring of hair, like the rest of his hair had sacrificed itself to make the hat fit better. Digger then tossed a crowbar to Bradley and opened the door. "Cam on, dat ringing means one's awake, and dey not known for being patient."

Bradley jumped to his feet, the crowbar held firmly in his hand, and quickly followed after Digger. He hadn't noticed it until it was pointed it out, but now Bradley soon could hear the soft ringing of a bell from somewhere to the east. He had to run to catch up to the old man who was moving much faster than his years should allow.

"Who are 'they' and why are they ringing a bell?"

"You not too bright are you boy? Do you know da term 'dead ringer'?"

Oddly enough, this was a phrase Bradley had looked up in school. He had an English teacher who insisted that you knew the meaning behind every cliché and colloquialism you used and Bradley wanted to write about a pair of women being 'dead ringers'; but he had come across a few different meanings of the phrase. His favorite went back to the old days when people were wrongly thought to be dead and buried alive. Once they realized this was happening, they would attach a piece of string from within the coffin to a bell on the headstone so if the person woke up in the coffin they could pull the string to ring the bell and call for help, hence "a dead ringer"

"Well, when I get a special in here, I rig up da bell so dey can tell me when dey are back."

"Back? From where?"

"From da dead. You hearing me at all boy?"

Bradley stopped in his tracks. Could this crazy old man really believe that there were vampires in the cemetery? That the bells he rigged up were chiming because of anything more than a blowing wind? But he remembered that look in Digger's eyes. That fire of purpose that was overwhelming to behold. This old man was either completely crazy, one of the best actors on the planet... or there were really vampires and that was not something Bradley was ready to accept.

Digger had come to a stop at a tomb a few yards ahead and was waving Bradley forward. Once there, he could see the small bell attached to the side of the tomb as it was still ringing away. He could also see the small piece of rope disappear under the stone lid. Digger gestured for Bradley to use his crowbar on the top while he used his own shovel to pry open the bottom.

"Do exactly what I do and dis should be no problem."

They slid the tomb lid off to the side and then cracked open the coffin. Inside Bradley could see a very scared woman, probably only a year or two younger than himself. She was alive. She had been entombed with no air but was alive just the same. Bradley gripped his crowbar tightly, not sure what Digger wanted him to do but ready no matter what.

"Now, now; just relax chere. We gonna explain dis whole thing."

Digger reached out his arm to the young woman, helped her out of the coffin and onto her feet. He spoke to her in a tone that was soothing and steady. Bradley watched as the woman listened to the old man, clinging to his every word.

"You feel funny don' you? Well, dats cause you something different now. But you need to take it slow. Da boy and I are here to help you."

The woman stumbled and Digger grabbed her by the arm. He explained her that she was weak since she hadn't had any blood yet. He told her about what she had become and how it would take her a few hours to get adjusted. He reached into his pocket and grabbed what appeared to be a hot water bottle. He pulled the cap off and held it out to the woman who sniffed it cautiously at first, then took a small sip that turned into a frenzy as she couldn't seem to pour the liquid down her throat fast enough. Bradley could see a small trail of blood rolling down the side of her mouth, verifying for him the bottle's contents.

At that moment, somewhere to the west, the chime of a different bell began. Bradley turned back to see the new vampire desperately trying to suck every drop of blood from the bottle.

"Damn. I hate being rushed."

Bradley was astonished at what he saw next. In a movement that could only be equated to a lightning strike, Digger spun around, bringing the sharpened edge of the shovel across the vampire's throat and in one fluid motion decapitated the ungodly creature. The body, dropping first to its knees and then flat on the grass, began to spew out its recently ingested blood. The head, in a morbid moment of irony, landed neatly back into the very coffin it had just risen from.

"You killed her! You acted like you were going to help… and then you killed her! Why the subterfuge?" Bradley was stunned and desperate to understand.

"Cause dey easier ta kill when dey are in bloodlust. Even just outta da tomb, dey could tear a man in half. Now we gots ta move."

The bell chimed louder in the distance. Digger grabbed Bradley by the arm and they began to run towards the sound. Bradley's heart was pounding so hard he was sure only his rib cage was keeping it inside. Even at full speed, he was having a hard time keeping up with the old man. The ringing was getting louder and louder and it seemed to be coming from just over the next ridge; but when they get to the top of the ridge the ringing had stopped. Digger held his hand up to Bradley as they both stopped dead in their tracks. The old man looked around the graveyard for a moment, then crept forward. He moved about another twenty yards and stopped, gesturing for Bradley to join him. Once there, Bradley could see why Digger had stopped; there was a tomb that has obviously been broken out from the inside. The heavy stone lid tossed about four feet to the side and the coffin lid was nothing more than toothpicks.

"Damn. Out on dey own. Let's go boy. We gots to find dem."

"To hell with that," Bradley responded, leaning back against the open tomb. 'I answered an ad for a job, not to commit suicide against a fictional monster."

"I could tell you were gonna be a problem from da moment I saw ya." Digger looked angry. "But no time for dat right now. You either with me or ya get your ass outta my graveyard and don be looking back."

Digger started making his way through the scattered tombs and mausoleums and was quickly out of site.

Bradley left LA because he had nothing left there to live for. When a drunk driver killed Janet, his whole life went on hold. Every passing car, every brunette walking by, they all reminded him of his lost love. Even two months later, he would find himself at a place the two had visited and it would take every ounce of strength he had to hold back the tears. He had to leave LA if he was ever going to get his life moving forward again. He picked New Orleans because of Mardi Gras... because Janet thought it was the most ridiculous event and never wanted to go. They had no past here so it was perfect. He came here to live again... not to die trying to fight the undead.

He stood up straight, resolved in his conviction to leave the cemetery immediately and take the job at the Book Palace by the mall. That was his plan... until he heard movement behind him... in the wrong direction from where Digger went.

Bradley turned his back to the open coffin and began searching for signs of movement. The night had become silent; not like a normal night where you still hear a distant car or an owl... but a silence so intense that it hurts your ears. The sound of your own pulse becomes like a bass drum pounding incessantly. A silence you only hear when you know you're about to die.

"What happened to me?"

Bradley spun around to see a man wearing a beautifully-tailored three-piece suit appearing from the shadows about five feet away. His pale skin almost shimmered in the moonlight. The man seemed agitated and confused. His hands were elongated into a deadly looking set of claws. But if nothing else looked different than the average guy on the street, his teeth would make you think "vampire" right away. The front two incisors were extended about twice as long as normal and honed to a very sharp looking point. The rest of his teeth also seemed to take on a more jagged appearance. If he smiled it would look like two rows of inverted picket fences.

"Why was I buried? Am I dead? Why do I feel so strange? Who are you?" The young man threw out questions at a rapid fire pace, each seeming to increase his own stress level ten fold.

"Now, just stay calm sir. I'm going to explain this whole thing." Bradley gestured with his palms, showing he meant no harm. He tried his best to imitate exactly how Digger had dealt with the first vampire. Mimicking his soothing and steady tone, even his choice of words. Hell, if he could pull it off, Bradley would have used that damn Cajun accent. As he continued to speak he could see the vampire beginning to relax; his hands losing some of their length. And then Bradley got to the part about the blood and he realized his mistake. The words were only part of it; distracting the vampire with blood was the key to killing it and the only blood Bradley had was his own... something the vampire realized at the same time.

The vampire dove at Bradley, knocking him to the ground and pinning him in one motion. The vampire leaned his head back and opened his mouth wide. Bradley could see his teeth begin to elongate into a set of fangs. The vampire let out a primal growl then started for the exposed neck. Bradley then heard a sound he would never forget... "THWANGGGG!" It was a sound one would get when hitting the flat part of a shovel against a skull with great force.

Digger hit the vampire cleanly across the face with the shovel, the clang echoed through the empty graveyard. The mighty blow knocked the vampire off of Bradley. Digger quickly followed it with a second shot to the head. The stunned vampire ended up flat on its back looking up as Digger thrusted the point of the shovel at its neck with all his might. The vampire reacted with lightning reflexes, snapping the wooden handle in two and sending the shovel head flying off into the distance. He grabbed the other half of the handle, the half Digger was still holding, and pulled the old man down towards him. The claws on his free hand lashed out and gutted the caretaker. Digger's body fell to the ground motionless, still holding on to the handle of his shovel.

Bradley raced towards the vampire, swinging his crowbar for the creature's throat, but the vampire caught it with ease. He tossed the crowbar aside and grabbed Bradley by the throat, lifting him off the ground. Bradley could see into the vampire's eyes, there was an intensity here too, but this wasn't the engulfing intensity of Digger's eyes, this was a frenzy of desire, the start of bloodlust.

"Now, you were just telling me how I need to feed on fresh blood."

The look on the vampire's face shifted quickly to shock. He released his hold on Bradley and looked down at his chest and the shaft of wood sticking out from the center. Digger had run the handle of the shovel through the vampire's back, and then he fell back on his knees trying to hold his guts in. The vampire turned towards the old man.

"If you were trying to kill me… you have failed, old man."

"But I won't!"

Bradley had the other half of the shovel and swung the point across the vampire's throat, slicing it wide open. The vampire's head fell back against its shoulders, but didn't come off. The body fell to the ground where Bradley knelt next to it, driving the shovels head into the remaining bone and cartilage, six, seven, eight time, until the head was finally severed clean.

Bradley crawled over to Digger's body. The old man was still alive, but only barely. His breath came in short wheezy gasps; his chest struggling to rise on each time. The intensity that so stunned Bradley when they first met had now softened. His face contorted into its first smile in decades.

"You all right boy. You gonna do jus fine." And with that, Digger closed his eyes for the last time.

Bradley buttoned up the old man's jacket then lifted the body up and laid it gently into the open coffin. He placed both halves of the shovel on top of the body like laying a knight to rest with his sword. Finally, he retrieved the old brown fedora and was about to toss it in as well, but then changed his mind and carried it with him back towards the old shack.

About half way across the cemetery, Bradley sat down between a beloved wife named Grace and her loving husband Earl. It was as good a spot as any to stop, since his legs were no longer working. All that he had just seen came rushing into his mind. The dead coming back to life. Vampires existing in the real world… not the romantic gothic type that Hollywood had made so much money on, but blood lust driven creatures of horror. He wasn't sure how to deal with any of it, but he knew that it would take an act of God to get him back to his feet any time soon.

It wasn't an act of God, though, that got Bradley moving. It was a much simpler thing… the sound of a bell in the distance.

Bradley sprang to his feet and raced towards the sound, not really understanding why he was sprinting to his possible doom. He hurdled a few small markers and even rolled over the top of one tomb, never changing his direction, a straight line to the sound. When he arrived to the spot, the bell still clanging, he noticed it wasn't a tomb with a string attached. The noise was coming from inside a mausoleum. Bigger than Digger's shack, the cement building had a solid metal gate on the front with an impressive looking padlock and chain to keep it closed. The ringing was coming from inside, or at least it had been when Bradley arrived, but as he caught his breath it had stopped.

He moved forward to see if anyone was inside. The moonlight shined down and lit the first few feet of the inside, but not enough to see the whole room. Bradley squinted to try to make out anything out of the ordinary. He wasn't sure, but he thought he saw a foot… a woman's bare foot.

"Hello." Bradley called out, shocked by his own voice cutting through the silence. "Is anyone there?"

"I'm here." A feminine voice replied. "But I'm not really sure where here is."

The woman took a step forward and then another. She came up right up to the gate where the moon caressed her with light. She was gorgeous. Not like the women in Hollywood that nipped and tucked their way into the shape of a Barbie doll. This woman was beautiful from the moment she took her first breath. Long red hair lay across her soft pale shoulders. Her high cheekbones framed her jade green eyes like they hung in a museum. Her lips looked like oval rubies laid gently upon ivory. She wore a thin, gauzy green dress that seemed to flow freely, yet hug her curves tightly.

"Can you let me out?" Her voice was smoky and soft, like she was whispering in your ear.

"I don't think I have the key." Bradley wasn't thinking at the moment. He would have opened the gate if he could… he wanted to pry the bars off with his bare hands. "What's your name?"

"Simone." She started at him, her eyes directly locked on his. "I'm a little scared right now and I don't quite feel right. Can you help me? I really would like to get out of here."

Bradley wanted to run across and pull on the lock till it gave way, but he stopped himself. Something in the back of his mind kicked in, forcing him to remember the truth. This gorgeous woman was in there because she died. And if she had returned to life, she wasn't human anymore.

"I don't think that would be a good idea." Bradley took a step back.

"Get me out of here, now!" Her voice went up a full octave and jabbed its way into Bradley's head. "Or so help me I will tear your throat out!"

Bradley looked around quickly for a weapon of any kind. No shovel, the crowbar was long gone. All he had with him was Digger's fedora, which wouldn't be any help. He looked back to Simone. She grabbed a metal bar from the gate in each hand. Her fingers began to elongate as she grasped the cold steel. Her china doll features began to twist as her brow protruded forward and her lips parted to give way to jagged fangs. Her jade colored eyes darkened till you could see nothing but black.

"I said I want out!" Simone pulled on the metal bars, snapping them in half like tooth picks. Then she bent the jagged bars forward until there was enough room for her to climb out.

Bradley scrambled over towards a tomb with a good-sized cement cross on top. It wasn't attached. He grabbed it with both hands and held it in between he and Simone. She kept coming forward; her features becoming more dark and menacing with each step.

"Why wouldn't you help me?" She was in a rage that would quickly lead to bloodlust.

"Because you aren't human anymore." Bradley started moving back, his cement cross not helping him at all. "You died. You were in there because you died and now you're a vampire."

Her response wasn't words, just a guttural growl as she leapt the distance between them. Bradley swung the cross with all his might, catching Simone across the face before should could reach his throat. She staggered back, still weak from having not fed. He swung again and connected, sending her spinning around and back towards the mausoleum. As she raised her head, Bradley ran forth with the cross in front of him. He caught her in the stomach and pushed her back with all his might. She was forced back two feet, three, four, and finally straight onto the jagged metal bars she had bent forward for her escape. The two points protruded out from her chest, pinning her in place. She screamed out in pain.

"Help me." She pleaded to Bradley. Her face had almost returned to normal.

He paused for a moment, almost taken in by her helplessness. Then he saw them, the two black eyes staring back at him. Whoever Simone had been, this was no longer her. He gripped the cement cross in his hands once more. It seemed even heavier than when he first grabbed it.

"Please don't." Her smoky voice asked for mercy.

"I'm sorry." His words came out as a whisper, like he was speaking to a confused child.

He swung the cross, bringing it solidly against the side of Simone's flowing red hair. He leaned back and swung again. And again. It took far more swings than he would ever have imagined to weaken the spinal cord enough to snap. Her head never came completely off, but dangled by muscles and sinew down upon her chest, pinned between the two jagged metal bars.

He left her body where it was. He didn't know how Digger disposed of the corpses after they had gotten up. He found the old brown fedora, swirled it in his hand a few times then carried it with him as he headed back to the old shack. Once inside, Bradley headed over to the old recliner, sat down and stared at the TV and waited for the dawn. The hours passed quickly as Bradley replayed the night's events in his head. A knocking on the door brought him crashing back to the here and now. Mr. Witzig walked into the shack; the morning sun creeping in through the open door behind him.

"I saw Digger lying in the coffin over the ridge… did they get away?"

"No, we got all three."

"Three? We've never had three in one night before." Witzig looked at Bradley with a new level of respect. He could see an intensity in Bradley's eyes that told him everything he needed to know.

"So… I guess you're the new Digger."

Bradley stood up, put on the old brown fedora, and pulled it down so the brim is just above his eyes.

"Looks that way. But I'm going to need a new shovel… and a color TV."

Vampire Hunter Dean

by J.C. Vaughn

DO THE undead feel awkward if they read fiction aimed at the Young Adult market? I mean, doesn't it just remind them of what's been taken from them? If they're more or less frozen in time at the point they're turned from humans into vampires, and if that means they stay the same as when they were bitten, doesn't it remind them that they'll never attain Young Adulthood, they'll never enjoy in normal terms their Young Adulthood, or they'll forever be tormented that they cannot enjoy Young Adulthood ever again?

Would they, in fact, feel awkward if caught reading Barry Lyga's *Boy Toy* by another vampire?

I'm not saying; I'm just asking. These aren't questions I feel comfortable asking my nieces, both of whom are in that target audience. I don't have all the answers and I'm certainly man enough to admit it, but those are the kind of things that keep me up at night lately. That and the fact that I've taken to sleeping during the day because it's the only time I'm not worried about vampires.

You see, I'm in the vampires' target audience. And they're in mine. And while saying that probably marks me as crazy in your eyes, I can live with that, at least as long as I get to live.

First, a few important observations of things I now know to be true:

1. Most of the clichés about vampires are true.
2. The people who make up stories — particularly in movies — where the rules have changed are just trying to be clever or serve a darker purpose. Mostly they're just wrong.
3. Vampires don't like garlic.
4. They don't like mirrors and they can't bear sunlight.

5. They have to be invited in, but that doesn't count outside.

6. They hate the Cross and burn at its touch.

7. A wooden stake through the heart will kill them. And just about anyone else you might be inclined to try it on.

8. Holy Water actually works.

9. The appropriate, creative application of high explosives will solve most problems.

10. You can actually kill a vampire with a steak (no misspelling). I'll explain that one later.

Some of these things I learned the hard way, on the run and in desperate circumstances. Others I confirmed through trial and error after the first few worked. The steak thing I learned out of necessity, but again, more on that later.

I realize that some of the truisms I've just imparted could fly in the face of your beliefs or lack thereof. Sorry about that. I'm not here to offend, but I'm not going to pretend I don't know what I know. You can meditate on that or choose to ignore it, your choice, but until you've had your life saved by a cross, I just don't think you're any more qualified to speak on the subject than I was before it happened. I'll just tell you my story and you can do with it what you will.

The first vampire I ever encountered, at least that I know of, was at a club in Miami. We were there for the annual HVAC (heating, ventilation and air conditioning) association convention with my boss, David "Scuba Dave" Donovan, and the husband-and-wife owners of the company, Vance and Nance Morrison. Vance and Nance had a well-deserved reputation as cheap-ass bastards (even Nance) for 51 weeks out of the year, but they almost perversely treated everyone on the staff like royalty when it came time for this convention each year. They closed the office and sprung for hotel, travel and meals, at least as long as the host city was some place Nance had read about in *Vanity Fair*, *Cosmo* or *Us*.

After she talked to the hotel's concierge, she insisted that we all go as a group to Club Flamingo, supposedly one of the hottest nightspots in the city. We followed. It was almost like walking into the very concept of retro-futurism. From an art deco base, the amenities were strictly twenty-first century with huge flat-screen monitors, LED-laced floors, strategically placed "random" video cameras and so many speakers that it couldn't possibly matter.

Dee-Dee, our accountant, turned out to actually be sort of stunning away from the office (as I had long suspected and seriously contemplated more than once) and she just about blended right into the trendy, colorfully dressed

---

crowd, thumping music and too-cool-for-the-common-folk atmosphere. The rest of acclimated ourselves like the bunch of tourists we were, which is to say we didn't even begin to fit in. As long as Nance thought it made us cool, though, she was paying the tab.

"Dean, you just enjoy yourself! This is the hottest venue in all of Miami and next week we'll be back in Dormont, PA and up to our armpits in HVAC and HVAC-related problems and solutions," she yelled in my ear, more or less deafening it for the next couple of days.

Except for Dee-Dee it was hard to imagine how we could have been more out of place (Nance, God bless her, was oblivious to this and Vance just went where Nance told him to go). I suppose we could have worn signs that designated us as future victims of pickpockets, robbers, and hookers, but other than that we stuck out just fine on our own.

I was tired and would have been just as happy to hit the hotel bar or go for a walk on the beach before turning in, but Nance did have a good point. When you're someplace new, it's cool to go out and at least try to take some of it in. With that mantra in mind, I made my way to the edge of the dance floor and looked for some other tourist to take a spin with before I headed back to my room. I had no aspirations of discovering some semi-blind vixen with the body of a goddess and the mind of a flight attendant to spend the night with. I just wanted to be able to look back and say, yes, when I visited Miami that time I did indeed sample the night life. I even danced at Club Flamingo, the famous hotspot.

There were, as it turned out, a lot of beautiful women there. Most of them looked vacant behind the eyes, the kind of radiating neediness that gervgf3tts really annoying after a long weekend and toxic after about two weeks, but that didn't stop them from being popular. I watched and waited. I saw a couple of out-of-place women on the other side of the dance floor, but they were either coming or going from the ladies' room and they didn't look like any fun anyway. I was contemplating what sort of different Miami experience I could have elsewhere when she reached out and touched my forearm.

Now I'm not technology-phobic or anything stupid like that, but I wouldn't have known who Sara Varone was or what she looked like if my old Army buddy, Kevin, down in Texas hadn't emailed me a link to several images of what he called his latest *obsession du jour*. If you don't know what she looks like, Google her, but she's an Italian fantasy come to life. I don't speak Italian, so I don't know what she's supposed to be famous for, but she's famous for being a beautiful and well-endowed young woman who seems comfortable enough being famous for those reasons. I say all of this so that you'll know when I say that the gentle, electric touch I felt on my arm came from a woman who looked just like Sara Varone.

"Would you like to dance?" she asked, her eyes sparkling and deep. It seemed for a moment like her voice was quieter than the music but carried above it.

"A-bwah," is the closest I can come to approximating my immediate response.

"Pardon me?" she said.

"That sounds great," I said over the echoing music. "My name's Dean. Dean Marklin."

"Dean Martin?" she laughed and yelled back.

"No, Marklin," I replied, "but it doesn't matter. What's your name?"

"Jocelyn Elder," she yelled, grabbing my hand and pulling me onto the dance floor. "We can talk later. First, we dance!"

So here I was on the dance floor with a devastatingly hot goddess who had the same name as perhaps the most bizarre Surgeon General in the history of the United States, and the chances of anyone believing me later about this had already officially reached negative numbers. If she talked about safer bullets, Eric Clapner, or masturbation, I would probably have to kill myself.

But, man, was she stunning!

We danced for four songs in a row in styles I didn't know to music I'd never heard before and I'm sure I looked like a total idiot. It was not one of those scenes where the awkward guy gets out on the floor with a luminescent beauty and suddenly knows all the moves. I was just me and she was just…

A-bwah.

No question, I had it right the first time, and I didn't care how I looked. Dee-Dee and a Latin-looking guy who was about ten years younger than her danced right by us. She was really getting into it and didn't seem to see us, though most of the crowd did. Pretty much everyone who wasn't plainly staring at this particular odd couple was at the very least sneaking glances in our direction. It's nothing I'd ever spoken about, but every average guy wants to feel that way sometime, and this appeared to be my turn.

For the record, I don't have any problem being "average." I'm healthy, make good money, save a chunk of it, have my place paid off, dress nicely when I'm not working, have a great bunch of friends, an okay car, and season tickets for the Steelers and mini-season packages for the Pirates and Penguins. I help my parents out financially and cut the lawns at my church. Sublimely and almost totally average, except for never finding the right woman. I'd found a few not-so-right ones over the years, but even they were only average in their not-so-rightness.

Jocelyn's dress was bright red and very short and anything but average. It alternately clung to her and flowed with the music in a symphony of teasing perfection. With plenty of reason to look at other parts of her, it was her eyes that continued to hold my attention. After the fourth song, though, I knew I needed a drink or I couldn't keep going.

"I have a table over there," she pointed to a semi-secluded portion of the room. She grabbed my hand and told me to follow her. We made our way through the crowd toward a section of the club obviously reserved for the rich, the famous and the hangers-on. A uniformed young man unhooked the velvet rope, admitted us, and re-hooked it after we passed through.

"I don't think I have seen you around here before," she said as we sat down. Before I could even reply, a waitress appeared from nowhere and took our orders. The pulsating music was still all around us, but it was much more like a current in this part of the club rather than the tsunami it was on the dance floor.

I told her the truth, and I watched her reaction closely as I did it. She seemed to take in stride.

"I don't know what I'd do without air conditioning," she said. "It's great to work up a sweat when you want to, but there's not much worse than sweating when you don't want to." I was hard pressed to disagree.

The waitress reappeared with our drinks almost that quickly.

"Bottled water isn't much of a vacation drink," she said to me as she sipped her frozen margarita.

I eyed my uber-trendy-looking $7.50 bottle of Pül Wasser suspiciously.

"Are you sure this is actually water?" I inspected the label and for a few minutes we made that kind of chit chat. She said she was an art dealer and had lived all over the world and that she moved to Miami a few years ago. This was her favorite club and she came there often to dance and meet people.

All through the conversation I just about couldn't stop looking into her eyes. Their magnetism was practically tactile. She was an excellent conversationalist, asking questions and then actually listening for the response rather than waiting for the next chance to speak (unlike most folks these days). We talked for quite a while and then danced for a couple more songs. As the second song ended, that's when she said it.

"How about we cut out of here and I show you some of Miami's real hotspots?" she whispered in my ear. Aside from feeling as if the bottoms of my shoes had suddenly melted to the floor, I was ready to go. My legs were a little sluggish and there was a tingling in my brain that told me none of this was real, but I didn't listen. This was happening way too fast and that just wasn't my style.

"Sounds great!" I heard myself say.

I looked around for my group. Nance and Vance were still at their table, soaking in the atmosphere and ordering large quantities of assorted large frozen drinks. Scuba Dave and the rest of the gang were nowhere to be seen. Dee-Dee and her Romeo were still on the dance floor and I suspected they'd never been off it. They probably wouldn't miss me and I was old enough to take care of myself. I followed Jocelyn out a side door and into an alleyway.

"I love that place, but it can get pretty loud," she said when the door closed behind us and substantially muted the music. She stopped, turned around, and looked straight at me. Then she kissed me. Like you might expect, I was startled that this knockout celebrity lookalike danced with me let alone wanted to unleash any sort of passion.

But who was I to argue. I ignored the "This makes no sense!" alarm going off in my brain and just enjoyed the moment.

"I really want to show you something," she whispered in my ear. I murmured my assent and kissed her again. Then she held me tight and kissed my neck. And then —

I do not know how this happened. I'd love to say my instincts kicked in, but if they did it was definitely not on a conscious level. If it was instinct, it was really, really deep rooted stuff. I'm much more inclined to accept "divine intervention" as the answer, but regardless, this was the moment my life changed.

As she suddenly and violently bared her fangs and went for my throat, I jammed my wrist into her mouth. She bit down and bit down hard, right through the fabric of my shirt and into the big, honking watch Vance and Nance had given me during our last company trip for being the number one HVAC repairman on the team for five years running.

"Son of a bitch!" she screamed in frustration and pain, staggering back a few steps and bringing her hand to her mouth. "That hurt!"

Since I didn't believe in vampires, I stood there in the alleyway wondering what this chick was and why she was snarling at me. In the movies this is where the bad guys always say something like, "You'll pay for that!" or some such. She just grabbed me by the shirt collar and threw me into a row of garbage cans. I knocked them over, but they mostly broke my fall.

She leapt at me. I made like Captain America and threw a garbage can lid at her. It would have been a lot more spectacular back in the days of metal trash cans, but even with hard plastic it was a beauty of a shot. The rim smacked her in the face and hit her dead, so to speak, in the teeth. She yelled and doubled over for a moment, hands to her mouth. I took this as my cue to run.

Whatever she was, Jocelyn wasn't human. If I had been at home and this happened, I would have run for my car. Outside of the big commuter cities, I think that's what most people would have done. But I wasn't at home, so I ran to where people were.

The first door I tried was the one we came out, but it was one of those ones without even a handle on the outside, like the exit doors from a movie theater. The next one was about thirty feet down. I opened it, ran in, and suddenly found myself face to face with the kitchen staff, all of whom looked up at me for a moment as if I was crazy, then went back to what they were doing. I tried to act normal and walk through the kitchen as if I was supposed to be there. For whatever reason, I didn't even think of telling the workers there what had happened.

Because I didn't know what had happened.

I made mental checklist: I danced with a beautiful woman. She said she wanted to show me the town. We went outside. She kissed me and wanted to bite my neck with some freaking huge teeth. There was probably more to the story, I figured, but those were the salient facts. I forgot about walking and started running.

And I ran straight into her on the opposite side of the kitchen. There was no way she could have gotten there ahead of me, but she did.

"You broke my tooth!" she yelled.

"Sorry!" I yelled back, looking straight into her now fire-filled eyes. I didn't know at the time what a rare but frustrating thing that is for a vampire. I mean, sure, it's not pleasant for anyone to break a tooth, but I was a little less sympathetic than I might have been because she was actually trying to kill me with the tooth in question when I broke it.

She hit me with a lightning fast backhand that lifted me off my feet and sent me flying back across the tile floor.

"You broke my tooth!" she yelled again.

A waiter entered from the main area of the club, saw what was going on, turned around and walked back out. The cooks and the rest of the kitchen staff tried to scatter. I only stopped sliding when I hit the front of the stove, which I'm thankful to say was closed.

I might have lingered a moment to get my bearings, but the surface was warm enough that it snapped me back to the potential danger at hand. Good thing, too, because after Jocelyn had sent me sailing she grabbed a couple of impressive looking knives and threw them my way. I moved to the side and they clanged off the oven.

She started running toward me. Two busboys with fully stacked trays came out of a little side area and stepped right in front of her. Dishes went everywhere when she smacked into the unsuspecting young men. She grabbed the nearest one before he could get back to his feet, stared at him uncomprehendingly for a second, and tossed him aside like a rag doll. The other busboy was trying to scramble away. She caught him by the collar and yanked him back to her. He kicked and screamed as she lifted him off the ground. She smacked him twice and then he hung limp and I figured he was unconscious. She leaned and positioned herself to take a taste of his neck.

The sane thing to do would have been run and try to get some help like some of the other kitchen staff had done, but I couldn't get over the feeling that this poor guy had just accidentally stumbled into my fight. I looked for anything I could use as a weapon. I spotted one of the knives she had thrown at me, picked it up and put everything I had into my throw. It imbedded in her back.

The Hollywood moment would have had her roar in pain as she dropped the defenseless busboy. Reality was, to me, far more frightening. She did drop the guy, but when she turned around and looked at me, her face said "How annoying can you be?" more than anything else. The remaining kitchen staff ran.

The blade had struck her between the shoulder blades and was hard for her to reach. She did manage to get just a little feel of the handle.

"Ah, plastic," she said. She stepped over the fallen busboys and moved to the nearest wall, all the time watching me.

"You don't dance very well," she said.

"I know."

"And how exciting can working on air conditioning be?"

"It's not exactly adventure-filled, if that's what you mean, but most folks are happy when we get their AC working in the summer or their heat going again in the winter," I said. I was looking for anything that could stop her and I wasn't coming up with anything.

"Okay, I admit it. That comment wasn't fair," she said. "Everyone has to have a job and I'd die without my air conditioning."

With that, she threw herself backward against the wall with enough force that the tile behind her was spider-webbed in cracks. A good bit of the blade now protruded through her chest. She grabbed it with her bare hands and pulled it out the front and examined it closely. There was actually blood, but not as much as you'd expect if a normal person had just done that.

"Wow, that's actually pretty gross," she said to herself.

"Sorry about the dress," I said, even though I was distinctly trying to not say anything.

She dropped the blade and it echoed in the suddenly silent kitchen.

"I'm almost sorry I have to kill you now, but you did break my tooth," she said as if genuinely reluctant. It was at that point that I wondered if time had stopped or something because where the hell where the cops? Where were Don Johnson and Philip Michael Thomas or Ponch and John, the SWAT guys or even Sting and the boys for that matter? How was it that we had been fighting in the kitchen of what was supposed to be one of the trendiest places in one of the trendiest cities in America, and the police had not shown up yet?

Jocelyn shoved the metal counter in the middle of the kitchen out of her way and sent food all over the place. It cut off my main avenue of escape, so now I had to either go back out the door I came in or through her and out into the club. Neither choice seemed that spectacular, but she was walking toward me and that definitely didn't bode well either.

The next thing I knew I was sailing through the air upside down. A wall graciously stood up and stopped my flight, and the floor was equally polite in catching me. I tried to shake it off, but in a moment I was airborne again. In general, I have no problem with flying, but at that point I was beginning to have my doubts. The next wall, not to be outdone by its brother across the kitchen, offered a kind cessation to my aerial activities, and the floor again welcomed me back with its gentle embrace.

I didn't know what was going on. Again, I tried to clear my head. I faded between blacking out and seeing Jocelyn coming toward me again. I was in darkness when I felt her grab me by the shirt and yank me to my feet. My legs were like rubber, so at this point it was probably good that she was holding me up.

"Do you hear me?" I heard her demand.

"Now I do," I said, though I was still trying to figure out who was talking.

"What?"

"I missed the bit before that."

"We don't have the time for me to make this really worth my while, so I'm just going to kill you. I'm going to bounce you off a couple more walls and then I'm going to rip your heart from your chest," she said, "and unlike in the movies, you don't get to see it beating. It just kills you."

"I hate that idea," I said.

"Too bad," she said as she flung me through the air once more. Trans-

Kitchen Airlines flight 001, you are cleared for take-off. Despite my less than optimum mental condition, this time I managed to not only land short of the wall, I rolled up and jumped to my feet.

"Don't tell me. Martial arts training?" she sighed.

I was about to say something snotty back to her when I spotted it on the opposite wall, toward a corner, running up toward a junction box the jutted out from the surface. It was mounted all wrong and I was immediately annoyed with the lack of craftsmanship. This time when she came at me, I ducked under her grasp, shoulder-rolled behind her, and sprinted to the offending junction box.

Irritated, she raced toward me, growling. In the past, people had snarled at me, but never actually growl. As she neared, I snapped off the main cable leading into the junction box. The lights and pretty much everything else in the building immediately blinked off including the music and the AC. The emergency lights came on. If my move hadn't worked, I would have just handed the one person in the place with indecently good night vision a distinct and probably lethal advantage, though I didn't know it at the time.

My effort, though, did have its rewards.

As she reached me, Jocelyn grabbed for my throat. I just slightly sidestepped her lunge and applied the open end of the main cable to her midsection. In hindsight, she actually started smoking pretty quickly, but at the time it seemed like it took forever. First, sparks shots out of hair and eyes. It was spectacular in its own way, but then her dress caught fire. She managed to break the connection, then she jumped back and started beating out the flames. She was smoking hot, literally. She stumbled backward a bit. This was my first opportunity to do more than evade her.

"Sorry about the dress," I said, "again."

I spun and kicked her in the head. She staggered backward, but I reversed and kicked on the other side. Again she stumbled. As I kept up my barrage, I silently thanked the good Lord for martial arts training and looked for something to finish her off with:

Kitchen utensils? No, knives had proven ineffective.

Salads? Not unless they had a lot of garlic. No Thai food was to be seen.

Dishes? No.

Dishwasher? Hobarts were a force to be reckoned with, naturally, but not a readily apparent threat to vampires.

Oven? Only if I could induce her to climb in, and Hansel and Gretel were nowhere to be seen.

There were meals in various stages of preparation and the components of meals not even started staged in parts of the kitchen. Our little recreation of Rock 'Em Sock 'Em Robots had sent most of them flying.

Another roundhouse kick almost toppled her, but the reverse actually kept her standing. I knew if I let up I was done for, and I also knew I couldn't keep it up much longer. Almost just as I was coming to that realization, she blocked my next kick. It wasn't enough to stop it, just deflect it. The force still caused her to stumble back further.

Right out the door into the main area of the club.

I'd like to believe I would have done the same thing if the patrons consisted entirely of strangers, but who knows? My friends and co-workers were out there, and I had just unintentionally exposed them to danger. I charged after Jocelyn.

Out in the main area of the club, just as in the kitchen, only the emergency lighting was on. Whether the kitchen staff had informed the management of the titanic struggle taking place in their culinary center or not – and whether they in turn had informed the authorities – was not readily discernable. At least the patrons were headed toward the door in a semi-ordinary fashion. A huge bald guy wearing a sports coat and an "I Love Mr. Zero" T-shirt was motioning the path out of the club with two flashlights like the ones they use to wave in airplanes at their gates. I immediately hoped that Vance, Nance, Scuba Dave, Dee-Dee and the others were either in the outbound procession or already outside.

That hope lasted about nine seconds or until I saw that Dee-Dee and Scuba Dave were doing what most of the people on this side of the room were doing, which was staring at the scorched and still smoldering, angry, almost-naked, growling lady on the dance floor.

"I think maybe we should go," I heard Scuba Dave say to Dee-Dee.

She was about to agree, however, when it hit her.

"Hey, is that Dean?" She pointed me out and he saw me, too.

That was about the instant that Jocelyn hit me like a freight train, sending us both sprawling through the door and back into the kitchen. She landed on top of me, but when we landed I managed to use our momentum to catch her with my feet. Instead of her pinning me down, I caught her in the stomach and sent her flying over my head. Turnabout, fair play, all that.

As she got to her feet, I spotted it, a large wooden cooking spoon. I didn't even have time to break off part of the handle into a point before she was on me again, so I swung it up hard as she tried to pull me in. It broke the skin and went in a bit, right over the heart, but not enough to do any real damage. It did seriously freak her out, though.

Her sooty features weren't improved by her new, bluish hue. She looked positively ill, and she shook nervously as she stared down at the spoon dangling out of her. At any time she could have pulled it out, but instead it hung there like those darts they stick a bull with at a bullfight. She couldn't decide what to do.

It was barely a flesh wound, no matter how close it had come to killing her. I looked for a frying pan, a tenderizing mallet, anything with a flat surface that I could put some power behind. In the end, I grabbed the only thing in arm's reach and made my play.

Why on earth anyone would freeze a perfectly good cut of meat is beyond me, but there was a solidly frozen rib eye sitting on one end of the prep cook's table. I grabbed it and swung. It connected and drove the wooden spoon into Jocelyn's so-called heart. A look of utter disbelief and horror came over her face. Her skin went from blue to gray and started cracking with age. Her beautiful figure fell apart with the rest of her, and she dropped to the floor a brittle and ashen old husk.

I stood over her, my heart pounding, expecting her to get up and throw me around some more. I watched and she didn't move and I watched some more. Somewhere in the back of my head I noted the sirens in the distance and getting closer. I kept staring at Jocelyn's corpse.

"You'd never know it to look at you, but you really know how to party," said Dee-Dee from the other side of the kitchen. Startled at the sound, I jumped back from the figure on the ground.

"This isn't what it looks like," I said.

"Don't figure it could be," said Scuba Dave.

I stared at Jocelyn again.

"What happened here, Dean? One minute the two of you are dancing, the next moment she's all smoking and you're killing her with a steak and a spoon," Dee-Dee said.

"You guys better get out of here. The police are on the way and I'm sure I'll have to talk with them. There's no need for you to be a part of that," I said.

"What are you going to tell them?" Scuba Dave asked, and I certainly didn't have a good answer for that one. What was I going to tell them? I couldn't even bring myself to use the word "vampire" around my friends yet, so what was I going to tell the cops about why I killed the 357-year-old woman (just guessing) at my feet?

Dee-Dee suggested adjourning to the hotel before the constabulary arrived. We went out the kitchen's back exit and into the night.

It took me a long time to understand what had happened, but it didn't take any time at all for me to know my life had changed forever. Even if I never met another vampire as long as I lived, I still had met one, and that's easily 493 percent more vampires than I ever expected to encounter.

Scuba Dave and Dee-Dee came back to the room with me and I recounted the details of the portion of the fight that they hadn't witnessed. It really helped that they had seen the end of the brawl since that made the other parts pretty believable. They were very supportive.

"I've seen some pretty weird things in my life," Scuba Dave said, "but that was some weird-ass party you had going tonight, Dean." He told us about coming face to face with a Great White shark on a diving trip and how the lead diver had narrowly saved his life.

"The thing is, you have to expect a shark to try and make a meal of you. It's not supposed to be that way on the dance floor," he said as he looked out the window into the Miami night sky.

"As much as that's a set-up line for a really great one-liner, I'll let it go this time," Dee-Dee said and almost smiled. She hooked her arm in mine and put her head against my shoulder. "He's right, though. This is officially the most weird-ass vacation I ever took." On the craziest night of my life, it felt good to have her holding onto me.

After exhausting my mini-bar, Scuba Dave decided it was time to turn in and headed to his room. Even though it was only a few doors down, we stuck our heads out and made sure he made it okay. We saw Vance and Nance and some of the others coming out of the elevator and ducked back in so we wouldn't have to talk with them.

"Well, that certainly wasn't what I was expecting," we heard Nance say.

We sat down on the edge of the bed and I clicked on the TV to see if there was anything about it on the news. Dee-Dee put her head back on my shoulder and looped her arm through mine.

"I have to ask you something, Dean, and I don't want you to take this the wrong way, but that was a vampire you were dancing with tonight, right?"

I was forced to agree.

"Why weren't you dancing with me?" she asked, studiously watching the channels I was flipping by.

"Biggest mistake of my life," I said.

"Good. I'm glad we cleared that up," she said. "Now what are we going to do about it?"

Over the next few months, I learned that I had a lot more to learn and came up with a second set of observations:

1.   Vampires are strong, but they generally rely more on the element of surprise than on astonishing strength to take advantage of their intended victims.

2.   They can indeed turn into wolves or bats.

3.   They seem to get along well enough with rats.

4.   They don't, though, have a strong sense of smell.

5.   If they did, they'd realize that they really, really stink.

6.   A few of the more sophisticated ones I've met have been serious collectors of things ranging from rare newspapers and cast iron mechanical banks to Nazi paraphernalia and comic books.

7.   If you do it right, you can distract the dumber ones with their own blood.

8.   If I was a vampire, I'd be really unhappy that NBC couldn't do any better than Carson Daly.

9.   Their breath is horrible, but those fangs really will kill you.

10. I know that she's not a vampire, but I swear that Oprah really sucks that life right out of me. I knew at least one vampire who felt the same way.

But I'm getting ahead of myself.

A few nights later we were all in the gate area at Miami International Airport, waiting to catch our return flight to Pittsburgh. Nance had plundered what good times there were to be had and forced the rest of the group to do the same, but the HVAC and HVAC-related demands of Dormont and the surrounding suburbs could wait not longer. Dee-Dee was rather openly at my side (getting those odd sort of looks from those who noticed) and Scuba Dave lingered close as well.

I meandered into the bookstore there in the gate area. As airport bookstores go, it wasn't too bad. I found myself in the horror fiction section with a book in my hand. It had been made into a movie by a director who put his name in front of the title but missed the real soul of the book (and you think vampires are a problem? Don't get me started). It got some of it right. I put it back and tried another. Bits and pieces. The more I read, the more it was like that.

After thumbing through a dozen titles, I was at the edge of the Young Adult section. At the far end I noticed a teenage girl pointing toward the latest cool thing (I don't mean to suggest that I know what it was) and her mom promised it to her if she was good on their trip. Then I noticed the woman who was standing next to me. She was very attractive, but looking through a copy of Barry Lyga's first YA novel, *The Astonishing Adventures of Fanboy and Goth Girl*, which was clearly a bit under her age range.

"Don't worry," Jocelyn said. "You're in no danger." She was wearing sunglasses, had her hair pulled back and had a fairly nondescript white top and khaki slacks ensemble going on and she still managed to be devastatingly beautiful.

"You'll forgive me if I'm a bit suspicious." My hand went instinctively to the empty jacket pocket where I had been carrying wooden stakes for the last few days, right up until we reached the security checkpoint.

"I'm not going to do anything with this crowd," she said

"That didn't exactly seem to slow you down you before," I said. I started looking around the store for a makeshift weapon and didn't see much beyond a few heavy-looking Harry Potter books and a Tom Clancy novel.

"True, I have to admit you didn't catch me at my best. I take my teeth pretty seriously," she said.

"I can see that, and I suppose I should admit that you look very nice this evening," I said, trying to look like I was taking in the offerings, that I was calm and confident. "Particularly when you consider that I killed you. Why are you here?"

"I wanted to talk to you," she said, still pretending to look at the book in her hand. Dee-Dee and Scuba Dave were just out of earshot on the other side of the store. They were looking at a pop-up book featuring the famous celebrity killings in the greater Miami area.

"No, I mean, *why* are you *here*?" I looked up at her eyes. "I killed you."

"Oh, that!" she laughed a small, almost genuine laugh. "Some moron pulled the stake out. I'm eternally grateful."

"Just like that?"

"Sometimes it is," she set down the book. She pulled down her sunglasses so I could see her eyes clearly. "Listen, I was getting a little sloppy, a little complacent. You showed me that, hence our little truce here. And that's what this is, a truce. If I was at the top of my game, you wouldn't stand a chance. Next time, it will end differently."

"Thanks, I guess," I said.

"Don't thank me. It's just a matter of respect. In your own bizarre way, you did me a favor. Now I'm returning it by telling you the word's out on you, Dean Marklin. And in this day and age, the word travels fast, even for those of us who only come out at night," she said and pushed her sunglasses back up her nose. She turned to leave.

"Wait!" I shout-whispered. She stopped. "I want to know one more thing." She turned back to look at me.

"Don't push it," she said. "I don't like you that much."

"Why did the police take so long to get there? Why weren't they on the place immediately if it's such a big hot spot?"

She stared at me. Behind her dark lenses her eyes took me all in. It was one of those moments that hung there. Then she tilted her head very slightly to one side.

"Certain parties who were beholden to some of my friends were aware that I hunted there," she said, then leaned forward and whispered in my ear. I flinched but held my ground. "Consider that when you're looking for people to believe you, people to trust in your little crusade," she almost hissed.

"What are you talking about? What crusade?"

"We'll talk about that next time," she turned to walk away again.

"What next time?" I asked.

"Of course there'll be a next time. You're a vampire hunter now." She was gone as if she was never there, and of course she was right.

Vampire Anonymous

by Nancy Kilpatrick

Vampire Anonymous

Mortals! Enter freely and of your own free will!
All may post in the section marked
VICTIMS
with absolutely no assurance that
your post will ever receive a written response!

To post on this site:
VICTIMS will be accepted after personal info is submitted:
Name: _____
Address: _____
Phone number: _____
Email Address: _____
Age: _____
Internet Name: _____
Gender (not optional): _____

VICTIMS:
"Hey man, cool site so far! Cool images. Well, cool fangs, anyway. Looking forward to some chillin' words 'o wisdom from the great Undead!" *Your Boi Georgie*

 "I find the idea of a new vampire blog intoxicating. I just hope you don't resort to the mundane clichés so many pseudo vampires do. In darkness…" *Lucrezia*

"I am SOOOOO lovin' this! Hozit feel ded? LUV 2 B U! xxooxx" *Lisa*

"Not too many blogs have a chat function for the general public. WTG!" *Your Boi Georgie*

"This is the *stupidest* blog I've ever seen. Fuck off!" *Nightmare on Elm*

"I've yearned to be a vampire. And now *you're* here! I can tell just from the visuals that my dreams are coming true!" *Dark Angel*

"Nightmare on Elm, you obviously don't possess the sensibilities for this blog. Perhaps U should go elsewhere for entertainment. Maybe there's a Freddie blog somewhere." *Lucrezia*

"Screw U bimbo!" *Nightmare on Elm*

"Vampires Anonymous rules! Bitchin'!" *Your Boi Georgie*

Testament #1

Those perusing this site will surely wonder if you exist. Out there. In here. You do not wonder where is 'here', meaning this cyber world. It is a place for hiding, a realm of disguises, the realm of the *Giaour*. Or, as your contemporary Edgar Allan would have put it, a veritable *Masque of the Red Death* virtual ball. Hence no *Facebook* or *My Space* but a unique invention where you remain anonymous and yet your *VICTIMS* reveal all! After all, one who dwells in the land between *Heaven and Earth* cannot remain surreptitious when forced to expose details, and this *is*, after all, your blog!

But OTOH, you must reluctantly acknowledge that the world of phosphors isn't exactly foreign terrain. Anyone in doubt can read the poem *Darkness*. Reality is a fine weave of the senses, is it not? The five mundane senses, and that elusive sixth. You can frolic in any of those arenas, yet most often you are relegated to what is not seen, heard, felt, touched or tasted. You are the intangible. Others know you exist, but may not admit it. For lack of a better word—which they likely find unpronounceable—they call you *The Vampyre.*

Enough tedious philosophizing. In this, your first blog entry, you must cater to the *VICTIMS*, who are—your tongue-firmly-in-your-cheek—dying to learn something of you. Here it is, a tidbit. A veritable bloody morsel, gouged from your beatless heart and offered on this microchip plate: You were born in 1788, just five years before the French Revolution, not that you are French, nor have you ever been revolting, as it were, at least not to your own mind. Mileage varies as they say. Some may beg to differ.

There! A British-ism has crept into that previous paragraph, betraying your ancestry. You are not ashamed of your past. Why should you be? All creatures born must adjust to their circumstances, or die. But sometimes they die anyway, when circumstances prove unnatural or, if the *VICTIMS* prefer, supernatural. Die and revive. As did you. Fate is a bitch.

But you were birthed during the long and diseased reign of the vegetarian king George III, who suffered porphyria. Anyone who has found this blog is a true vampyre, or a wanna be, and in either situation knows about the 'vampire disease'. For the uninitiated:

The Symptoms: sensitivity to sunlight, receding gums (all the better for the fangs to show!), bloody urine, etc. etc. Oh, and the incessant talking. They say George Three once chatted non-stop for fifty-eight hours! Half the time reciting *Childe Harold's Pilgrimage* and other assorted poems. But enough of this tedious medical trivia. You are not an encyclopedia. Anyone desiring to know the symptoms of porphyria can bloody well go look them up!

You met George 3 in his dotage. George, with whom you shared a first name. It wasn't long after the turn of the 19th century, years before your 'official' death, but not before your death to life as it is generally understood. The monarch, then in his 80s, had been exiled to Windsor Castle where he was more or less left to his own devices. He'd gone both blind and deaf. The first night as you entered the castle at his invitation, it was clear to you that no one looked after the old bastard. Indeed, his eldest son had already been named Regent, anticipating the ancient one's demise. George had gone quite bonkers. He mistook you first for the wind, then a ghostly friend. Only the insane seem to notice the presence of your kind. Isn't it peculiar that the lucid tend to rationalize cold drafts, fleeting shades, barely heard whispers, while those who have lost their marbles see more clearly the shadows? The insane and the bards of this world, and perhaps visual artists, but you digress.

Poor George had stopped shaving for quite some time and sported a scraggly, wiry beard that brushed the middle of his chest, about heart level. Sleepless, he wandered the dank castle halls garbed in a regally purple dressing gown with his Garter star pinned to his chest. You did not believe he knew that his wife Charlotte had died, but then he did not seem to have a clue that his own demise was eminent. At your hands.

Yes, before the unsettling thought enters any mortal heads, you want to make it perfectly clear that back then you still retained vestiges of human emotion and felt sorry for perhaps the kindest, most fair-minded of British monarchs. In your lifetime no one would have called you selfless. In fact, your reputation was the opposite. Still, due no doubt to *Hours of Idleness*, you helped George to his end as a generous if yet selfish act. To this day, you still remember the texture of his parchment skin, and the sour taste of his thin blood, the coppery element common in human vitae all but missing from the liquid weakly spurting from his aorta, replaced by something more acrid. His skinny chicken neck and the prolapsed veins and arteries proved difficult to work with and, back in the day, you found this not esthetically pleasing. Still, these aspects of George to the third power did not prove insurmountable, but the process of piercing him became extended. Oddly, his rummy eyes found yours as you moved in close to bite him. He smiled with his eyes and his lips and murmured something endearing which you've forgotten, though you do recall that he whispered Sarah, a reference no doubt to the lovely Lady Sarah Lennox of whom George was enamored in his youth—before his mother bollixed that romance.

Never mind *The Dream*. Sentiment be damned. Your dagger-sharp incisors sliced through the emaciated flesh to allow what blood he possessed to trickle like hot treacle between your eager lips, quenching the dire thirst which has since become perpetual, that drives your every waking moment. *When We Two Parted* and it was done and his corpse lay crumpled on the floor at your feet, you, who sported the title Lord, who loved and was loved by many including your sister, you who enjoyed early fame if not fortune in the realm of realms literature, you came to a startling discovery: blue blood is not nearly as satisfying as red blood. It was at that moment that you decided you would, once your death had been staged in Greece, move to America.

VICTIMS:
"This old one is soooo amazing! I really want to meet YOU." *Lucrezia*
"Y R so real, VA! Keep the stories commin' xxooxx" *Lisa*
"Man, there's like SO many people on here now. Get a life, folks!" *Nightmare*
"Why don't YOU get a life, Nightmare!" *Lucrezia*
"I'm new here. I'm not sure what's going on." *Harry Lewis*
"Well, Harry Lewis, you've hit the pit of hell where all these morons are talking about vampires. Get out before the stake swings in your direction!" *Nightmare*
"Welcome, Harry. You are fortunate to be here and we are fortunate to meet you. We are in the presence of an Old One who has lived many centuries and shares with us his dark history. George Gordon Byron." *Dark Angel*
"Lord Byron? The poet? Impressive." *Harry Lewis*
"Yeah, right!" *Nightmare*
"I've waited one entire month for another entry. Please, kind

vampire sir, the esteemed Lord Byron, bestow upon us another tale!" *Lucrezia*

"How come you talk like you're in some Anne Rice book?" *Nightmare*

"Where's Your Boy Georgie? He hasn't posted lately." *Dark Angel*

"No idea. xxooxx" *Lisa*

"People come, people go. Only those of us with deeper sensibilities remain." *Dark Angel*

"Like you, airhead?" *Nightmare*

"Honestly, I don't know why you're still here! You think its all crap, so just go somewhere else." *Lucrezia*

"Hey, I'm hangin' to see just how stupid you people can get!" *Nightmare*

Testament #2

You observe that your list of *VICTIMS* has grown. Furiously they post between your monthly entries, when *la luna* fills, when you fill. Let them speak with one another! You have no need to respond. That is not your concern, although you will miss *Your Boi Georgie* who seems to have... vanished. *Arrivederci, bello!*

Still, what a strange phenomenon, human beings desperate to befriend a *vampiro*. And after centuries on this Earth, you thought you'd seen it all!

If you are *nuovo*, you have arrived at *Vampire Anonymous*, where the undead speak and the living listen. Come one, come all! Enter freely, but enter at your own risk (especially you, lovely *Lucrezia*.)

All have been warned! What more can you do?

One *VICTIM* in particular you find intriguing, at least the photo—those long dark tresses, eyes obsidian almonds accentuated by black kohl from the Orient, lips as red as virgin blood, skin corpse white. Si, *Lucrezia*, you are a look-alike for she for whom you are named. An homage to the Renaissance beauty Valencian Borgia, famous for her poison rings. Do you own a poison ring? What type of poison does it contain? Would you let me touch your ring, taste your poison?

Ha! Lucrezia Borgia. Her beauty was renowned. Her lips red passion, her breasts fruits for your lips ... You remember her well. How could you not remember your sister?

Back then, you carried the mortal name of Cesare, bequeathed by your despotic 'padre', Pope Alexander VI. Yes, at that time, *Papa* equated with

King, and this office incorporated a different meaning than it does today. At least you believe so. Be that as it may, ultimately, you were forced to kill your father, an all-too common action. Then. Now. Oedipus Rules!

You were fortunate to have been born *un vampire* and did not need to suffer the transition to this eternal existence. Naturally, you were a beautiful child who grew tall and handsome, dark wavy locks swirling down to your shoulders, hypnotic black almond eyes that lured everyone—hair and eyes like your sister's, like the lovely *VICTIM Lucrezia*.

Your parentage remained somewhat obscure, at least on the paternal side. But full of ambition, you were destined for *grandi cose*. At the tender age of fifteen, you were appointed Bishop of Pamplona, and at eighteen Cardinal. Of course, you were more or less forced to resign that last post, becoming the first Cardinal in history to do so. This, at the 'request' of your father, who needed you to head the military when your oh-so-beloved brother Giovanni met his untimely end. An end that involved your teeth at his throat!

Leaving the church for a more mundane if volatile profession had its perks. For a brief time you employed Leonardo da Vinci as an architect and engineer, although that didn't last long. You found the artist, like all artists, annoyingly arrogant. His blood, though, contained a certain heady quality, like a *vino* grown with fat antique Sicilian grapes.

During your military career, you also had occasion to meet and befriend Niccolò Machiavelli, a brilliant analyst, who resided at court for just over one year until you brought him, too, to an undead state. You wonder how many *VICTIMS* recognize that his seminal work *The Prince* is largely based on your military and political strategies?

In any event, it was the French King Louis twelve aka the Duck of Orleans—he of The Crusades, and the defeated in the four decades of pointless wars with Italy—it was he who dubbed you Duke of Valentinois, hence your nickname Valentino. Is it possible that any *VICTIM* recalls your reinvention in the early part of the twentieth century as a fabulously famous film star of the silent screen? A mesmeric star, hypnotic, especially the eyes. *Si, bello*, the vampiro charm! Yes, you have gotten around.

Suffice it to say that you had always been a Prince of Darkness. Sadly, though, your body 'died', at least officially, yet you resurrected and your unnatural state became permanent during a siege at the age of thirty-one. Had you not been so near dissolution of mortality already suffering symptoms of third stage syphilis, you most certainly would have fought courageously to preserve not just the physical body, despite its pathetic condition, but also the *anima immortale*. But mortal death would have happened eventually. And logic was always your strong suit. Better to leave with a pleasing body intact, which is a state you bestow on your food sources. Live fast, die young, leave a corpse you would be proud of! But, as they say nowadays, *ciò è la vita*: such is life. Or, in your case, living death. One cannot predict nor do much to change Fate. You had always found acting out the role of undead to be a humorous enterprise.

But of course the *VICTIMS* are modern and bored with history and long explanations and want nothing more than to know the connections, for example, to sweet poisonous-ringed Lucrezia, your sister. She became your lover at an early age—relationships like that happened back then. She even birthed your child. And you birthed both of them to a new existence, an eternal life that the church fathers had not envisioned.

VICTIM Lucrezia entertains thoughts of being your lover. Perhaps she is your sister, now living incognito in Kalamazoo, Michigan, as her personal information states. She would like you to taste her blood and compare it with your darling sibling's, trace memories of which still linger within you. Shared DNA. Sharing so much more! Blood is thicker than any important liquid. It travels through the centuries and finds its way to you again. Ah, but fantasy is everything, is it not, *il mio amore Lucrezia*? Tantalizing fantasy, meshed with the reality of the *vampiro*. Come! We are *famiglia*. Take my hand, *sorella*! I desire to taste your blood. Again…

VICTIMS:
"Where's Lucrezia?" *Lisa*
"She hasn't logged on in weeks!" *Morticia*
"Maybe she finally got a life!" *NoE*
"She's probably busy," *Harry Lewis*
"Yeah, playing Vampire the Masquerade!" *NoE*
"Perhaps she's stepped over into the Other Realm?" *Dark Angel*
"Is that not what you did? Sorry for my English, I'm Swiss." *Nosferatu*
"Of course not! I have not yet been called." *Dark Angel*
"You mean excuse you being Swiss!" *NoE*
"That's racist!" *Harry Lewis*
"You mean nationalist, doofus!" *NoE*
"Guys, chill!" *Lisa*
"Hi! I'm new!" *Sin-de*
"And oh-so-perky!" *NoE*
"Leave her alone! Don't listen to him, Sin-de. He's out Resident Evil.. Welcome!" *Dark Angel*
"Welcome." *Harry Lewis*

"Wavin'" *Lisa*

"I'm new too," *Vampira*

"Hi!" *Lisa*

"Hiya!" *Harry Lewis*

"This place is so crowded!" *Sin-de*

"We are the regular posters but there are others." *Dark Angel*

"So, who's this guy posting this vampire stuff?" *Vampira*

"It is all in the posts." *Dark Angel*

"It's all in the Prozac." *NoE*

"What's NoE? North of Erie?" *Sin-de*

"Nightmare on Elm." *Lisa*

"Nightmare on Elm." *Harry Lewis*

"Nobody Owns Elvira." *Dark Angel*

"Wouldn't you like to know?" *NoE*

"Duh, that's why she asked." *Vampira*

"Guys, chill!!" *Lisa*

"We must be respectful of the blogger's space. Or as Lucrezia would say: Why is it only girls are human?" *Dark Angel*

"Hi. I'm Elizabeth. But you can call me Black Lily." *Black Lily*

"More females, yes!" *Nosferatu*

"When's the next post? I'm bored." *NoE*

"He posts on the full moon, as anyone intelligent could figure out." *Dark Angel*

"Hi Black Lily. Welcome to hell!" *Vampira*

Testament #3

So many *lány*, so very little time. I am amazed at how the gentler sex finds it way to me, *lepkék -hoz egy láng* or, as the English speakers say, moths to the flame. There! I have already tarnished my reputation as a high-born Lady by littering this site with clichés. I am an educated woman, an exceptional creature for the place and time of my birth—Hungary, 1560. Destined to be a Countess or to carry some other elevated title, I learned at my mother's knee to read and write four languages and a smattering of three others at a time when women received little or no education. But this damned English language! It stymies me now, so lacking as it is in innuendo. In any event, I am known to all of you already, I am quite sure. Countess Erzsébet Báthory, aka the Bloody Lady of *Čachtice*. And now you will hear the truth!

How can I convey my extraordinary life to you <u>VICTIMS</u> who speak with one another electronically and share but an image that may or may not reflect who you are? I can only tell each of you, my precious little ones, that four hundred and fifty years ago life was primitive by today's standards, even for those of us of noble birth. Primitive and dangerous.

Luckily, I was somewhat protected. For the daughter of parents directly related to two distinguished *vivodes*, or warlords, of Transylvania, and niece of the King of Poland, how could it have been otherwise? In fact, I was next in line to be Queen of Poland, a task for which I was eminently suited and one which met my ambitions.

At the tender age of eleven, I was were already betrothed for political reasons to a rather rough soldier named Ferenc Nádasdy who stank of garlic morning, noon and night. My parents sent me to Nádasdy Castle in Sárvár. It was not against my will. Perhaps you cannot grasp the concept of an arranged marriage. Such unions were the practice everywhere among the wealthy and this one spoke to the goals of my parents as well as my own. Betrothal is not marriage, and even as a young girl I was keenly aware of the difference. A charming peasant in the village—a blacksmith as I recall— took my maidenhead—oh did I bleed! My first enrapture with blood! From that union I suffered a stillborn daughter. The gods owed me!

You must indulge me. I love talking about myself. So much has been written about me, and I think you should all know the truth. And where better to hear it than from my own, perfect lips!

Yes, you guessed it, I was an exquisite girl, my beauty legendary, and the times were such that four years later Nadasdy, smitten with me, forgave my indiscretions and married me anyway. Perhaps the best part of the marriage was his wedding gift to me, his home Čachtice Castle, situated in the Carpathian Mountains near Trenčín, together with the Čachtice country house and seventeen adjacent villages.

Ferenc was reasonable for a man, but a soldier to the core, and a beautiful, young, intelligent wife could not hold the attention for long of a man who longed for battle. Three years after the nuptials he was appointed chief commander of the Hungarian troops and off to war for much of the remainder of the marriage. I'll just say that I was not heart-broken.

Managing such a vast estate and being charged with protecting our lands, especially during more than a decade of war, took up much of my time, yes, but not all. There were servants, many, to be managed. The role of Countess is exhausting, yet I fulfilled my responsibilities, even intervening in the causes of peasant women who needed help for one thing or another.

Then, one day, I had a rude awakening. In my silvered hand mirror I found a shocking sight. My flawless porcelain skin, famous in four countries, showed signs of aging. A wrinkle here, a sag there... How had I not noticed before? But I did now, and the awareness hit deep in my chest. At that very moment a *szolga* or servant girl had been brushing my hair and allowed the boar's bristles to tangle in my dark tresses, yanking my head back sharply. Instinctively, I slapped her, hard enough that a drop of blood splattered onto my cheek. Mesmerized, I stared in the mirror, watching the vitae drip down my skin. Impulsively, I rubbed the glistening ruby liquid into my cheek. And it seemed to me then that the flesh on that side of my face took on a new hue, a glow of vitality.

This discovery led to musing and long discussions with several of my most trusted and loyal servants, including Dorka who was closer to me than the others. We came to the conclusion that the blood produced an alchemical transformation. Blood was the answer, the elixir guaranteed to stave off the ravages of time.

One thing, as they say, led to another. At first, with Dorka's help, I drew blood from the servants, but the stupid girls resisted my humane methods and quickly we resorted to the whip. Dorka used the hide liberally and I admit that from time to time I took a turn flailing. The blood of the screaming peasant girls who unfortunately often perished in the experiment was gathered and applied to my face and, astonished, I immediately saw the change occur. Suddenly I looked younger, as if I had discovered the Spanish explorer Juan Ponce de León's Fountain of Youth.

I acknowledge to you all now that perhaps I allowed Dorka and the others to go too far. They not only whipped but they burned, froze, starved and bit girls, needles under the fingernails, and mutilation of faces and genitalia, all in an effort to, as they assured me, 'excite the *vér* and render it more potent' which, at the time, seemed a reasonable avenue to pursue.

Several years passed and it occurred to me that what worked magic on the face and the neck would transform just as well skin on the entire body. I knew that in order to achieve the desired effect I needed a constant supply of girls. Too quickly I ran out of expendable servants and was forced to bring in female peasant from the villages, lured to the castle with the promise of well-paid work as maidservants. The job required living at the castle full-time, no days off as you modern workers are offered. Consequently these girls never returned home. No one missed them. They were hung upside down, their veins sliced open, their precious offerings caught in my bath. My skin stayed lovely and fresh as the day I'd wed Ferenc. For a time, all was well.

Then, on another fateful day, I stared in my damned mirror lamenting that I was no longer the fairest in the land, despite daily treatments with the magic potent. I became furious and threw the mirror against the wall, shattering it to bits. Dorka, as always, comforted me. She brought me to the realization that it was some basic coarseness in the blood of these *paraszt* that left my skin unnourished. Dorka insisted that I required refined blood, and the only way to have that would be to acquire refined donors.

Through my many contacts I was able to invite the daughters of nobles to my home, ostensibly to be trained in the ways of the aristocracy. I generously offered to be their mentor, assuring these young women would possess the manners, skills and intelligence needed to function at the level of society to which they aspired—one level up. I was overwhelmed with requests to take in these well-born girls and tutor them. You can see that I had little choice in the matter. Fate called me to preservation.

I procured a house in Bucharest on a small street that has today come to be called Blood Alley. This is where I met these refined girls as they came to the city. With the help of a German clockmaker, I created a design, ingenious if I say so myself, and far ahead of its time. I called it the Iron Virgin—a later design which imitated my own was known as the Iron Maiden. But I named this Virgin for I had realized rather early on the exquisite and dramatic effects of virgin blood which far outweighed that of non-virgins. Anyway, the device allowed me to imprison a girl in a sarcophagus then hoist the apparatus to the ceiling. Within this iron structure with its painted blue eyes, the yellow hair of one of my prettier princesses and the white perfect teeth of another, were long spikes that, as the door slammed shut and automatically locked, pierced the flesh in such a manner and in so many places that the blood was permitted to flow freely down to a tub below in which I was immersed. With a small leap of the imagination I am certain you can imagine my ecstasy. Any woman could.

I can still recall the sharp, sweet aroma and the tangy-sweet taste as the vitae engulfed my flesh, the hot blood burning through my skin, altering it with its magical properties, transforming what had become old and tired and revitalizing my body. I reveled in the blood. It filled my mouth, my nose, and I gulped it down greedily, allowing it to burn away from the inside the dross of age and reveal the hidden, nearly lost beauty of my youth. Call it an early acid-peel. Botox!

I am certain that each girl *VICTIM* understands my pursuit, my desire to stay attractive at any price. And if you do not now understand it, you will!

These noble girls performed a service for me. I took possession of their youth gratefully and they gave up their lives in the same way, gratefully, at least in their hearts. A symbiosis. A sacrifice. For the greater good. Isn't that obvious?

In any event, I continued in this way for many years, retaining my beauty to the amazement of many in my social circle. During this time, at age forty-four, I became a widow, barely noticing. Ferenc had been absent for some years. He died at the hand of a general, or having been killed in battle, or murdered by a prostitute in Bucharest whom he refused to pay—take your pick. I had little interest in his fate. And upon his demise I inherited his wealth and consequently had no shortage of suitors lured as much by my youthful beauty as by the hope of marrying my money and power. But I barely tolerated these leeches. Especially now that I was in direct line for the throne. I was, you see, on the verge of becoming the Queen of Poland! And now, sweet *VICTIMS*, you understand the greater good, do you not?

Alas, nothing continues forever. Mine was a political era and rumors abounded about illicit practices involving witchcraft at my estate and at my house in Bucharest. While the deaths of peasant girls were tolerated or ignored, the offspring of nobles was duly noted. Eventually, in 1610, I was brought to trial, found guilty of twenty-five years of abuses. Three of my most trusted servants were burned alive as witches, including Dorka. From my window I watch her body blacken, her dark hair catch fire and and all the while her screams pierced my ears.

I was charged with bringing about the deaths through sadistic torture of 650 girls, an absurd number. Although I kept no written records, I did compile a tally in my head and the numbers had been triple that, at least!

During this sham trial, I refused to respond with the regret or remorse expected. After all, I was a Countess and did not deign to address their ridiculous accusations. Consequently, without being found guilty because of my station, I received the harshest punishment—I were walled up alive in the tower of my own castle where I remained for the next three years, being fed through a slot like an animal. Were the powers-that-be concerned with the deaths? Of course not! The entire charade of a trial was a strategic move on the part of the then heads of state to usurp my land and my wealth, which they did, and to keep me from ascending to the throne. A woman then had few legal recourses.

Ah, but did I not have the last laugh? You see, the blood not only changed my skin but it altered every aspect of my being, body and soul. Not only did I return to youth, but that youth became eternal, and my taste for blood infinite.

When I stopped eating, they finally opened the tower door. But I was not there! My body, you see, has never been found. The pathetic *paraszt* who resided near Nádasdy Castle have insisted for centuries, to this day in fact, that they can hear the wail of girls being tortured to death, and my sparkling laugh as I delight in the voluptuous richness of their young blood. Me, whom these cretins call *vámpír!*

So many young and pretty girls here! And of course you understand. There are far more important concerns that those of a petty nature, what might be deemed 'personal' problems. The greater good must prevail!

You are not *VICTIMS* but lovers of history, of tradition, of fate. Surely, my pretties, you would like to meet me? Ah, to surrender to a larger fate, what better destiny? ...

VICTIMS:

"Awesome!" *Harry Lewis*

"That story chills my bones, man." *Nosferatu*

"Where's all the chicks? How come they aren't posting anymore?" *NoElm*

"Maybe they got tired of your stupidity!" *Harry Lewis*

"Hey, how's it going? Thought I'd check this out." *Vampire of Dusseldorf*

"Hey V of D. Good to meet you!" *Harry Lewis*

"Yeah, man, it's getting lonely here without chicks." *NoElm*

"Doesn't matter to me. I'm gay. And German." *Vampire of Dusseldorf*

"That's a problem." *NoElm*

"Being gay?" *Vampire of Dusseldorf*

"Being German!" *NoElm*

"Groan!" *Nosferatu*

"Don't you think it's weird that every time this guy tells a story, VICTIMS disappear? I mean, the missing people are like the people in the stories!"

"It's coincidental, man. Do I have to remind you we're on the Net. There *aren't* any vampies here!" *NoElm*

Testament #4

Landsmann! A *Deutsch* amongst the *VICTIMS*! *Vampire of Düsseldorf.* Düsseldorf. Northwest of *Köln, ja*? I am familiar with your small city. *Und* your reputation!

Have you not heard of me? My name is Fritz. Fritz Haarmann. Like you, I have been identified for eternity. They call me The Hanover Vampire, The Butcher of Hanover, oh, so many names! We are alike, you and I, but different. But you have a taste for girls while my predilection is for boys. Not for you but for me, there are many now here amongst the *VICTIMS*...

Dracula: Long Live the King

by C.J. Henderson

The room was a devotion to crimson, a master's thesis built around a complete and utter knowledge of scarlet and all its secret emotions. From floor to ceiling, from the fixtures to the floor boards, blood and bodies had been swirled and dabbed, brushed and spat and just plain flung— callously used as something less than art, but more than a decoration.

The desecration of the chamber had, in fact, been a statement, a manifesto—of sorts—and ultimately, the opening salvo in a war of subjugation, one that would be fought relentlessly to overwhelming success. Anyone skilled in reading the signs knew that retribution and hate would soon mingle once more, with the end effect of spreading their bastard children across the face of the planet once more so the streets could run ankle deep in bile and blood.

And that would just be the beginning.

"So, tell me ... why do you think they chose to start this whole thing in such a cherished place, anyway? A place practically guaranteed to bring the wrath of the world down on them?" The man being questioned whispered his response.

"You don't understand even that much yet," he said, a tone close to pity in his voice. Not the mean-spirited, I'm-so-much-better-than-you type of pity so common in the world, but the type a mother feels for her child when the poor youth cannot find the obvious even though it is so clearly right there in front of them.

"Let us go back, review everything from the beginning," the quiet man added softly, almost as if hoping not to embarrass the questioner any further. "Let us think back to that, oh, so horrible, morning of blood and despair, and see if it all cannot be made clear for you."

The morning in question was an easy one to remember. Most anyone living on the face of the Earth could focus on that one slice of time with instant clarity. The way an older generation remembered the announcement of Victory in the Pacific, or the moment the youthful president was gunned down in Texas, or when that pair of planes struck those buildings in Manhattan. They were, all of them, moments in time which so completely riveted the world's attention that few could forget what they were doing when they were made aware of them. That morning in question, that was one of them.

Indeed, as all the world agreed, that was the worst of them.

Gold Shield Daniel Madsen had been one of the detectives assigned to the case when the crime scene had first been discovered, nearly a day before it had become the defining moment of a race. As he exited his unmarked car in the church complex's parking lot, he saw a number of familiar faces. None of them were acting in any of their familiar manners, however. There was no humor on the air, not even the black and morbid chuckles of the damned that most law enforcement types easily shared with ambulance drivers, doctors, nurses, lawyers and all the other professionals whose job it was to keep scrubbing away under the massive fat roll of society to keep infection from setting in too greatly.

No, the attitude of those standing around outside the Catholic high school's gymnasium was one of horrid shock. Men and women stood with wide, unblinking eyes, wishing for tears, understanding they had moved past them. Some of them, anyway. Others wept uncontrollably, again—men and women both. Some balled their fists, shook them at the sky, cursing the God that would take such ill care of his most devoted children. Others cursed themselves for not being able to provide the protection which was part and parcel the reason for their existence. All of them died a bit inside, however, and it was this fearsome pallor which hung in the air, filling the newcomer with apprehension.

"Why, welcome, Detective Madsen," came the coroner's voice, rasping and far-away. Looking past the officer, through him, his hands moving absently, wiping at blood long cleaned away, he asked in a burst of dry humor, "What brings you out on a night like this?"

"Look again, Elliot," Madsen shot back. "It's morning."

"I guess it is somewhere." The detective stared at the older man for a moment, wondering how to interpret his comment. There was a tired, hollow sound to the man's voice, a level of weariness Madsen had never heard before—not from the coroner, not from anyone. He almost questioned the sound, then stopped himself, not wanting to risk offending his co-worker.

Hell, he figured, whatever it is, I'll be seeing it for myself in a minute.

Madsen was correct.

The detective made his way into the Catholic high school gymnasium slowly, stopped at every checkpoint and made to shown identification. The requests annoyed him, especially when coming from officers who knew him personally. Some apologized, some seemed not to hear him when he groused. By the time he made it to the gym itself, he found himself too keyed up, too filled with anticipation as to what he was going to find on the other side of the metal doors. He did not like that feeling.

It meant he was already forming impressions, prejudices about the case before he had any real facts. That worried him for he valued his objectivity. It also worried him that he could not even begin to fathom the mood of those already on the scene. He had seen the like previously—at sites holding the bodies of slain fellow officers. But this was different. Such crime scenes were much cleaner psychically, easier to define—more righteous anger, more palpable hunger for revenge in the air.

This was different. Indeed, if anything, people seemed as if they were not acting in any easily defined manner because they were seeing something they had never witnessed before. Something beyond their ability to catalogue emotionally. Something unique.

Well, thought Madsen, once his hand was poised to open the door before him into the gymnasium, whatever the big deal is, its secrets are about to become mine. And, with that thought, Daniel Madsen open the door before him and stepped into Hell.

Madsen managed five steps into the room before the stench of the blasphemy swirling around him filled his nostrils and focused his eyes. Despite the number of people in the room, detectives and uniforms, politicians and medical examiners, their minor, everyday chatter and task-attendance could not muffle the horror upon which they concentrated.

"What in fucking Christ ..."

Everywhere Madsen looked he saw blood. Blood dripping from the slaughtered bodies of nearly two score nuns. In every corner, hanging from the rafters, stretched across the bleachers, smashed and broken and ripped apart, ravaged and slashed and torn into bits, female bodies and the uniform of the wives of Jesus lie in vulgarly soiled disarray. It was heart-freezing. Revolting. Terrifying. Madsen was not a Catholic, but he was a human being. He stood for a long time—staring, as had everyone that had proceeded him into the room—before finally being able to move once more. When he did move, it was to stagger, his head turning from side to side, limbs jerking, as he tried to bring the numbing horror around him into focus.

"Okay," said Madsen to the quiet man there in the room with him. "I remember the first day, the opening shot. I was there—it's not like I'm going to forget that anytime soon. So, what's your point?"

"How did you feel then," asked the man. "How did the sight of such a slaughter affect you? You personally? This is the key to your question, so take a moment and concentrate, and then tell me ... when you saw what you saw ... how did it make you *feel*?"

Daniel Madsen did not need a moment. Stalling only long enough to conquer his surprise that anyone would think he would need to think about his answer, he told the quiet man;

"It made me want to kill them. To find whoever had done such a thing and exterminate them. St. Augustine's, for Christ sake. The nuns of St. Augustine's ... how could anyone think that wasn't going to bring some kind of wrath to play?"

Detective Madsen was correct, of course. The slaughter of the nuns so recently returned from their missionary work in Africa set off a wave of anger around the globe. One of the best known symbols of Christian charity in the world thanks to a relentlessly obvious media, an organ too lazy to jump further than the nearest bandwagon, the slain Sisters of Charity became a universal rallying point for calls to revenge.

Just as mindless news machines had made the kind sisters a symbol for all that was giving and wonderful in the world, so to did they then build the murder of those same poor souls into the crime of the millennium. The howls for swift and brutal justice were endless, plastered across every front page, puffed from the lips of every talking head to be found around the world in all the languages of man.

Of course, as one would expect, the reaction was as anticipated. Outrage from all corners pumped amazing results. One thing that had amazed, and to some extent annoyed, Madsen was the overwhelming amount of money and manpower that was instantaneously pumped into finding the St. Augustine killers. This was not because he did not want to see such monsters brought to justice. It was more that he was offended by peoples' notions over who deserved avenging and who did not.

Still, if the money had not poured in, if the public outcry had not only prompted private contributions, but also forced public officials to throw manpower at the problem, it might have taken the world far longer to discover not only who the killers were, but *what* the killers were. It took those who made the determination quite some time to believe their findings. Tests which normally would have been believed without question were run multiple times. Facts were reviewed by expert after expert, each of them being turned out and another summoned until so many of them had reached the same conclusion that those guardians of the public trust overseeing the search had no choice but to believe.

And, when the news was released to the world as to what had been discovered about the true nature of the killers, nation after nation reeled from the information. The peoples of every continent were staggered, first shouting down those telling them what had been discovered, calling them liars and fools—then screaming to the rafters for something to be done. It was perfectly understandable, however, for the villains in the world's latest drama were practically beyond the understanding of humanity in general.

You see, until the attack on the nuns of St. Augustine, most people really did not believe in vampires. Indeed, after the initial reports went out, at first most people still did not believe in vampires. How could they? They were an old wive's tale, a myth, a superstition. Something for grandmothers to frighten children with, at least until the vast world of entertainment got their hands upon the idea. Over the decades, after scores of bad movies and worse books, the concept was a joke.

Oh, there were the men willing to give the idea credence so far as they could use it to live out childish power fantasies. And, there were plenty of women, especially in the more decadent cultures where they had scads of idol time—time to lose themselves in adolescent sexual daydreams. But this was not believing in vampires, this was simply using the concept to prolong the time before accepting maturity.

No, for the most part, in the opening days after those conducting the investigation into St. Augustine's revealed the insane truth to the world, the vast majority refused to believe what they were being told. It was, when all was said and done, simply too bizarre, too fantastic. Aliens from another world they could have accepted. Satan come to Earth would have been more reasonable. But, vampires?

The tide of public acceptance was turned quickly, however, as further attacks were launched across the globe. After a while, a pattern was established. The attacks came every eight days. No one could say why. Each time they came in a different country. They shifted from hemisphere to hemisphere as well, and from the day side of the world to the night. Every eight days, some horrible blood-letting came that stunned the world.

Every time it left a mound of corpses drained of their blood. Some of it might be left around at the scene for effect, but never again like at St.

Augustine's. No, that amount of waste had been used for effect, to make an impression—to start the cattle thinking in a certain direction.

Then, after eight days had passed eight times, the number dropped to seven. Suddenly only a week was required. Only a week before another busload of children, or all the workers on the night shift at a bread factory, or the patrons of a small nightclub, or all the sailors on a war ship were slaughtered. Every seven days people could lock their doors and pull the covers over their heads and pray they were not in the path of whatever was coming for whomever it was coming for.

And, as you might of concluded, after seven sevens had been achieved, the waiting period dropped to six. Six days only before a retirement village would be murdered, or a school would be left lifeless, or a sporting event would find its players would not be entertaining anyone that afternoon because they would not be leaving their locker room ever again.

It was during the sixes that everything began to change. Well, to be fair, things had been changing all around the globe since the first word of the St. Augustine's attack was dispersed. But, the changes—real changes—to the way things unfolded were stiflingly slow, at least, until the attacks dropped into the Six Cycle.

With the sixes, people began to believe not only in vampires, but in the inevitability of them. They could not be found. They could not be stopped. Month after month, attack after attack, not one of the creatures was stopped. Not one was even located. None were even seen. Wild rumors sprang up. The internet was awash with ideas that governments were simply ridding themselves on unwanted citizens, or that it was all part of some massive conspiracy to start a one-world government—many of the others were even more outlandish. The problem was, whether or not people believed in the existence of undead creatures of the night, one way or another chaos was descending over the face of mankind.

By the time the Five Cycle arrived, as thousands were slain, throats ripped open, blood drained from their bodies, the nay-sayers were quieted. By that time, people were more than willing to believe, but as acceptance came, so did the inevitable questions? What did the creatures want? What were their attacks all about? There were no demands being made, so why were they doing what they were doing? Was it simple extermination? Why, after being among us for years, would they start something that would turn the entire world against them?

And worse yet, what exactly was this new "them?" What was it that people were supposed to believe in? Even if the world was suddenly supposed to accept that there were vampires, what kind of vampires? Turn into smoke vampires? Change into wolves and bats vampires? What were the extent of their powers? How could people protect themselves? These questions were screamed from the rooftops, and soon most governments were scrambling to determine the best way to release what they knew. Or, more importantly, how they knew what they knew.

"Really," the quiet man half-whistled his response. "You wanted to kill them? Because of what they were. I see—so, you're telling me, you weren't actually one of the ones who _knew_. I can scarcely believe it."

"Yeah, a big laugh for you, I guess."

"No," the questioner assured Madsen, his tone most genuine, "I mean it; you're statement catches me completely off guard. From the beginning, when we first encountered one another. You've always been so completely competent. I supposed I made the fatal mistake of assuming you were in on 'the secret.' So many were, you know."

Madsen shook his head at the words, for they reminded him as to how the uproar over the question of vampires and the nature of their abilities had left the world's politicians, police, religious leaders, et cetera, in a terrible panic. Despite the paranoia that had gripped the world since the beginning of what by that point was already becoming known in some circles as "the Great Unraveling," there were really not that many who had concluded that the simple truth was, their leaders had known about the existence of vampires all along. They tried to hide it, of course, and many did to one extent or another. But, during the fives, as the cycle played quickly down to the inevitable fours, the news did finally come out, and the frightened masses of the world did not take to it well.

A number of European Union members were found to have agreements going back hundreds of years not to reveal the secret that vampires walked the Earth. Most of those governments fell rather quickly in bloody revolution as their frightened citizens saw no point in doing otherwise. Leaders who felt it was best to sacrifice those they were sworn to protect to monsters to stay comfortably in power were not people anyone felt much sympathy for in those days. But still, as human beings continued to die around the world, another group slaughtered with cold deliberation every time the correct number of days cycled through again, the world screamed for answers.

Just what are these things, people wanted to know, and how can they be stopped? Surprisingly, it turned out that those making deals had been tricked all along. No two groups who had struck such satanic bargains— not the British House of Lords, not the oil billionaires of the Middle East or the oh-so-dignified men in red of the College of Cardinals—had the same information. They had all been given conflicting sets of facts, told different tales, been lead down false paths. When this was discovered, panic around the world doubled, and the Three Cycle saw hysteria growing to where it threatened the fabric of civilization.

And that was when the Americans captured Dracula.

To be fair, the ultimate master of the creatures of the night was not actually captured by the Americans, but rather brought to them. The vampire lord's subduer was an Englishman, William Delbourne, a scholar and scientist more home-produced than university-taught. It was Delbourne who alerted the United States that the greatest vampire of them all had been brought to his knees. He also let them know that he was willing to allow them to question the monster, as long, that is, as he was well-compensated for the privilege.

Those in the American State Department, all of them people of who only existed in the real world, did not waste anyone's time by attempting to appeal to Mr. Delbourne's sense of decency or humanity or any other such whimsical notions. If anything, there was an immediate recognition between Delbourne and those he had contacted as kindred spirits. Thus, with only minimal proofs, those rubbing their hands with glee over such a fortuitous turn of events were made more willing to believe that a single man could have succeeded where all the planet's law enforcement agencies had not simply because of his ruthless nature.

It took the newly formed mutual admiration society little time to come up with a figure and matching set of amenities that closed their deal. A military transport was dispatched to bring Mr. Melbourne and his prisoner to the United States, and some twenty-seven hours after his initial call, Melbourne was comfortably ensconced within his new mansion, and the legendary creature known as Count Dracula was in the custody of the American government.

For obvious reasons, the deal made between Melbourne and the Americans was classified as top secret—to be kept from the rest of the world, and that meant even the rest of the American government. For one thing, part of the deal demanded Dracula not be harmed. Melbourne wanted to study the vampire when the Americans were through with it. The notion was understandable—their own teams wanted to study it as well. And besides, what harm could there be in such a price tag? The device which restrained the creature caused it such a hideous level of pain whenever it even considered trying to escape that the monster had agreed to tell those with their hands on the controls anything they wished to know.

Of course, the Americans were suspicious. Raised as children on comic books and simple-minded movies, spending their adult lives moving from one shadowy, black ops scenario to the next, they were geared for suspicion. Mistrust was a casual part of their daily existence. You did not get to work in the State Department without that level of paranoia coursing through your veins.

But, the results the classified deal garnered the questioners were so immediately spectacular, their collective doubts were vanquished almost at once. Dracula proved to be a never-ending fount of valuable, intricate information—all of it accurate. All of it deadly to its own kind. For one, garlic actually worked. It was not so much the plants, but concentrated bursts of the pungent scent of their bulbs. As the vampire had instructed;

"Most humans think of garlic only as something to aid in cooking. They know nothing of its medicinal values. These properties are monstrously destructive to the undead. As, I assume, you can see for yourself."

Indeed, observing the vampire, hooked to the machine that kept a never-ending trickle of a garlic-laced plasma flowing to his veins, it was hard to argue. Delbourne had provided photographs of the vampire before his capture. The monster had been staggeringly handsome then, tall and lean, dark and beautiful. His eyes had been piercing, illuminated as if by their own inner light. Hooked to Delbourne's machine, however, he was a sunken, debilitated creature, shrunken and wrinkled—old, harmless.

Of course, those selfsame photos had set off a controversy themselves. Were not vampires non-reflective things—unseen to mirrors, to cameras?

"Piffle," was Delbourne's answer. "Complete and utter dreck."

The adventurer/scientist quickly brought his American teammates up to speed. On this point, he instructed them that the human eye was as reflective as any camera lens. If we could see a vampire, then so could anything else. It was a shockingly simple thing, but it was just one of those bits and pieces learned at the beginning of the education—obvious only after it was revealed. Being good students, the Americans took notes which they rapidly began to dispense to the rest of the world. And, the list of things considered noteworthy seemed endless.

Vampires could be seen in mirrors. Vampires could be photographed. Vampires could even eat meals in restaurants like anyone else, and sustain themselves on such fare for years on end if necessary—hold the garlic, of course. They could also go about during the day, if necessary. They did not burn away to dust and ashes at the first touch of sunlight.

"Sunlight does not strike us as does a laser beam," Dracula had told them. "It is debilitating, yes. But not deadly. Wheel me to the window—I will show you."

This was not done immediately by any means. Overwhelming levels of paranoia become accepted job qualifications for a reason. Doing anything the vampire suggested was hotly debated each and every time, and that time was no different. While Dracula waited patiently, captive in its restraint-laden wheelchair, arguments were hurled back and forth. This time, the fear motivating the nay-sayers was that they felt the king of the monsters was attempting to commit suicide. Those in opposition replied with scorn, countering that no matter what one might think of the creature, it was practically impossible to think of it as the type that could seek such a cowardly exit.

When the psychiatrists studying the monster concurred with those in favor of following the suggestion—their opinion of their subject being that it was not in the thing's nature to sacrifice itself for any reason—the test was made. Dracula was wheeled to the window and left in the freely streaming noontime sun. And, as the vampire had told them, the rays of the sun did nothing noticeable to the exposed portions of its body. Its skin did not crack or blister or boil, steam did not burst from its body, its eyes did not melt, and no part of it whatsoever disintegrated into dust.

After some five minutes, a period during which the Count kept its eyes tightly closed, the monster did remind those watching its pitiful form that despite the lack of Hollywood effects, it was still being affected in subtle, and somewhat painful ways, and if all had been satisfied that it would prefer to be taken out of the sunlight. Once safely back in the room's specially darkened corner, the lessons continued.

Sunlight, striking a vampire's skin, caused internal problems. Dracula explained it as their version of cancer, as it were. If a vampire desired to be abroad during the day, it was not an insurmountable problem. If its kind simply wore suitable clothing, moving about during the day was not much more than a minor inconvenience. Yes, of course, their eyes were especially vulnerable, but strong sunglasses could compensate if worn diligently.

"Naturally," the questioner said in his quiet, whispering voice, "as you might suspect, the more they learned, the more they wanted to know."

Dracula was such a willing accomplice that it did not take all that long before the suspicions over its motives began to lessen. After all, when the party of the first part does nothing but cooperate, it is generally hard for even the most frightened and cautious of souls to continue to question their every word or suggestion. No one put forth the idea of removing the monster's restraints, or lessening the dosage of garlic being administered to it. Everyone involved in the project understood completely that they were dealing with a thing that had existed on the blood of its, at least, one-time, fellow human beings for hundreds of years. The creature claimed to have been born in the 1200s. What the exact day was, it had no idea. Nor the year. It only knew that by the time 1300 had rolled around it had already lived too long.

There were some that noted a sense of irony in the thing's words—a self-awareness that almost humanized it for them. Although no one was letting their guard down, still, as long as the answers flowed freely, what harm was there in not treating the thing with at least a modicum of respect? They planned on working the creature hard. Keeping its cooperation was of paramount importance.

So, when it narrowed their understanding of the effects of sunlight on vampires, that lead directly to the topic of when did vampires rest? Did they need rest at all? When they did rest, did they need coffins filled with dirt? Did they have to sleep during the day? And so it went. Yes, they had observed Dracula for some time, but it was a captive—locked into servitude by Delbourne's machinery. Like a wild tiger held in a small city zoo, the way the public saw the beast might not actually be how it would perform its tasks if left to its own devices. Once more, their slow-speaking captive revealed the answers to all they wanted and more.

"We sleep when we wish. Most vampires sleep during the day because it is easiest. They do it to avoid the sun, and, well, as you might suppose, because the night is the most exciting time to hunt. It is also the easiest time to cover up such actions as well. But, you will find little to help you in your struggle following this avenue. When we sleep, we do so where we please. We do not need to lie in the dirt of our homeland, or in coffins attired for the opera with our hands folded over our chests. We do not hang from the ceiling. We simply sleep."

As the fascinated scientists, politicians and military men questioned Delbourne and his amazing captive at length, around the world, of course, the battle still raged, escalating further with every passing hour. The effects of the knowledge that vampires were real had on mankind were simply devastating. No one had been prepared for it. And, the more information the Americans released, instead of being comforted in any way, the people of the world only became more frightened.

The toppling of small governments across the globe had only been the beginning. Despite their violence and the insanity they almost always released, those had practically been controlled reactions compared to what came next. The riots that followed came close to allowing the human race to destroy itself. On each continent, in every country, sooner or later someone was accused of being a vampire who escaped for a moment the brutal mob that leveled the accusation.

Dodging that first mad rush, however, the accused would then find themselves on the run, a situation which would only bring more of the desperate and the frightened to bear on them. Entire towns were destroyed by fire and gunplay as people, terrified for their very souls, began to slaughter anyone they did not trust, anyone who looked different, whose canines were a touch too pointed, or who only came into view at the wrong moment.

"What did you think of the violence then?" The quiet man tilted his head to the detective, his look one of sincere curiosity. Madsen sighed, remembering the insanity, the pointless blood letting, the God-only-knew-how-many-of-millions who died needlessly because of their neighbors' fear. But then, if they were not to die that way, there were so many other ways coming.

Less than three months after St. Augustine's, more than half the world's employees—from farm hands to CEOs, to counter clerks, nurses, cigar rollers, beer bottlers, television stars, drug dealers, and so forth—were not showing up at their collective workplaces. Many of them would come in on occasion, two, possibly three days a week, fear-filled attempts to keep some cash flowing and to hang on to such rapidly disappearing notions as medical benefits. But that was all. Hardly anyone found it worth it to leave their homes for anything but the most serious of emergencies.

By the time the Three Cycle was nearing, many non-essential businesses were facing disaster. Movie theaters were the first to feel the pinch. Indeed, already suffering from the onslaught of the home entertainment juggernaut, the film palaces of the world began closing by the hundreds. The mere fact that they were invitations to walk into a large dark room and sit down with strangers had much to do with it, but not everything.

The simple fact was, it was not something a person needed to do. Only the most ardent film fans continued to seek out movie halls. And so it went from business to business. Laundromats closed their doors as people began doing their wash at home. Even if they had no washing machine, they still owned bath tubs and sinks. It would do. Drug stores, groceries, hardware stores—businesses like these were able to limp along if they delivered. Those that did not were forced to close their doors.

Mega-stores closed early on. Bargain warehouses could not afford to deliver goods. They would be faced with too many orders, and with no one to fill them. No one wanted a job where they would be out on the streets all day. It was not worth the pennies such employment paid. It was not worth most people's lives.

No, as the threes approached, chaos was looming on all fronts. Money was becoming worthless. People were already bartering for what they needed with neighbors. Banks and the world's various lending institutions began to close. So did cruise lines, and air lines. So did many sporting franchises. Suddenly, even the most rabid sports fans did not see the need to go to a stadium—to be outside, in the dark, watching millionaires play a children's game. Not if it meant risking their life.

"What did you think of the world's chances in those days?"

Madsen looked across the table, trying to remember. He felt compelled to answer honestly. Staring into the quiet man's eyes, he cleared his throat, then said;

"Not a lot, to be honest. I mean, most cops are pretty cynical by nature, at least ... on the outside."

"What do you mean?"

"Well, you know ... you see so much more death and pain and evil than the rest of the world, you need to get your guard up against it. Shield yourself. You see violence every day, murder every day, drugs and thieves and rape ... every *goddamned* day—it gets to you."

"Oh, I understand that principle well enough. But, the shielding— why bother? Why not open yourself up to it? Let the feel and flavor of it penetrate? How can you combat something you don't understand—that you hold at arm's length?"

"What can I tell you," Madsen answered honestly. "I don't have to think like a rabid dog to know I want to put a bullet through its head rather than let it bite me."

"But," the whispering man asked, his voice holding the slightest trace of humor, "haven't you ever wanted to know what it feels like ... that rabid freedom to throw off the rules? To do exactly as you desire?"

The Three Cycle began with a less than spectacular attack. The Vampire Legion, as many in the media had begun calling those responsible for the world-wide slaughters, struck a trailer park in southern Ohio. Oh, there was a large enough body count, and the touch of torching the largely plastic bodies of the scores of trailer homes, sending the resultant black oily clouds of smoke into the air to mark the event was considered by many with the distance to judge such things as a stroke of genius.

Still, it was a feeble cycle opener compared to many of their other launches. Despite its lack of elevated drama, it did sent a clear message to the human race. All right, it said, since you've decided to simply hide in your homes, we'll just have to start killing you there.

But, the Vampire Legion had not counted on one thing. They had not considered the possibility that the greatest of them would pass out their deepest secrets. And, those closely guarded bits of revealed information were not confined to the general powers and weaknesses of the species. No, after Dracula had told the Americans all he could on ways to detect and destroy vampires, then he asked if there was any interest in where they might be found.

He could not, of course, give them the addresses of every rank and file vampire in the world, nor was that what he had been suggesting. What he had to offer was a series of likely headquarters for those who had planned and were making this attack on humanity.

"You mean you know where they are?" The questioner had growled his words in a dark and threatening voice. Laughing softly, despite what seemed considerable pain, Dracula answered the man.

"I mean that I can give you some ideas on where to find the ringleaders of this foolishness. Surely you must have considered that I might be able to. I volunteered the information because, well actually ... I was wondering why none of you had asked."

The shrunken figure of the monster chuckled, its eyes locking with those around the table. There was nothing any of them could say. They had not asked the question. Indeed, when they thought about it, they had not asked all that many questions. Dracula had continued to volunteer so much information that they had spent most of their time listening, taking notes, then trying to verify what they had been told. Sighing at their own folly, those running the show admitted that they would indeed like to hear anything the vampire had to say on the subject of possible locations where they might find the vampires responsible for the attacks on humanity. With the unrestrained sense of cooperation which had been its trademark so far, the monster told all it knew.

It gave them names of those individuals most likely to be leading the campaign and where they might be found. It identified secret meeting halls and safe spots known to the hidden broods in country after country. Its memory for such things was remarkable. Of course, once it had told all it knew, the question was, once again, was it telling the truth? Madsen had been one of the people in on deciding the answer to that question.

The detective had been one of the first outside of the State Department to be pulled into the inner circle. His unwavering dedication to duty since St. Augustine's had kept him on the government's short list of law enforcement people to keep an eye on for when the moment to retaliate appeared. He had actually been recruited at the end of the Five Cycle. At this point, he and the thirty-eight other outsiders from around the world were joined by one hundred and sixteen more. The "firsts," as the thirty-eight had come to be known, were asked to bring the "seconds" up to speed.

Once they did, the question of whether or not to believe Dracula was poised along with a follow-up—if we do believe him, what best could be done with the information? The many answers offered boiled down to a single response to both questions:

Verify.

The plan met with no dissent. Around the world, teams would be put into place to watch the sites in question. If any of the individuals Dracula had named as being likely leaders of the Vampire League were spotted, it was to be assumed he was once again telling the truth. If the information panned out, task forces would be assembled. Raids on as any of the dens as possible would be made in one great synchronized push. Yes, it was true that Dracula might have named non-vampires—anything was possible. But, so many of those on the monster's list were known criminals, were people who could so easily be vampires, that following the path of least resistance once again simply made the most sense.

And, after two days of observation, nearly every single site bore the hoped-for fruit. Almost all of those Dracula had named were spotted at the sites in question. When the Three Cycle hit its second date, and all the inhabitants of an apartment complex in the suburban countryside beyond the city limits of Dusseldorf were slain, the watchers had all the proof they needed. Those sites nearest the buildings attacked were hotbeds of activity just before the incident. Those others becoming rallying points soon afterward, with suspects coming from far and wide to watch the news reports—like football fans filling a sports bar.

And thus "the plan" was conceived.

"Were you actually one of the ones who helped orchestrate 'the plan,' detective Madsen?" When the officer nodded, the other said, "Sorry, it was a confusing time then, so much happening. I couldn't remember. So, what do you think of the results?"

"We don't have them yet. Why do you ask?"

"Come now, detective. Really ... how long do you think the world will want to keep me around after tonight?"

Madsen turned to Dracula and pondered the question. The detective had to admit to himself he had not thought about what would be done with the vampire if that night's raids went well. Yes, the monster had been promised to Delbourne for study—or, more exactly, the promise had been made that the vampire would be studied, and that the Englishman would have access to both the facility as well as all of its findings.

"I don't know what to tell you," the detective answered honestly. "I'd think, like any criminal, you'd be given the consideration your cooperation deserves. I mean, on the one hand, you're a murderer who's come down the ages living on the blood of human beings. On the other hand, these other vampires have brought the world to the brink."

"Really," the monster said with mild interest. "How so?"

"Things are bad out there," Madsen confided. "I mean, even if tonight's raids are a success, there's no guarantees that mankind is ever going to recover."

"Surely you don't think of civilization as so fragile, do you, detective?"

"I don't know. There's panic in the streets out there. Ten, fifteen countries are having civil wars. Tribalistic conflicts have broken out across Europe, mostly in the east. All of Africa, a lot of Asia ... and I'm not saying we're doing all that better."

"You don't think America could fall, do you now, detective? Not the great and wonderful, all-powerful, shining city on the hill known as the United States ... heavens ... you wouldn't want to upset me, would you?"

And then, suddenly Madsen felt something within the back of his mind that made him stare at the vampire. He had asked for the duty of staying with the monster. He was offered the chance to lead any of that night's raids, but something had made him decide he would rather be in charge of those who watched Dracula. Since everyone else connected was vying for spots on the assault teams, he had found little opposition to his choice of duties.

Now, staring at the monster, he played the thing's words over within his head. The creature's tone had changed since the evening began. Acting as if he was only performing his routine duties, Madsen checked the garlic drip, making certain it was still working, that the level had been adjusted upward to make certain the vampire was not acclimating to that which was supposed to keep him subdued. The machinery checked out. All the monster's restraints were tightly in place. The wizened creature seemed no threat to anyone or anything.

And yet, thought the detective, there was something in his tone, something that ...

And then, before Madsen could ponder the situation further, the State Department official who had first brought him into the entire affair entered the room. Filled with an uncontrollable glee, the man blurted;

"We did it!" Striding over to Dracula, the man grabbed the monster's head with actual affection and tousled his hair. "You beautiful bastard, you sure called it. You certainly did!"

"Mind filling us in?" The man caught himself, understanding the detective's request. Putting his hands up while bending his head downward, he explained, "Everything he told us panned out. We've got 'em on the run."

"The vampires?"

"Fuck yes, the vampires. Who else? Reports are pouring in from around the world. Everything you told us worked. Those garlic bombs—ingenious. Ate the skin right off 'em. Boiled their eyes out."

"Well, that's terrific news," said Madsen, suddenly nervous, not knowing why. Turning toward Dracula once more, the detective studied the monster intently. Looking at it as he would any prisoner caught and sitting on a station house bench, Madsen sized up the monster with a professional eye. He did so for only a handful of seconds, then put his hand to the State Department official's shoulder, moving him toward the door.

"Let's not bother the prisoner now, shall we? Why don't you go tell the others? Get the party started."

"But, don't you want to hear how well we're doing?" Suddenly the government man felt uncertain. He knew something was happening, but he did not know what. Feeling left out, and deciding such was an assault on his dignity, he said, "I'd think anyone would want to know that."

"I do," answered Madsen. Desperate to silence the man, not knowing why, he tried, "But Dracula has expressed concerns about how he's to be treated. And you're talking about the extermination of his race. Let's not give the bleeding hearts the 'insensitivity' ticket to play against us."

"Oh no," called out Dracula, his voice stronger than it had been all night, "I'd like to hear? How are things going out there in ... the real world?"

"Great!" The official shouted his answers, glee filling his voice at finding a receptive ear. "Over two thousand targets confirmed as taken out. Dead, gone, finito! And that's just from the first third of the reports. They weren't expecting a thing. Caught flat-footed around the globe. It's a miracle!"

"Yes," agreed Dracula, his smile growing wider. "I could not think of a better word."

And then, to make Madsen's problems worse, the door opened then, admitting Delbourne and a half-dozen more State Department men. Looking to the Englishman, the vampire called;

"Mr. Delbourne, I do believe our work here is done."

And, so saying, Dracula snapped its bonds with but the merest of shrugs. At the same time, the monster released all of itself that it had been holding in, its strength and weight and terrible presence. In less than a blink, the withered skeletal form was replaced by a deadly-looking thing, one appearing to be made more of iron and fire than simple flesh.

As it rose, those within the room stared with unbelieving eyes. Quickly, understanding his part, the Englishman shut the door, trapping all coming noise within. Reaching forward, the vampire drove its clawed hands deep into the chests of the men nearest it and tore their hearts free with a single motion. As some of the others turned to run, the horror moved among them with a blinding speed, snapping necks, cracking spines, tearing out jugulars. By the time Madsen had his service automatic in his hand, he was the only human left standing outside of Melbourne.

"You can shoot now if you like, detective." Madsen put up his weapon.

"Something tells me it won't do me much good."

"I so appreciate a clever adversary. So, Mr. Melbourne, was the oaf correct? Are things on schedule?"

"Absolutely, my lord. Civilization is crippled. Delivery of services has almost completely fallen apart. Starvation is rampant in all major cities. Reports of cannibalism are everywhere. Wars are raging on every continent, some of them being fought with kitchen knives and rocks."

"And my bastard children?"

"Taken care of. The upstarts are all destroyed." Sitting once more at the table, eyes unblinking, hands gripping each other so as not to shake, Madsen spoke, asking the vampire;

"You ... you did it all, didn't you?" When Delbourne made to answer, Dracula cut him off. Walking across the room toward the detective, licking the blood from its hands, the monster challenged Madsen.

"You tell me, detective. What are your educated guesses?"

"I think like any criminal who's had a long run, you've made a lot of enemies. In your case, you literally made them. You're the first vampire, aren't you?"

Dracula nodded, his expression pleased.

"And all the nut jobs that have been doing all this killing, they're boys and girls you turned to the dark side over the centuries. But some of them have been breathing down your neck lately. So ..." and then, a horrible realization forced itself to the front of the detective's mind. It was an outrageous, hideous assumption, one that turned Madsen's blood cold. But, stealing a glance into the vampire's eyes, he realized the worst he could think of was probably not horrific enough. Still, he ventured—

"You, you planned the Vampire Legion attacks. You stirred this whole thing up so the world would do your dirty work. Take out all your competition at one time. And that wasn't all of it ... was it?"

"Master," interrupted Delbourne, "it might not be wise to tarry too long." Dracula turned to its accomplice.

"Are you questioning me?" Its voice had gone back to the whisper it had used all night, making its meaning frighteningly clear. The Englishman went noticeably pale. As the vampire turned back toward Madsen, the detective said;

"You could have accomplished that with our help in a lot of ways, though. So the question is, why did you choose this one? Why let people know you existed? Why do what you did to the world? And the answer is, this is the world you wanted."

"You see," said the monster with a smile. "I told you this one was smart. Just watching him at Augustine's, I knew I wanted him here. So tell me, detective, why would I want the world to be reduced to the state it is now?"

"Because," answered Madsen with confidence, "what do you care if bread gets baked, or movies get made? Something tells me you're not a big HBO fan. My guess is that you're sick to death of this plastic world, this pathetic waste people have made of civilization. You've seen empires come and go, but you've probably never seen one where every sack of shit was revered, and every innovative thinker was silenced."

"Detective," answered Dracula, actually giving Madsen a smattering of amused applauds, "I would love to discuss this with you further. But, my servant here is correct. It most likely is best not to tarry too long." Turning to the Englishman, the monster tilted its head slightly as it said;

"Come Delbourne, you've waited long enough. It is time for your promised reward."

Light filling his eyes, the Englishman crossed the room, stripping off his tie, pulling his collar widely free from his neck. Bending to his lord and master, Delbourne accepted the vampire's bite, sighing with contended glee as his humanity was stripped away with his blood. And, after taking the precise amount required to transform and not kill, Dracula asked;

"How do you feel, William, now that you are vampire? Any regrets? Was it all worth it to you?"

Feeling the swelling power beginning to grow within its body, the newly created vampire nodded its head eagerly, practically dancing as it answered;

"Oh, yes master, yes. It was all worth it. Of course it was worth it."

"Betraying your own kind? You feel no regrets? You are happy with all your decisions in this matter?"

Delbourne laughed, as if Dracula could not have made a more hysterically funny comment. Facing each other, the oldest vampire on Earth looking into the eyes of the newest of its kind, Dracula smiled, nodding its head with an almost kindly warmth. If it had still been capable of such, the Delbourne thing would have shed tears of joy. That denied it, the freshly created monster reached out to its father.

Taking its son in its arms, Dracula drew Delbourne close, and then reached up, grasped the Englishman's head, and twisted it violently, shattering its spine and killing it once more. Sitting at the table, Madsen actually laughed out loud.

"What an idiot," the detective sputtered. "You just went to all this trouble to slaughter all the other vampires in the world, and this nut job thinks you're going to let him into the club. Oh, that's rich."

"Do you disapprove, detective?" Madsen shook his head, still chuckling. When the vampire inquired why he did not, the detective told it;

"Hey, the moron got what he deserved. Both for selling out humanity, and for being such a goddamned idiot. I mean, seriously, how could he not see this coming?"

"Men have always been easily blinded to truth by self-interest."

"It's true," Madsen admitted. "What was it Hoffler said, 'We lie loudest when we lie to ourselves.'"

"I believe that's correct," answered Dracula, seemingly impressed with the detective's sudden erudition. "Or as my old friend Oscar Wilde once said, 'I have nothing to declare except my genius.'" Madsen chuckled. As he did, the monster across the table from him said;

"It is going to be a terribly cruel world out there from now on, yes?"

"Oh, I'd say you've seen to that. And your point...?"

"The worst thing about immortality is the loneliness. I like you, Mr. Madsen. That being the case, I put the following to you simply ... would you care to watch what happens to this planet from the spectator's gallery, scrambling with the maggots and flies for your daily bread, or would you care to take your chances as companion to the master of world?"

The detective raised one eyebrow unconsciously as he mulled over the options presented to him. Bobbing his head for a few seconds, shaking and nodding it at the same time, he finally answered;

"Well, as they used to say, 'The king is dead. Long live the king.'"

Accepting the human being's answer, the master of the world strode forth toward the door. The chaos trembling its way through the hallway beyond did not bother it. The smell of fire and blood coming from outside the building, however, did offer it a moment of intrigue. Smiling as Madsen turned the knob and opened the door for it, the monster stepped forward into the beginning of the newest Dark Age, thinking;

It's going to be another wonderful millennium.

About Our Creators

L. A. Banks is the recipient of the 2008 Essence Storyteller of the Year award has written over 35 novels and contributed to 12 novellas, in multiple genres under various pseudonyms. She mysteriously shape-shifts between the genres of romance, women's fiction, crime/suspense thrillers, and of course, paranormal lore. A graduate of The University of Pennsylvania Wharton undergraduate program with a Master's in Fine Arts from Temple University, she writes full-time and lives in Philadelphia.

Elaine Bergstrom — A horror, suspense, and fantasy novelist, Elaine Bergstrom has been taking her readers into under-explored realms since beginning her career in 1985. Her books on the Austra Family, her signature series, ventured a new twist on the world of vampires. Elaine is currently working on a new book for the Austra series, and has contributed to other Moonstone anthologies *Kolchak: the Night Stalker Chronicles*, and the previous Moonstone Monsters book, *Werewolves: Dead Moon Rising.*

Dave Dorman was born in the same town, and the same year, as the somewhat well-known vocalist and exhibitionist, Madonna. He learned to surf, while a youth, living in the beautiful Pacific islands known as Hawaii. He has never been convicted of a felony, no matter what anyone else has said. He also paints a bit.

P.N. Elrod has sold over twenty novels, an equal number of short stories, and is best known for *The Vampire Files* featuring undead detective Jack Fleming. Elrod has co-written three novels with actor/director Nigel Bennett, edited and co-edited several genre collections, and is an incurable chocoholic. More news on her toothy tales may be found at www.vampwriter.com

C.J. Henderson is the creator of the Teddy London supernatural detective series, and the author of some fifty other books and novels. He has also had published hundreds and hundreds of short stories and comics, as well as thousands of non-fiction pieces. Called everything from "the literary master of the hardboiled" to "that guy, over there," he is one of the most brilliant fictioneers of our age, and will happily tell you himself if asked. To do so, go to www.cjhenderson.com, where there are always free short stories to read. Tell him Moonstone sent you.

Nancy Kilpatrick is an award-winning author and editor who has published 17 novels, about 200 hort stories, 5 collections, and has edited 8 anthologies. Her most recent books include the horror anthology *Outsiders: An Anthology of Misfits* (co-edited with Nancy Holder, Roc/ NAL); the novels *Jason X: To the Third Power* and *Jason X:Planet of the Beast* (Black Flame Publishing / New Line Cinema); and the non-fiction opus *The Goth Bible: A Com-Pendium for the Darkly Inclined* (St. Martin's Press). Look for these recent or upcoming short stories: "Going Down" in *Mondo Zombie* (edited by John Mason Skipp, Cemetery Dance Books)); "Heart of Stone" in *Monster Noir* (edited by Steve *Savile*); "The Age of Sorrow" in *PostScripts* (edited by Peter Crowther, PS Publishing); and the novel *Hunted* (Orion Publishing / Neon imprint). Nancy was a Guest of Honor at the 2007 World HorrorConvention. Check out her website at www.nancykilpatrick.com.

Paul Kupperberg has written hundreds of comic book stories for DC, Marvel, Charlton, and others (including his own creations, *Arion Lord of Atlantis, Checkmate,* and *Takion)*, as well as novels, short stories, non-fiction books, essays and humor for a variety of publishers. He has been an editor at DC Comics, as well as the late, lamented *Weekly World News* and for World Wrestling Entertainment's *WWE Kids Magazine*. His book *Jewjitsu: Hebrew Hands of Fury* (Citadel Books) was published in November 2008.

Bill Messner-Loebs was born in Ferndale, Michigan, of poor, but honest rocket-scientists. He graduated from Oakland University with honors in History. Almost immediately he discovered that General Motors wasn't hiring consulting Historians that year. He sold art supplies, built catamarans, homesteaded along the Canadian border, taught in Jackson Prison, wrote radio mysteries for the telephone, and oddly enough discovered all this had given him the ideal training for writing and drawing comic books. He is the creator of *Journey — the Adventures of Wolverine MacAlistaire,*

Bliss Alley — Alchemy At Street-Level, *Epicurus The Sage* and *The Bunny of Death*. He has written Jonny Quest, Flash, Batman, Dr. Fate, Atom, Wonder Woman, Superman, Jaguar, Thor, Mr. Monster, The Maxx and Spider-Man. His awards include: The INKPOT, the GLAAD award and this year *Rue Morgue* magazine declared his book, *The Necronomicon*, best horror comic of the year. He lives in Livingston County, Michigan with his wife Nadine and several fungi from Yith.

Martin Powell — Eisner-nominated Martin Powell has been a professional writer since 1986 and is perhaps best known for *Scarlet In Gaslight,* the Eisner-nominated graphic novel featuring *Sherlock Holmes* and *Count Dracula.* Martin's unique style of comic book scripting has also been showcased at *The International Musuem of Cartoon Art* at Boca Raton, Florida, in a special celebrated exhibit. He lives in a creepy one hundred twelve year old haunted house in Minneapolis, with artist Lisa Bandemer, their two nearly human dogs and five diabolical cats. http://www.myspace.com/martinpowellphantomshadow.

J.C. Vaughn is the creator of Moonstone's *Zombie-Proof* (with Vincent Spencer), *McCandless & Company*, *Antiques: The Comic Strip* (with Brendon and Brian Fraim), *Twenty-First Century Romances*, and the upcoming *Dead Inspector* (with Filip Sablik). He co-wrote *24* for IDW and *Shi* for Crusade, Avatar and Dark Horse Comics, and contributed to *The Wicked West 2* and *Whiskey Dickel, International Cowgirl* at Image Comics. His work has been profiled in *TV Guide*, *Emmy* magazine, *24 Magazine*, *Wizard*, and other publications. He is the Executive Editor and Associate Publisher of Gemstone Publishing, home of *The Overstreet Comic Book Price Guide*, Disney comics, and *The EC Archives*.

Dan Wickline has been writing comics for over a decade, starting with his own imprint Hardline Studios and moving to freelance work in 2001. He has done work for Avatar Press, Humanoids Publishing, IDW Publishing, Image Comics and Moonstone Books. More information can be found at www.danwickline.com.

Ken Wolak has been working as an artist/illustrator for the past twenty years, known mostly for his horror work and use of eerie color schemes in his paintings. He tries to convey a feeling of actually being in the work or art itself. Presently he works with many comic publishers and still does fine art paintings for a loyal group of patrons. For more on Ken, visit www.wolfheadstudiosart.com.

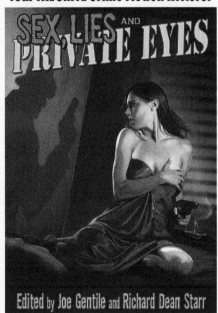
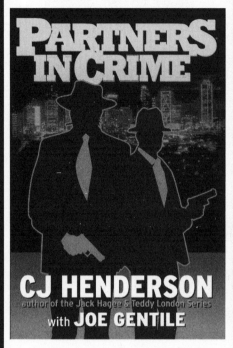